INSPIRING GLORY

INSPIRING GLORY

David T. Lee, M.D

XULON PRESS

Xulon Press
555 Winderley Pl, Suite 225
Maitland, FL 32751
407.339.4217
www.xulonpress.com

© 2024 by David T. Lee, M.D.

All rights reserved solely by the author. The author guarantees all contents are original and do not infringe upon the legal rights of any other person or work. No part of this book may be reproduced in any form without the permission of the author.

This novel is a work of fiction. Names, characters, places and incidents either are the product of the author's imagination or are used fictitiously. Any resemblance to actual events, locales, organizations or persons, living or dead, is entirely coincidental and beyond the intent of either the author or the publisher.

Unless otherwise indicated, Scripture quotations taken from the Holy Bible, New International Version (NIV). Copyright © 1973, 1978, 1984, 2011 by Biblica, Inc.™. Used by permission. All rights reserved.

Paperback ISBN-13: 979-8-86850-577-5
Ebook ISBN-13: 979-8-86850-578-2

Dedication

To my sons, Christopher and Evan, who through their energy, wisdom and creativity have inspired me to write this book.

Chapter 1

BRANDON AND EMMA WERE nearing the destination of their four-hour trip from Cincinnati to Cleveland to visit Brandon's mom. The temperature outside was below freezing, and there was a light blanket of snow on the ground. The interior of the car was warmed comfortably by the bright sunshine flooding through the windows. Emma closed her eyes, lifted her face toward the sun, took a deep breath and basked contentedly in the sun's rays. The wellspring of Emma's serenity was actually the result of the recent rekindling of her once-promising romantic relationship with Brandon. Following his successful recovery from multiple addictions, Brandon was gradually regaining Emma's love through a fresh foundation of trust and faith.

"I haven't asked you in a while," said Emma. "How are you doing with processing your dad's death?"

"It's now been four-and-a-half years since his accident, and overall, my loss seems less painful. My faith has really helped with my healing, but of course, I still miss him. I also still wonder about how my life would've been different if he hadn't died."

"Don't torture yourself with those thoughts," suggested Emma.

"What I regret most is the chain of events after my dad's death that derailed our relationship, Emma. How is your healing from all that going, and how do you feel we're doing?"

"As you know, Brandon, your actions wounded me deeply, especially your deception and your shunning of me during our pregnancy. Like you, my faith has helped me to heal more quickly, and I fully understand that your behavior was driven by your addictions. I have completely forgiven you, and my love for you is reawakening."

"Thank you for your forgiveness, Emma."

"Returning to Cleveland, where we went to high school together, is bringing back a lot of the pleasant memories and emotions we shared in the earlier days of our relationship. I hope you'll continue to be patient with me, though, because I still want us to move forward slowly."

"Of course. Please take all the time you need. I'm just so encouraged that we're together again."

"I agree," she said as she looked at Brandon and they exchanged warm smiles. "By the way, how did your first workout with Dylan go this morning?"

"It went great! I really enjoyed seeing Dylan, and it felt so good to be out running around on a football field again. I can hardly wait to get my hands on the old workouts my mom found that Dad prepared for me when I was about Dylan's age."

Dylan was an eleven-year-old boy who Brandon and Emma had encouraged when Dylan was undergoing treatment for leukemia about five years ago. At that time, Brandon was a star running back on Ohio State's football team, and Dylan idolized him. Dylan, completely cured of his leukemia, was now showing early promise as a running

CHAPTER 1

back. He had recently asked Brandon to give him personalized workouts and coaching sessions every Saturday morning, much like Brandon's dad did for Brandon during middle school and high school.

"I'm really glad to hear that the workout went well, Brandon. I know how excited Dylan was about seeing you again and how much he was looking forward to your time together. Is he talented?"

"It's a little too early for me to judge his skill level as a football player, but it's apparent that he's a natural athlete just by how gracefully he moves."

Brandon continued, "Hey, did I mention that Mike Nelson is going to join us at my mom's house this evening?"

Mike Nelson was a college roommate and lifelong friend of Brandon's dad, and he was a sportswriter for the *Cleveland Plain Dealer*. He had attempted to remain in close touch with Brandon after his dad died.

"That's great," replied Emma. "I really enjoy being around Mr. Nelson. Is he coming for a specific reason?"

"Mr. Nelson has always encouraged me in my faith, and he played a key role in helping my dad become a Christian. I invited him to join us today in hopes that he can also encourage Mom to consider a personal relationship with Jesus."

Suddenly, the traffic on the highway in front of Brandon instantly became a sea of red brake lights. As Brandon narrowly avoided hitting the vehicle in front of him, his mind instinctively recalled the accident scene on the night of his dad's fateful crash.

Chapter 2

MIAMI CENTRAL HIGH SCHOOL, with six state championships, had a rich history as a football powerhouse in Florida. Through the years, the school had groomed many outstanding players who had gone on to stardom in college. Press conferences for their football players to announce their college selections were commonplace, but none of them had as much fanfare or national media attention as the one for Tristin Garner. Not since LeBron James played high school basketball in Ohio had a high school athlete so dominated the other players in his sport like Garner.

Tristin Garner swaggered into the room. A table was draped with a tablecloth featuring the logo and colors of his high school, as well as a backdrop behind it bearing the same look, as the school wanted to capitalize on the publicity opportunity for such a sought-after athlete. He sat down at the table, and seated beside him was his mother. He had never met his father. Lined up on the table in front of him were baseball caps from Georgia, Michigan, Alabama, Notre Dame, Ohio State, Clemson and Penn State. In the packed room were over 200 attendees, including teammates, classmates, coaches, teachers, local reporters and members of the national media. As the crowd waited in hushed, excited anticipation, Tristin basked in the attention

CHAPTER 2

knowing that all eyes were on him. He reached out over the hats, hesitated for a second to build suspense, then confidently selected the Ohio State cap and placed it on his head while displaying a smug grin for the cameras. The room erupted in exuberant cheers and applause.

As Garner leaned toward the microphone to share with his audience the reasons behind his selection, an expectant silence blanketed the room.

"I'm very excited to commit to The Ohio State University as my choice to begin my collegiate football career. Ohio State has not had a truly elite running back like me since Brandon Campbell played there four years ago. My plan is to win the Heisman Trophy my freshman year and become the first freshman running back to ever win it. I'll get it again my sophomore year and join Archie Griffin at Ohio State as the only other two-time winner. More than likely, after that, I'll transfer to another school that offers me the best chance to earn the Heisman during my junior year, and become the first player to win it at two different schools. After my junior year, I'll be ready to take over the NFL."

Tristin's mother had a pained expression on her face. Except for a few of Garner's teammates who began cheering, most of the audience sat in shocked silence. Even the national media members, who were accustomed to immodest, self-centered elite high school athletes, were taken aback by the level of conceit displayed by Tristin Garner.

On the ride home after the press conference, Garner's mom, Eloise, drove in silence for about ten uncomfortable minutes before she spoke to her son. As she tried to restrain her emotions, she said in a measured voice,

"Tristin, I'm really disappointed in what you said at the press conference."

Tristin, who thought that he did exceedingly well, was genuinely surprised by his mother's assessment. "What're you talking about, Mom?" he demanded.

As calmly as she could, she said, "You are so full of yourself, Tristin. That is not how I raised you. All you talked about was how you planned to use college football for your own personal glory."

"Football is a dog-eat-dog world. You're either the lead dog, or you're another puppy in the pack. I wanted to make it clear that I'm the alpha dog, because I'm the best high school football player of all time."

"Tristin, it's admirable to be confident in your ability, but you are so arrogant that it offends others. In order for you to be successful, you need the support of your coaches and teammates. They're going to be less likely to play hard with you if they don't like you. And right now, you are hard to like."

Tristin quickly dismissed his mother's remarks, and the two of them rode the remainder of the way home in silence.

Chapter 3

BRANDON'S VIEW OF THE road was completely blocked by the semi trucks in front of him. When the traffic failed to move in either lane for a few minutes, Brandon turned off his engine and stepped out of his car to investigate. Just a short distance in front of him, a three-vehicle collision had just occurred. Apparently, a deer had run onto the highway in front of a pickup truck and caused the pickup truck driver to brake suddenly. The car behind it also tried to stop, but the semi behind it was not able to come to a complete stop in time, and the semi pushed the car into the pickup truck. The driver of the car anticipated the impact from the semi, and tried to steer onto the right shoulder to avoid the impact. He was only partially successful, however. The impact of the collision was absorbed entirely by the driver's side of the car.

As Brandon cautiously approached the wreckage, he quickly realized that the accident had just occurred and that no first responders had yet arrived. He also noticed that the drivers of the semi and the pickup truck had climbed out of their vehicles and appeared to be uninjured. The car in the middle had absorbed nearly all of the impact, and the airbags had been deployed. Brandon approached the car from the passenger side. He saw a young man who was awake but appeared dazed. There was an older man in the driver's seat who was unconscious and likely very seriously injured. Brandon also noticed a pool of gasoline under the car, and perceived the risk of a fire. Most of the glass in the car was broken out, including the passenger side window. A small group of bystanders had begun to form, and one of them shouted, "I just called 911!"

Brandon approached the young man purposefully and asked, "Are you hurt badly?"

"No, I don't think so, but my dad may have saved my life by swerving to the right at the last second." In that instant, the mental cobwebs began to clear, and the young man remembered that his dad had been driving. He glanced for the first time at his unconscious father sitting in the driver's seat next to him. He audibly gasped, then he immediately began sobbing.

Brandon, sensing the precarious urgency of the situation, said to the young man, "The best way to help your dad is to take care of you first. I'm Brandon. What's your name?"

"Patrick."

"Patrick, I tried to open your door, but it's jammed shut. With my help, do you think you're able to climb out the window?"

"I think so."

Brandon reached into the car and released Patrick's seat belt. He then helped lift Patrick's head and shoulders through the open window. Fortunately, Patrick was slender and flexible, and with Brandon's assistance, he was able to slither out through the window. They both became aware of the sound of sirens, signaling the approaching

CHAPTER 3

ambulance which arrived a few seconds later, along with several police cruisers.

Brandon said, "Patrick, it's going to take the emergency team a few minutes to assess your dad. Let's sit over here off to the side and out of the way." Brandon helped Patrick sit on the grass just off the shoulder of the highway. "Are you a person of faith?"

"Yes, I'm a Christian," answered Patrick.

"So am I. Can I pray for you and your dad?"

"I could really use that right now," Patrick said with a heavy heart as he glanced at the wreckage and the emergency team working to extricate his dad.

Patrick was still stunned and disoriented from the accident, and was struggling to come to grips with the severity of his dad's condition. Yet, he had a supernatural trust of this stranger who was helping him.

"What's your dad's name?"

"James Cutler."

Patrick and Brandon sat near the shoulder of the highway with eyes closed and heads bowed, as Brandon prayed, "Dear Heavenly Father, we love you and trust you. Even though we don't know why you sometimes allow us to endure crises like the accident this afternoon, we are comforted by your presence and have faith that you will use today's events to accomplish your good and perfect plan. Father, we lift up James to you and ask that he not only survives but that he recovers quickly from his injuries. I also ask that you relieve all fear from Patrick about his dad and help him to depend on you completely during this difficult time. Finally, Father, please oversee the work of the emergency team. Please guide their actions and keep them safe.

May you be glorified in the aftermath of this tragedy, Father. In Jesus' name we pray. Amen."

"Amen" was repeated by two other voices – the one of Patrick, as well as the sweet voice of Emma, who had silently joined them as they prayed. Brandon said, "Patrick, this is my girlfriend, Emma. Emma, this is Patrick. He was in the passenger seat of that car." Brandon nodded toward the wreckage and continued, "And his dad was the driver that the medical team is still attending to."

Patrick's eyes welled up with tears as he looked at the wreckage and saw the EMTs feverishly working to remove his dad from the car.

Emma said suddenly, "Patrick, you look familiar. I think I've seen you studying in the medical school library at the University of Cincinnati. Are you a medical student there?"

"No, but I'm a freshman engineering student at UC, and I often study in the medical school library in the evenings. It's really quiet, and I don't have to worry about bumping into someone I know and getting distracted."

"Is Cleveland your hometown?" asked Brandon.

"Yes. My dad picked me up at UC this morning, and I was going to spend the weekend with my parents. My dad and I are really close, and it's been a tough adjustment for him since I've left for college. He was homesick to see me and insisted that I spend the weekend in Cleveland with him and my mom."

"Do you think we should call your mom and let her know about the accident?" asked Brandon compassionately.

"Yes. I was hoping to know a bit more about Dad's status before I called her, but it looks like that may be a while,"

CHAPTER 3

said Patrick as he glanced at the wreck with tears rolling down his cheeks. "I better call her right now."

Patrick slipped his phone out of his pocket and touched the number for his mom, as Brandon and Emma stood near him.

"Hi, Mom." Patrick, suddenly wracked with sobs, could no longer speak. Brandon quickly intervened, and gently took the phone from him as Emma stepped in to embrace Patrick.

"Hi, Mrs. Cutler. My name is Brandon Campbell. There has been an accident involving Patrick and his dad on I-71 on the south side of Cleveland. I was in another car just behind the accident. Patrick appears to be uninjured, but his dad is unconscious and being attended to by EMTs. I'll stay with Patrick and let you know as soon as we learn where they'll be taking your husband."

"Oh! That's horrible," said Cathy Cutler, as her voice broke with emotion. "Thank you so much for looking after Patrick. I'll contact James' sister who lives near me so that she can go with me to the hospital. I'll await your call."

"I'll call you as soon as we have more information, ma'am." At the conclusion of the conversation, Brandon immediately added Cathy Cutler's number to his own phone. Patrick's sobs were beginning to relent as Emma continued to console him. It was a skill she had expertly developed as a pediatric oncology nurse.

One of the EMTs approached Patrick. "Hi, I'm Will Jacobs, and I've been trying to help your dad. I understand you were a passenger in that car," he said while pointing at the Cutlers' car.

"That's right," Patrick responded solemnly.

"Are you injured at all?"

"Not really. Just a bit shaken up. How's my dad doing?"

"He's still unconscious, but he has a strong pulse and his blood pressure is good. We won't really know the extent of his injuries until we get him to the hospital."

"Where are you taking him?" asked Patrick.

"He's going to the Level One Trauma Center at University Hospitals Cleveland Medical Center. We're ready to take him there right now."

Brandon spoke up and said to the EMT, "Emma and I will follow you and bring Patrick to meet you at the hospital."

Brandon asked Emma to drive to the hospital so that he could make some phone calls on the way. He first called Cathy Cutler to let her know where James was being taken, and that his pulse and blood pressure were good even though he was still unconscious. Brandon also shared that Patrick was with him and that they were on their way to the hospital.

Brandon then called his mom, Lydia, and explained how their trip had been waylaid because of the accident. He shared that he was driving the unhurt accident victim to join his injured dad and his family at the hospital. He told her that he and Emma would not likely get to her house until later that evening.

Brandon was now ready to devote all of his attention to Patrick, who was seated in the back seat blankly watching the world go by through stunned, tear-filled eyes. Little did Brandon know that the love and guidance he would provide Patrick was going to have a dramatic impact on the direction of his own life.

Chapter 4

WHEN BRANDON, EMMA AND Patrick arrived at the hospital, they were told that Patrick's dad was being admitted to the Neurocritical Care Unit. After they walked through the hospital corridors to the unit, they were advised that James was being evaluated and that a physician would speak with them once the assessment was completed. In the interim, they were asked to take a seat in the waiting area.

Brandon sensed this would be a long vigil, and as a way to help distract Patrick, Brandon initiated a conversation with him. "You mentioned earlier that you are an engineering major at UC, how do you like it?"

"Although I've only finished one full quarter and part of a second one, I'm enjoying it a lot."

"Which engineering discipline are you planning to study?" asked Emma.

"I'm going into chemical engineering. I've always enjoyed chemistry, and my chemistry teachers in high school were really good."

"Where did you go to high school?" asked Brandon.

"I went to Washington High School."

Brandon and Emma looked at each other and smiled. Patrick, noticing the glance between them, asked "Did one or both of you also go to Washington?"

Emma answered, "We both did."

"How long ago did you graduate?" inquired Patrick.

"It will be seven years this spring," replied Emma.

"I would've been in the sixth grade then," remarked Patrick with a faint smile as he recalled a simpler, very contented period of his life. "I don't think I caught either of your last names, Brandon and Emma."

"I'm Emma Brooks, and this is Brandon Campbell."

The look of recognition slowly spread across Patrick's face as his eyes widened, and he said, "As in Brandon Campbell, the football player?" As Brandon nodded affirmatively with a sheepish smile, Patrick enthusiastically exclaimed, "I remember when I was in middle school and you were chasing the state rushing record. I didn't even know much about football at that time, but our whole school was excited about the team winning the state championship. You were bigger than life in those days. I remember that you played football at Ohio State and had some ups and downs, but I don't recall the details. If you don't mind me asking, what happened?"

"My dad died in a car accident at the start of my junior year, and I struggled to recover. I haven't played football since."

Patrick's brief respite in talking to one of his childhood heroes vanished in an instant as he recalled his dad's dire situation, and tears again began welling up in his eyes.

Brandon looked deeply into Patrick's eyes and said, "Patrick, I don't know what God's plans are for your dad, but I'm going to help you get through this."

Just then, Patrick's mom, Cathy Cutler and aunt, Sally Jamison, arrived at the waiting area. Patrick shared a

CHAPTER 4

long, tearful embrace with his mom and then with Aunt Sally. He then introduced his mom and Aunt Sally to Emma and Brandon.

"Thank you so much, Brandon and Emma, for looking after Patrick. I really appreciate your kindness," said Cathy.

"We believe that God put us on that highway at that moment to take care of Patrick," said Brandon.

"I'm glad to know God was looking after Patrick through you. And I'm confident that God is also taking care of James. Has there been any news from the doctor yet?" Cathy asked Patrick.

"Not yet, Mom. We were told the doctor would talk with us as soon as Dad has been evaluated."

A few minutes later, the receptionist at the desk for the Neurocritical Care Unit called out, "Is the family for Mr. Cutler here?"

Patrick, Cathy and Sally simultaneously rose to their feet bearing anxious expressions, and the physician who was standing beside the receptionist approached them to have a private conversation. She was slender, dressed in scrubs, and looked to be about forty, with very kind eyes.

"Hi, everyone. I'm Dr. Jennifer Hammond, the neurosurgeon who is taking care of Mr. James Cutler. Are you his family members?"

Introductions were made quickly, then Cathy asked, "How is my husband doing, Dr. Hammond?"

We've done a CT scan of his brain and multiple x-rays. He has a number of rib fractures, and the CT shows that he has some moderate brain swelling, which we call cerebral edema. This is entirely consistent with the type of injury he sustained. The good news is that we don't see any bleeding in his brain."

"Is he still unconscious?" asked Patrick.

"Yes, and we will keep him sedated with medication for a few days to help decrease the swelling, so we won't know if he will regain consciousness until we withdraw the sedative. We also have him on a ventilator, even though he is able to breath on his own."

"Why is that?" asked Cathy with concern.

"There are several reasons, but the most important one is the ventilator allows us to control his breathing. By actually causing him to breathe faster than he needs, which is called hyperventilation, we can reduce the pressure on his brain."

"Can he recover from this, Dr. Hammond?" Patrick asked the one question to which they were all aching to know the answer.

"Yes, he can, but it will be very touch and go, especially over the next forty-eight hours. He will get another CT scan tomorrow so we can monitor the status of his brain swelling. He is also at high risk to develop pneumonia. Even if his brain swelling recedes, we are still uncertain as to how much underlying brain damage he may have. Like I said, he can possibly recover from this, but there are a number of potential obstacles in his path. We will have a better handle on his prognosis over the next two to three days."

"Thank you, Dr. Hammond. May we see him now?" asked Cathy nervously.

"I believe so. I'll check with the nurses to make sure they have him ready for visitors, and they will come out to escort you back to the unit to see him."

CHAPTER 4

"Thank you, Dr. Hammond," they all said in unison.

As Patrick's eyes again welled up with tears, he exclaimed, "Although much of what Dr. Hammond said was scary, it was still a relief to hear that he at least has a chance. When I first looked at him sitting next to me at the crash site, I thought he was dead." As Patrick began sobbing, his mother wrapped him in a tight embrace.

Emma and Brandon recognized that it was best to give the Cutler family some private time, so they discreetly moved to another part of the waiting room. As Patrick began to calm down, everyone exchanged mobile phone numbers, and Brandon promised Patrick he would be in touch later that evening. Brandon called his mom, Lydia, to let her know they were on their way. Emma and Brandon then left the hospital and headed for the home of Brandon's mom in suburban Cleveland.

It was shortly before 7:00 PM when they arrived at Lydia's house. Brandon's mom was so delighted to see him after the harrowing experiences Brandon had endured over the last several years following the death of his father. Even though he had gained some weight since his days of narcotic addiction and homelessness, he was much more slender now than in his days as an Ohio State football player.

"Your timing is perfect," said Lydia. "Mike Nelson will be here shortly. Thanks for your call earlier to let me know you were delayed. Because I wasn't sure when you were going to get here, I just decided to have pizza for dinner. I ordered it right after you called to say you were leaving the hospital, and it should be here soon. What do you think about eating in the basement around the fireplace?" Lydia asked.

Brandon and Emma said excitedly in unison, "That would be great!"

Brandon added as he smiled at Emma, "It would be just like old times, and we already know that it's the perfect spot for a spiritual discussion." Brandon and Emma had hung out on the couches in front of the fireplace in Brandon's basement nearly every Saturday night while they were in high school. During their senior year, they often included Sam Gilmore, one of Brandon's football teammates, and Sam taught them about Christianity and encouraged them in their faith. Tonight, Brandon, Emma and Mike hoped to have a similar conversation with Lydia, who had recently discovered that her husband, Rob, had accepted Jesus into his life shortly before his fatal car accident. Upon learning this through a letter she'd found written by Rob shortly before his death, Lydia had expressed interest in knowing more about her husband's decision.

"Before we go down to the basement," Brandon's mom said with a grin, "there's someone I'd like you to meet." Brandon looked at her quizzically, and Lydia continued, "I've been telling her all day that she gets to meet you today, and she's about to burst with excitement. I'll go get her." Lydia hurried off excitedly toward her bedroom, as Brandon and Emma waited in silent anticipation in the kitchen.

The next thing they knew, they heard commotion coming from Lydia's bedroom, followed by the approaching sound of claws clicking at full speed on the hardwood floor in the hallway. Suddenly, a medium-sized goldendoodle came charging into the kitchen, and she was the most

CHAPTER 4

beautiful dog Brandon had ever seen. She was the color of a toasted marshmallow, and her beautiful shading varied between areas of white, light tan and gold. Her belly and tail had long feathers that nearly touched the ground, and she also had prominent feathering on her ears and the back of her legs. Like her coloring, the texture of her coat varied from straight and soft as a kitten, to slightly wavy or even curly, especially along her back. Her most endearing feature, though, was her expressive, intelligent brown eyes which reflected so much love to the people around her.

When she spotted Brandon, she bounded up to him, her tail wagging nonstop as she walked in circles at his feet and leaned against him, making excited sounds. She enthusiastically received his attention and petting. Brandon's mom came into the kitchen and delightfully savored the first meeting of her son and her cherished puppy. "I see that Daisy has introduced herself," said Lydia with a smile. Daisy eagerly went to greet Emma next.

Brandon was speechless and couldn't take his eyes off Daisy. Emma gushed, "She's gorgeous! When did you get her?"

"Three and a half years ago. It was about a year after Rob died, and shortly after Brandon left home and moved to Cincinnati. I was lonely, and I needed a companion. She's been wonderful company and such a joy in my life," Lydia said with a sparkle in her eye. "Hey, what do you say we all go down to the basement and get comfortable while we wait for Mike and the pizza to arrive?" Not surprisingly, Daisy took a spot on the couch next to Brandon, laying right up against him as he gently and contentedly stroked her soft fur.

A few minutes later, Lydia, Mike, Brandon and Emma were enjoying the pizza on the leather couches in the basement in front of a roaring fire in the fireplace. They spent some time chatting and catching up. Brandon said, "Mom, thanks for having us over tonight. And I just want you to know how much I appreciate the emotional and financial support you've given me as I'm getting my priorities in order."

"Of course, honey. I'm just so glad you're getting your life back on track. I'm proud of all that you've overcome."

Then Lydia commented, "Emma and Brandon, I'm so sorry you got caught up in the mess surrounding that accident today."

Brandon replied, "Mom, I used to think that way, too. I looked at every inconvenience or interruption as a nuisance, but now I know better. When the accident occurred right in front of Emma and me, I became very aware of how God wanted to use us in that situation. I have no doubt that it was God's will that Emma and I come to the aid of Patrick Cutler today."

Brandon continued, "God is sovereign, meaning that he oversees all of the details of our lives. That doesn't mean that he necessarily causes unfortunate events to take place, like the traffic accident today, but he uses those situations for the good of those who love him. I've come to realize there's no greater joy than being in harmony with God's will."

"Why do you think that God wanted you to be involved?" asked Brandon's mom.

"I don't know, Mom, and I may never know, but I can think of some possible reasons. Maybe God just wanted me

CHAPTER 4

to be there to comfort Patrick. Possibly, he wanted me to pray with him to show him the importance of turning to God first in a crisis. Perhaps he wanted someone else who was at the accident site, and struggling with something in their life, to witness us praying together. Maybe God is preparing Patrick to be in a similar role in the future as a bystander at an accident where he needs to be the one to help. And possibly, God arranged it for my benefit, such as helping me to heal from Dad's accident. More than likely, Mom, God is using that accident to help multiple people."

"That's a fascinating perspective, Brandon," commented Lydia. "It portrays God as being loving and caring for us, rather than the image of being angry and punitive, as some people describe him. Can you please answer the question that I posed to you last evening? In your dad's letter, what does he mean by 'accepted Jesus'?"

Brandon and Mike shared a glance, and Brandon said "Mike, do you want to take this one?"

Mike responded, "I'd be happy to. What Rob meant by that phrase is that he has accepted Jesus as the Lord and Savior of his life. He believed Jesus is the Son of God and that he died on the cross for the forgiveness of our sins. Three days later, Jesus was resurrected from the dead and will live eternally. By accepting Jesus, it means you believe that Jesus died for your sins, reconciled you to God, and promised you the gift of eternal life. That is the Savior part. Stating that Jesus is also the Lord of your life means you trust him, depend on him daily and always seek to be obedient to his will."

"That sounds like a huge commitment," exclaimed Lydia. "How do I know it's the right decision?"

"Mom, God has offered us a free gift of grace," Brandon shared. "Grace is getting what we don't deserve. It's an opportunity to have all of our sins forgiven – past, present and future. All that it requires is our faith that we believe Jesus is who he said he is – the Son of God who died for the forgiveness of our sins. Once we understand the magnitude of the gift and how much Jesus endured, then we can begin to comprehend how much God loves us. It's then natural for us to love God in return and also to love others as an outpouring of our love of God."

"You're saying it all begins with me putting my faith in Jesus?" inquired Lydia.

"That's right," said Emma. "As I began reading the Bible regularly, going to church and spending more time with other Christians, I began to understand with both my mind and my heart, and it eventually became clear to me that I wanted to dedicate my life to Jesus. Going through a retreat a few weeks ago helped to further deepen my personal relationship with the Lord."

"Mom, I'm embarrassed to say that I'm clearly much more stubborn than either Emma or Dad. Looking back, I had many people in my life who were encouraging me to accept Jesus. Even though I knew in my mind it was the right thing to do, I continued to delay making my commitment. Instead, I made one bad decision after another as I tried to lead my life under my own strength, independent of God. Fortunately, though, God continued to pursue me, and my faith is actually deeper as a result of the trials I endured. Please don't misunderstand. I'm not suggesting you take the difficult path that I took. In fact, I recommend

CHAPTER 4

the more enlightened, less headstrong path that Emma and Dad traveled to find the Lord."

Mike added, "Lydia, I'd be happy to teach you in much the same way I guided your husband. We met weekly, and I shared with him the basic beliefs of Christianity and the Bible verses upon which they are grounded. Our time together was spent much more in discussion rather than me giving a lecture. Anyway, I think it really gave Rob clarity, and I'd love to have a similar conversation with you."

"That's really kind of you, Mike," said Lydia, "and I accept your generous offer. Clearly this meant a great deal to my husband, and I want to know more for myself. When do we begin?"

"How about next Saturday?"

"That sounds perfect."

As Mike was preparing to leave, Brandon escorted him to the front door. "Thank you so much, Mr. Nelson, for offering to spiritually mentor my mom."

"It's my pleasure, Brandon. Hopefully, she reaches the same decision as your dad and dedicates her life to Jesus."

"Wouldn't that be wonderful?"

"It sure would!" Mike zipped his coat. "Hey Brandon, before I go, I have a question for you. Have you ever thought about sharing your story with the world about what happened to you after you left Ohio State?"

"Not really. Do you think anyone would be interested in it?"

"It's a powerful testimony, Brandon, about how God pursued you. Given your national stature as a former elite running back at Ohio State, there would be wide appeal to the story, and God could use it to influence people's hearts."

"That's all I needed to hear, Mr. Nelson. Let's do it! How would you like to approach it?"

"I suggest we schedule some time for you to tell me your story from your perspective. I'll ask you some clarifying questions along the way and possibly interview others to add some additional perspective. After writing the story, I'd want you to edit and approve the final version, and then we would try to get it published in a national magazine, like *Sports Illustrated*."

"I expect I'll be busy for the next few days with Mr. Cutler being in the hospital, but I'm very available after that. Hey, I have an idea! Jalen Pittman, my former Ohio State teammate, is coming to Cincinnati next weekend. What would you think about me sharing my story with both of you at the same time? I think it would be helpful to see how he reacts to it."

"That's a good idea, Brandon, and I'd love to see Jalen again. I'll contact you in the next several days to arrange the details."

"That sounds great, Mr. Nelson. Good night."

As Mike walked to his car, Brandon texted Patrick Cutler, *Hi Patrick, how are you doing?*

Patrick texted back immediately, *Fine. I'm settling in for a long night of keeping a vigil in the waiting room.*

Would you like some company?

That would be great!

I'll see you shortly.

After saying goodnight to his mom, and dropping Emma off at her parents' house, Brandon headed to the hospital. On the way, he called his close friend, Jalen Pittman.

"Hey, Jalen. I was calling to see if you're still planning to come to Cincinnati next weekend."

CHAPTER 4

"Absolutely! I can't wait to see you and catch up, and hear more about the rough times you had after you quit playing football."

"I'm really looking forward to seeing you again, man, and telling you my story is another one of the reasons I'm calling. Do you remember Mike Nelson?"

"Of course. The sportswriter, and friend of both your dad and mine."

"That's right. He wants to write the story about my hardships after I left Ohio State. We both thought it would be a good idea if I shared my experiences with you and Mike at the same time. It would be helpful to Mike to observe your reaction as you hear the details."

"That's great, Brandon. I'd also love to see Mike again."

"Mike is working out the arrangements, and I'll let you know them as soon as I hear from him. The last thing I wanted to talk with you about is Dylan Hubbard. Remember him?"

"The little boy with leukemia, right? I will never forget the look on his face when you gave him the game ball in the locker room. It was the ball you threw to me for a touchdown. How's Dylan doing?"

"He's eleven now, and he is free of cancer. He's playing football, and he's asked me to coach him every Saturday morning. We had our first session this morning. Anyway, I thought it would be really fun if you surprised him at our practice next Saturday morning. We meet at the Bloomington High School football field at 9:00."

"Count me in, Brandon. That sounds like fun."

"That's great, Jalen. It'll definitely be a fun reunion. I'll see you next weekend."

Chapter 5

THE LIGHTS WERE DIMMED as Brandon entered the waiting area outside the Neurocritical Care Unit. There were groups of family members scattered throughout the space, and Brandon found Patrick sitting alone in a corner. As he approached him, he said solemnly, "Hey, Patrick. How are you holding up?"

Patrick looked up at Brandon and a smile laced with fatigue immediately spread across his face. "Thank you so much for coming, Brandon. I'm doing okay. How did the conversation go with your mom?"

"It went great. She was receptive to what we shared with her, and she agreed to meet with a family friend regularly to learn more about Jesus. How's your dad doing?"

"There's been no change. I'm glad he's holding his own. Brandon, you mentioned earlier today that your dad died in a car accident when you were in college. Would you be comfortable telling me what happened?"

"Sure," said Brandon, as he allowed his mind to revisit that difficult time. "My dad had a late business meeting in Pittsburgh, and he drove back to Cleveland after midnight with plans to travel to Columbus early that morning with my mom to attend my pre-game festivities. He apparently

CHAPTER 5

fell asleep while driving and hit a tree. The police thought he died instantly."

"I'm so sorry, Brandon. I vaguely remember your career at Ohio State ended prematurely, but I don't recall the details. Was that because of injuries, or your dad's death, or something else?"

"I had two seasons that were cut short by injuries, but after my dad died during my junior year, I lost all my desire to play and dropped out of school."

Patrick suspected there was much more to Brandon's story, but he sensed that it wasn't the appropriate time to ask him more about his life after football. Wanting to change the subject and also to be distracted from his current tragic situation, Patrick asked, "What was your senior high school football season like as you marched toward the state championship?"

It was the perfect question at that moment. For the next four hours, Brandon gleefully recounted the details of each game of that magical season as Patrick listened in awe. Brandon's eyes danced as he conveyed the highlights of each regular season game, building up to the playoffs. He then described the drama of the playoff games in even more detail and with escalating excitement.

Brandon saved the best for last, however. His masterful portrayal of the state championship game was told simultaneously from the perspective of an eyewitness, a participating player and an investigative reporter. He shared Coach Caldwell's rousing pre-game speech, the emotions of the players, the heckling between opposing players on the field, the sights and sounds in the stadium, and the multiple lead changes that had occurred prior to the pivotal last three minutes of the game.

"We were down 35-31 with about two-and-a-half minutes to go. We needed 25 yards for a touchdown, and Coach called for us to run the halfback option pass as our next play. It was a play where I would receive a backwards shovel pass as I rolled around the right side. Once I caught it, I had the choice of either running the ball or passing it to our wide receiver who was going deep. We practiced the play all the time, but we had never run it in a game because we were saving it for just the right moment when we would most likely surprise our opponent."

Brandon continued, "I'm going to share something with you that I've never told another human being, Patrick. You remember that I was close to breaking the single season rushing record that season?"

"Everyone in the state was aware that you were on the brink of breaking it," Patrick exaggerated. "Of course, I remember."

"My dad and my coaches had encouraged me to put the pursuit of the rushing record out of my mind and keep my focus completely on winning the game. As hard as I tried not to think about the record, I just couldn't help it. I was attempting to keep track of my yardage in my head throughout the game. When that crucial play of the halfback option pass occurred, I didn't know exactly how many rushing yards I had at that point, but I was pretty sure I was getting close to the record. Here's the part I have never shared with anyone else. When I received the shovel pass and had to quickly decide whether to pass it or run it myself, I saw our receiver wide open near the end zone. It

CHAPTER 5

would have been an easy pass, but the temptation for personal glory was too strong. I decided to run the ball myself, hoping to get the rushing record. Unfortunately, I fumbled the ball and almost lost the game."

Patrick understood why Brandon had never shared his secret with anyone before, because that moment revealed Brandon's underlying selfishness which prompted a disastrous decision. However, instead of Brandon's revelation lowering Patrick's impression of him, it actually fostered emotions of respect, admiration and even endearment because Brandon had shared such an unflattering secret with him.

In the wee hours of the morning, a nurse approached the corner of the waiting room where Patrick and Brandon were sitting. She said, "You're Patrick Cutler, right?" Patrick nervously nodded yes and braced himself for whatever might come. "My name is Ellen, and I'm the nurse taking care of your dad tonight. There's been a change in his condition, and I think it may be a good time for you to see him."

Patrick swallowed hard while thinking of the worst. Brandon saw the fear in Patrick's eyes, then glanced at Ellen who smiled almost imperceptibly at him.

Patrick asked, "Can my close friend, Brandon, go with me to visit my dad?"

"He sure can," responded Ellen. "Please follow me."

As Patrick entered his dad's ICU room accompanied by Ellen and Brandon, he saw his dad propped up in bed, and his eyes were open! He looked at Patrick as he entered the room. The tears of relief and gratitude came immediately and in abundance as Patrick rushed to his father's side. Because of the ventilator, James was unable to speak.

Ellen explained, "When I came into his room a short while ago to check on him, his eyes were open, and he tracked me as I moved around the room. He's still very sedated because of the medicine, but this is a very encouraging sign. We'll be getting another CT scan of his brain later this morning, and hopefully it'll show improvement in his brain swelling. We'll want to continue the sedation and the ventilator until we're certain that the swelling is improved. It's important that we don't get him too stimulated, but I wanted to give you an opportunity to see him while his eyes were open. Please take just another moment with him and then go back to the waiting room."

Patrick took his father's hand and said, "Oh, Dad. I'm so happy you're awake. Try and get some rest. You're in good hands. Mom and Aunt Sally and I have all been here for you, and we're praying hard for your recovery. We know how strong you are. I'll be just outside in the waiting room. I love you, Dad." Patrick said with a broken voice as his dad squeezed Patrick's hand.

As Patrick and Brandon got back to their familiar seats in the waiting area, Patrick could barely contain his excitement. "I thought I was never going to see my dad look into my eyes again. Wow, it's so good to feel hopeful again! Do you think I should call my mom? I know she'll be thrilled to learn the good news, but I imagine she's been awake most of the night, and I'd hate to wake her up if she just finally fell asleep."

Brandon suggested, "Why don't you text her and see if she responds."

CHAPTER 5

Patrick texted his mom as Brandon recommended, and within ten seconds, Patrick's phone rang. "Hi, Mom. I hope I didn't wake you."

"No, I was lying in bed thinking about you and wondering how you were doing, and also considering whether I should come to the hospital and join you."

"Mom, I've got some great news. Dad opened his eyes, and he clearly recognized me. I even spoke to him briefly. The nurse, Ellen, said that's a very encouraging sign."

"Oh, Patrick, that's fantastic," said Cathy excitedly as her eyes welled with tears.

Patrick continued, "Ellen said they'll do another brain CT later today to see if his brain swelling is improving."

"Do you think I should come into the hospital now?" asked Cathy.

"Mom, that's up to you, but like we talked about earlier, we may have a long road ahead of us, and it's important that we take turns so we don't get too run down. It's still really early, so I'd suggest that you either try to get some sleep or rest at home until mid-morning. It's unlikely there will be any news until then, but if there is, I'll call you. Besides, my good friend Brandon has been keeping me company and waiting with me all night, and he's been entertaining me with stories from his high school football days."

"Oh, that's nice. I knew the name Brandon Campbell sounded familiar. Is he the same Brandon Campbell who starred for your high school team about seven or eight years ago?"

"One and the same. He really helped to pass the time and take my mind off of Dad tonight as he shared the story of Washington High's run to the state championship," said Patrick as he glanced at Brandon and winked.

"That's such a blessing and a relief to know that he's with you, Patrick. I think I'll take your advice and try to get a little more rest before I come to the hospital. Is there anything you need, honey?"

"Just for Dad to continue to get better. See you in a little while, Mom."

As Patrick ended the call with his mom, he said to Brandon, "I can't thank you enough for all you've done for me today, Brandon, including looking after me at the accident site, praying with me, escorting me to the hospital and spending the night with me here in the waiting room. You also really touched me when you shared with me what was going through your mind when you fumbled in the championship game. Please know your secret is safe with me."

"It's kind of you to say all that, and I appreciate your discretion, but tonight has been very encouraging for me. Witnessing your dad open his eyes and seeing your hope restored has given me great joy."

"You said earlier tonight that you lost your desire to continue playing football after your dad's accident. Can you share what happened?"

Over the next several hours, Brandon shared the entire tale, beginning with the weekly workouts that he'd had with his dad since middle school and ending with his current relationship with Emma. He talked about the highs and lows of his Ohio State college career, and the trials of substance abuse, gambling and homelessness after he left Ohio State. He shared God's constant pursuit of him and Brandon's reluctance in making a commitment, which all

CHAPTER 5

culminated in the recent three-day Christian retreat where he dedicated his life to Jesus. During the telling of the story, Patrick was spellbound and mostly silent except for occasional gasps during the unforeseen dramatic twists in the plot. Just as Brandon was finishing his story, Patrick's mom arrived at the hospital.

With Cathy now in charge of the vigil, Patrick grabbed his mom's car keys, and then he and Brandon walked out of the hospital together with each headed to his respective home to shower, change clothes and refuel. They made plans to return to the hospital at noon to await the results of the CT scan and to keep company with Patrick's mom. As Patrick drove home, he reflected on Brandon's story and the obstacles he'd overcome. Patrick's heart told him that he was in the early stages of a lifelong friendship.

Chapter 6

AS BRANDON WAS DRIVING home from the hospital, he called Emma.

"Hi, Brandon. How are you doing?"

"I'm doing well, other than being sleep-deprived. I spent the night at the hospital with Patrick."

"That's so kind of you, Brandon. I have the sense you see a bit of yourself in Patrick with the common bond of both of your fathers being in tragic accidents."

"As always, your insight is on the mark. I shared my life story with Patrick last night, including all of the ugliness after I left Ohio State following my dad's death. I can't tell you how therapeutic it was for me, Emma. It feels like the burden of my dad's passing has been lifted from my heart. Part of the reason is because Patrick could benefit from my story, given that he may soon be facing the same situation."

"Is there any news on the status of Patrick's dad?"

"Yes, he opened his eyes overnight and clearly recognized Patrick. He's still not out of the woods yet, but the nurse said his waking up was an encouraging sign."

"That's great news, Brandon."

"I also called to let you know that I'd like to stay in Cleveland for at least another few days to support Patrick

CHAPTER 6

and his family, but I know you need to be back to work tomorrow."

"I'm way ahead of you," Emma interjected. "I anticipated that you might want to stay in town a bit longer, so I asked my dad if he would drive me back to Cincinnati this afternoon. He jumped at the chance to have four hours of uninterrupted windshield time with me. I'd like to drop by the hospital and see Patrick before I head out of town, though. When are you going back to the hospital?"

"I'm going to meet Patrick back there at noon."

"That sounds good," replied Emma. "I'll swing by there shortly after noon, before my dad and I take off for Cincinnati."

"That's great. One last thing before I let you go – how did you think the conversation went with my mom last night?"

"It was perfect. She seemed interested, inquisitive and open to what we shared with her, and she was genuinely excited about learning more from Mr. Nelson."

"Those were my exact impressions as well, Emma. I'll see you at the hospital in a little while. I love you."

"I love you, too. Bye."

Brandon and Patrick arrived at the waiting room within a few minutes of each other, and joined Patrick's mom.

"Any news, Mom?" Patrick asked.

"They just took him for another CT scan, so hopefully we'll get those results soon."

"Have you seen him since you've been here?" Patrick asked hopefully.

"They let me go into his room briefly, but he was asleep. The nurse told me that they've increased the dose of his sedative since he opened his eyes with you. They prefer to keep him deeply sedated to protect his brain until the swelling has improved. Otherwise, it sounds like he remains stable, and he appears comfortable, although it's still a shock for me to see him on that breathing machine."

As Patrick, Cathy and Brandon were talking, Emma arrived with a grocery bag filled with a wide assortment of snacks, including apples, bananas, cashews, carrot sticks, chips, candy and a box of Ding Dongs. Patrick immediately tore open the box and grabbed one for himself and tossed one to Brandon. While the guys relished their treat, Emma sat down next to Cathy and asked, "How is James doing?"

"About the same. He's getting another CT scan of his brain now, and we hope to hear the results within the next hour or two. By the way, thank you for the snacks." She smiled as she glanced at Patrick and Brandon who were savoring their Ding Dongs and laughing while sharing their childhood memories of them. "I understand you've seen Patrick around the UC campus. Are you a student there also?" asked Cathy.

"No, I work at Cincinnati Children's Hospital as a nurse on the oncology floor."

"You must see some heartbreaking situations."

"Yes, but it's more than balanced by the joys of the children who are cured. I'm praying that you and Patrick get to experience that joy with James' recovery."

"Thank you, Emma. We can use all the prayers we can get."

"I'm sorry I can't stay longer," said Emma, "but my dad is driving me back to Cincinnati this afternoon because

CHAPTER 6

I'm working tomorrow. I'll keep in touch with Brandon about James' status. Let me give you my mobile number, and please reach out to me if you need anything at all – including more Ding Dongs," Emma said with a smile as she glimpsed at Brandon and Patrick, who were engaged in their own conversation.

"Thank you for everything, Emma, and I hope to be reaching out to you within the next few days to share some answered prayers regarding James' condition."

Emma said goodbye to Brandon and Patrick and departed.

Brandon, Patrick and Cathy had been chatting for only a few minutes after Emma left, when Dr. Hammond approached and sat down among them. "I'd like to give all of you an update on James' condition and the game plan for his treatment. I have just come from radiology where I reviewed his CT scan with the radiologist. It shows dramatic improvement in his cerebral edema – the swelling in his brain. I'm very encouraged. Clinically, he remains stable, and no other complications have arisen. If he does well overnight, I plan to begin reducing the dose of his sedative tomorrow and allow him to hopefully begin waking up. We will watch his progress closely, and if he continues to improve, we will begin to gradually wean him off the ventilator in a day or two. It's still touch and go, but I'm cautiously optimistic after seeing his scan."

"That's encouraging news, Dr. Hammond. Thank you so much for sharing it with us, and for all you've done for James," said Cathy.

After Dr. Hammond left, Cathy and Patrick were giddy with relief. Their hope was surging that James might possibly recover from the accident. "Let's see if we can look in on him now," Cathy suggested to Patrick.

They checked with the receptionist in the waiting area, who verified that it was a good time for them to visit James. As they entered his room, he appeared to be sleeping comfortably, even though they both knew that his mental state was being controlled by the sedatives and his breathing was being sustained by the ventilator. Cathy studied him as he lay in the ICU bed and tried to imagine that he was instead taking a peaceful Sunday afternoon nap on the couch at home. As she watched him, she realized how close she came to losing him, and large droplets of tears silently began running down her cheeks. Patrick put his arm around her shoulders, and she tried not to think about the fact that Patrick could have also died in the accident. Her sadness began to evaporate as she realized God's blessing in saving both of them.

As Patrick and Cathy returned to the waiting room, Brandon said with a smile, "I have the perfect therapy for the two of you. As I was looking through the bag of snacks that Emma brought, I noticed that she slipped a game of Bananagrams into the bag. Do you know how to play?" Both Cathy and Patrick shook their heads no.

"It's easy," continued Brandon. "It's sort of like building your own crossword puzzle as fast as you can. Let's sit at the table over there, and I'll teach you how to play. I'm sure you'll pick it up quickly." Within several minutes, they were all engrossed in the game and laughing at each other for words they'd used that were made up.

CHAPTER 6

After playing multiple games over nearly two hours, Cathy said, "Lack of sleep is finally catching up to me. Would the two of you mind if I go home and get some rest?"

"Of course not, Mom. Brandon and I will hold down the fort, and I'll let you know if there are any changes with Dad."

After Cathy left, Brandon asked, "How are you holding up?"

"All things considered, pretty well. Like Mom, I think the lack of sleep over the last several days is beginning to take its toll, but the news about the CT results was such a great boost." Patrick paused for a moment in deep thought, and his eyes seemed to darken. "I so appreciate what you shared with me last night about the events of your life after your dad's accident, and it got me to thinking about how my life would change if my dad doesn't survive. How did you get through that really challenging period in your life?"

"It was only through the grace of God. I could have easily died or had a much different outcome."

"That's what has been bothering me, Brandon. How could a loving God allow your dad to die suddenly and then let you go through all that suffering in the aftermath? How could he let my dad also endure such a tragic accident?"

Brandon reflected for a moment to gather his thoughts and then shared, "I don't know the details or the reasons for God's plans, but in my Bible time this morning I was reading chapter 8 of Romans, which tells us that God works all things for the good of those who love him. I know that God was pursuing me at the time of my dad's death, but I was reluctant to commit my life to him. The very dark path that God allowed me to travel ultimately resulted in helping me recognize how much God loves me. It convinced me I want to spend my life glorifying him. So that's one way that God took those tragic events and used them for my good. A second way is that I can use my experience to help comfort you."

After pausing thoughtfully, Brandon continued, "Before tonight, I associated football with my dad and his sudden death. As a result, all of my football memories were painful because they reminded me of losing my dad. By recounting the fun of my senior high school football season with you, it has reminded me of all the joy of that time in my life and my dad's place in it. Those memories are once again generating pleasant feelings instead of painful ones. So, there's three ways that God has used our tragedies for good, and there are likely many more beneficial impacts he has orchestrated."

"I'm beginning to understand," Patrick said pensively.

"It took me a number of years and life experiences before I fully grasped it." Brandon paused a moment then exclaimed, "Jesus famously said 'Man does not live on bread alone', and a loose translation could be that man does not live on Ding Dongs alone either. I'm famished. What do you think about getting some dinner in the cafeteria?"

Patrick instantly brightened and enthusiastically proclaimed, "Let's do it!"

Chapter 7

BRANDON AND PATRICK FILLED their trays in the hospital cafeteria and found a table in a quiet corner. Brandon said a prayer before they began eating.

"Tell me about your dad and your relationship with him," Brandon inquired as they started dining.

"My most pleasant memory of my dad was when he was the coach of several of my youth soccer teams. We would talk strategy before the games and break down our team's performance afterwards. My dad would spend a lot of time with me in our backyard honing my soccer skills. He was my biggest fan on the field, but he was careful to not treat me preferentially. As coach, my dad was all about the team, and I think he enjoyed it more when I got an assist than when I scored a goal. Dad and I were really close in those days."

"Are you and your dad not as tight as you used to be?"

"That's a difficult question to answer, Brandon. The last few days have clarified for me how much I love my dad. I know that he also loves me very much, but our relationship is different than what it was when I was younger. My dad had a very rough upbringing. His parents were divorced when he was about ten years old, and his dad was an abusive alcoholic. His dad's father was also an alcoholic and a mean drunk. Although my dad has been openly determined to ensure that the cycle of alcoholism and abuse ends with him, the scars of his childhood are sometimes apparent. Most of the time, he's quiet and reserved, and he has difficulty expressing affection. At times, he's temperamental and quick to anger. He works as a financial analyst for a large company, and I know he's under a lot of pressure from his job. Having said all that, my relationship with my dad is no less loving, but I think the demons from his childhood and the stress of his job have made him more withdrawn and joyless over the last several years."

"I remember you telling me a few days ago that your dad was insistent that you come home for a visit this weekend."

"That's right. He's very proud of me, and I think he derives some joy by living vicariously through me."

"Is your dad a man of faith?"

"Sort of. My dad, my mom and I have gone to church fairly regularly all of my life. My mom's faith is very strong, and she has helped to instill it in me. My dad, on the other hand, hasn't seemed to embrace his faith very deeply. Instead of developing a personal relationship with Jesus, it's almost as if he uses church-going as a tool to ensure that he ends the cycle of abuse from his previous generations. I really wish he could learn to depend more on God, and less on his own strength, and to fully appreciate God's love for him."

"I know just the way to help your dad. Do you remember me telling you about the three-day Christian retreat that I attended about a month ago?"

"Yes, of course," replied Patrick. "You said it was the most powerful spiritual event of your life."

"That's right. The next retreat is in July. The host church is really close to the UC campus. Do you think we could

CHAPTER 7

convince your dad to attend if he has healed from his injuries?"

Patrick said excitedly, "I think I can, especially if I agree to experience it with him. Now all we need to do is help him recover!"

Patrick and Brandon again spent the night in the waiting room. Exhaustion and sleep deprivation had finally won the battle over both of them, as they slept through most of the night on the couches. Patrick was awakened early the next morning by Ellen, the ICU nurse.

"Good morning, Patrick. I was on duty last night and was again taking care of your father. We started easing off of his sedatives a few hours ago, and he is beginning to awaken. I thought you might like to see him. If he does well between now and noon, we may possibly begin to back off of the ventilator."

"Thank you, Ellen. That's an answered prayer," said Patrick gleefully as he quickly got to his feet. Brandon joined Patrick and Ellen as they entered James' ICU room, and they found him sitting up in bed with his eyes open and clear. He looked at Patrick as soon as he entered the room and immediately attempted to smile as well as he could with an endotracheal tube taped into his mouth. Patrick rushed to his bedside and threw his arms around his dad's neck in an awkward hug because of the ventilator. Tears of joy were streaming down Patrick's cheeks. As Patrick withdrew from the hug, he looked at his dad who noiselessly mouthed, "Where's Mom?"

"Mom's resting at home right now. She's been taking the day shifts, and I've been doing the night shifts, along with my friend Brandon," Patrick replied as he gestured toward Brandon. "As soon as I get back to the waiting area, I'll call Mom and tell her the good news. I expect she'll be here shortly."

James nodded his head with understanding and then glanced questioningly at Brandon.

Patrick, astutely interpreting his dad's expression, went on to explain, "Brandon was driving one of the cars behind us on the highway when the accident occurred. He helped me out of our car and has essentially been by my side ever since. Brandon was…"

Patrick saw his dad's eyes widen with recognition as he studied Brandon, and then James raised his right arm as if he were going to throw an imaginary football. He then raised his arms in the O-H positions, and Brandon, never more joyfully, completed the I-O portion of the Ohio State cheer.

Ellen began laughing, then said, "It looks like his brain is functioning pretty well, but let's allow him to rest a little more before we get him too active. My shift is almost over, but I'll get him prepared for your mom's arrival."

After returning to the waiting room, Patrick immediately called his mom who arrived at the hospital less than an hour later. For the rest of the morning, Cathy and Patrick alternately took turns talking to James while the doctors and nurses assessed whether it was safe to take him off the ventilator. After allowing him to breathe on his own without ventilator support through the endotracheal tube for an hour without any ill effects, the tube was removed shortly after noon. Although James' voice was quite hoarse, he was very glad to be able to speak to his loved ones who were at his bedside.

CHAPTER 7

"I remember having the most vivid dream," said James. "I dreamed I was involved in a severe accident, and I was searching frantically for Patrick at the accident site when I suddenly spotted him. Just as suddenly, he vanished, and I thought I'd never see him again."

"I wonder, Dad, if your dream correlates to you briefly waking up a couple of nights ago," said Patrick. "I was here, and you seemed to recognize me before you fell back to sleep."

"It's hard to say if the dream was related," said Cathy, "but I know how close I came to losing both of you. I am so, so grateful to have you both alive, and I will never take that for granted."

Brandon was relaxing in the waiting room when he got a call from Mike Nelson. "Hi, Mr. Nelson. How are you?"

"I'm great, Brandon. I sure enjoyed the time at your mom's home on Saturday evening. She seemed really receptive to learning more about Christianity."

"I agree, and thank you again for your willingness to mentor her."

"I'm happy to do it, Brandon. I'm calling to make final arrangements for our interview about your story. Are you still up for it?"

"Absolutely," said Brandon, "especially knowing it may be helpful to others in a similar predicament. By the way, Jalen Pittman is excited about participating as well. I have two others who may also provide some valuable perspective. The first is Sam Gilmore. Sam was not only my high school teammate, but he was a big part of my spiritual journey after high school."

"I remember Sam," said Mike, "and I think that's a great idea. Who's the second person?"

"His name is Patrick Cutler, and he's the young man who was involved in the accident on Saturday where his dad was seriously injured."

"Oh yeah, I remember you talking about him on Saturday evening. How's his dad doing?"

"He seems to be doing well. He's now awake, off the ventilator, and doesn't seem to have any serious brain injury."

"That's great, Brandon. Why do you think Patrick would be someone worthwhile to participate in the interview?"

"He also went to Washington High School and was in middle school when we won the state championship. I told him my story while we were spending the nights together in the waiting room outside of the ICU. I think his emotional reaction to certain parts of the story will give you some valuable perspective on how to craft it to maximize the impact. The other reason is that I feel a bond to Patrick, in part because of the common experience of our dads' accidents, and I would like him to meet my closest friends."

"That's good enough for me, Brandon. Please extend the invitation to Sam and Patrick. We will be meeting in the Graduate Hotel near the UC campus on Saturday at 1:00 PM. I've reserved a meeting room there, so just ask at the front desk when you arrive."

"That sounds great, Mr. Nelson."

"I have one more thing to share with you, Brandon. I had a conversation with my editor at the *Plain Dealer* about this story, and he gave me permission to pursue publication in a national magazine, such as *Sports Illustrated*, given the

CHAPTER 7

length of the story and the wide appeal. Take care, Brandon. I'll see you on Saturday."

"Wow, that sounds amazing. I'm looking forward to the interview, Mr. Nelson."

As Brandon was ending his call with Mike Nelson, Patrick returned to the waiting room. "Patrick, I've been thinking. Now that your dad's condition seems to be improving, I'm considering heading back to Cincinnati tomorrow if that's okay with you."

"Of course, Brandon. I really appreciate everything you've done."

"Do you know when you'll be going back to UC?"

"Assuming that my dad continues to make good progress, I think I'll ask Aunt Sally to drive me back on Thursday."

"Good. Hey, I have an invitation for you – only if it's convenient, and only if you weren't planning to come back to Cleveland next weekend to visit your dad. Mike Nelson, the sports journalist for the *Cleveland Plain Dealer*, is a family friend, and he'd like to write the story about my adventure after I left Ohio State – the same story I shared with you a couple of days ago. He's going to interview me on Saturday, and a couple of my friends will be there to fill in the details and give their perspective. You may remember me telling you about Sam Gilmore, my old high school teammate, and Jalen Pittman, my former OSU teammate. Both of them will be there."

"I'm honored to be included, but I'm not sure what value I can bring, since I didn't know you personally during that time."

"Mr. Nelson appreciates having a test audience as I tell the story. It allows him to assess the parts that are the most intriguing, shocking and engaging, and why. He uses that information to craft the story for its greatest impact. Also, I'd like you to meet my closest friends."

"Count me in, Brandon! By the way, will you be doing your practice with Dylan on Saturday morning?"

"Yes, why?"

"No reason, I was just wondering," said Patrick nonchalantly.

"Okay. Well, I'm gonna head out now. I'd like to spend the evening with my mom," said Brandon. "I'll drop by the hospital tomorrow before I head to Cincinnati. See you then."

After Brandon left, Patrick called Emma.

"Hi, Emma, this is Patrick Cutler."

"Hi, Patrick. How's your dad doing?"

"He's doing really well. He is awake and off the ventilator. Best of all, he doesn't seem to have any significant brain injury. Our prayers have been answered, Emma."

"That's great news, Patrick."

"I wanted to share with you how much I appreciate all that you and Brandon have done for my family. I was hoping to come to Brandon's practice with Dylan on Saturday and surprise Brandon with my show of support. Do you know when and where they meet?"

"You're so welcome, Patrick." Emma added, "What a thoughtful idea. They meet at the Bloomington High School field at 9:00 AM. Ironically, Bloomington was the school that Brandon's team beat in the state championship seven years ago. Since you're coming, I think I'll come too, and surprise Dylan. Also, Jalen Pittman, Brandon's former OSU teammate, is going to be a surprise guest as well on Saturday morning."

"It should be a lot of fun. I'll see you then, Emma."

Chapter 8

ON THURSDAY, FIVE DAYS after the Cutler accident, Coach Rodney Anderson was strolling down the hall of the Woody Hayes Athletic Center – the football complex at The Ohio State University. Coach Anderson was still the running backs coach, just like in the days when Brandon Campbell played at Ohio State. Coach Anderson encountered Kevin Perkins, the offensive line coach for the Buckeyes.

"Hi, Rodney. I haven't had the chance to congratulate you on landing that hotshot recruit from Miami, Tristin Garner," said Coach Perkins.

"Thanks, Kevin. Although I'm delighted we signed him because he has a world of talent, I have some reservations."

"Why is that?"

"Did you see the coverage of his signing day on ESPN?"

"No. What happened?"

"It was a circus, but the concerning part was his remarks after he revealed his selection of Ohio State. He talked about winning three Heisman's – two here and one at a new school during his junior year."

"Sounds like he has some lofty goals."

"My concern isn't so much about his dreams but more about his comments being so self-centered. His ego and attitude could really be damaging to the chemistry and culture of our team," said Coach Anderson.

"Do you remember when Brandon Campbell was a freshman and we were concerned that he would alienate his teammates because of all the accolades and publicity he received during his senior year in high school?"

"I do remember, and it turned out to be just the opposite. He was humble and earned the respect of the other players through his work ethic and performance on the field. Wait, Kevin, you've given me an idea. I wonder if Brandon would be open to joining our coaching staff in a role that would include mentoring Tristin. I haven't talked with Brandon in a long time, and I owe him a call."

"It would be nice to have Brandon around again. He just energized the team when he was here. It's tragic how his brilliant playing career was cut short by his dad's sudden death."

"So true. Thanks for giving me the creative idea, Kevin. I'm going to discuss it with Herb right now," said Coach Anderson.

Rodney Anderson found Herb Weaver, the head football coach, in his office.

"Hi, Herb. Do you have a minute?" asked Rodney.

"Always for you, Rodney. What's up?"

"I was just talking with Kevin about how valuable it would be to our team to have a coach whose responsibilities would include mentoring our players. We began talking about Brandon Campbell as a possible candidate for that role. What do you think?"

"I think it's a great idea. We have the dollars in the budget to create the position, and I love your suggestion of

CHAPTER 8

hiring Brandon Campbell to fill it. It would be really nice to reconnect him to Ohio State football. He was such an electric player and a tremendous influence on our team culture. I tried to reach him multiple times after he dropped out, but he never returned my calls. Good luck, Rodney. Please let me know what he says."

Later that afternoon, Brandon's phone rang, and although he only vaguely recognized the number, he took the call. "Hello?"

"Hi, Brandon. It's great to hear your voice. This is Coach Anderson."

"Hi, Coach! It's great to hear your voice as well."

"I realized that I no longer had your current cell phone number, so I called your mom to get it."

"I lost my phone about five months ago and had to get a new one." For a split second, Brandon recalled having to give up his cell phone during his destitute period of homelessness. He quickly shook off the thought and returned to the present moment. "I'm so glad you were resourceful in finding me."

"Brandon, I regret how your Ohio State playing career ended so abruptly after your father's accident. How are you doing now?"

"I had a really difficult time for a few years, but I'm much better now. You always encouraged me to be intentional about my spiritual life, and recently I committed my life to Jesus. That's been a huge part of my recovery."

"That's awesome, Brandon! While you were here, I had the impression that Jesus was pursuing you, so I'm really happy for you. Speaking of pursuing you, I have something that I'd like to discuss with you. Some of the other coaches and I were talking about the positive influence you had on the energy and culture of our team when you were here. I was wondering if you'd consider joining our coaching staff. We would still need to work out all the details, but one of your responsibilities would be to mentor some of our younger players. I discussed the idea with Coach Weaver, and he enthusiastically supports it. What do you think? Are you interested?"

"It's so ironic that you called, because you've been on my mind. I was going to reach out to you. I'm honored that you'd think of me for this role, Coach. Something really unusual took place this past week. I was driving to Cleveland and happened to be right behind an accident that involved a young man and his dad on the highway. The young man was uninjured, but his dad was in a coma for a couple of days."

"Oh, no. I'm sorry to hear that."

"He's now doing better, but for those few days, I spent a lot of time with his son at the hospital. We talked at length about the hard times I endured after my dad was killed in his car accident. It was very therapeutic for me, and it was as if a huge emotional burden was lifted from my heart. I once again can feel the exhilaration from my football memories, like the one when I threw that touchdown pass to Jalen Pittman on that halfback option pass. That's a long way of saying that this is the first time since my dad died that I have again felt passion about football. I've also been thinking about returning to Ohio State... but as a player instead of a coach."

"Are you serious?!?" exclaimed Coach Anderson excitedly. "What kind of shape are you in? Have you been working out?

CHAPTER 8

I know you didn't exhaust your eligibility, but I'll need to check with the NCAA, given your hiatus of nearly five years."

"I'm very serious, Coach. My desire for the game is back. I haven't been working out, but you're aware that I know how to get my body ready for football season."

"I can't make any promises on playing time, Brandon. You'll have to earn it like everyone else. But I'd love to have you back! I'll check on your eligibility with the NCAA, and also on availability of scholarship money. This conversation didn't go the way I expected, but you could possibly have even more impact on the chemistry of the team as a player than you would as a coach. I'll get back with you soon, Brandon."

"Thanks, Coach. Bye."

The call with Coach Anderson had happened so suddenly and so unexpectedly that Brandon felt a little overwhelmed as he tried to process it. He made a mental note to discuss it with Emma at his first opportunity.

Chapter 9

BRANDON LOCKED THE DOOR on his modest apartment, a place he'd rented with his mom's financial help, and headed to the Bloomington High School football field early Saturday morning for his practice with Dylan. As he drove, he reminisced about having the same practices with his dad every Saturday morning for years. All of the workouts that Brandon's dad had created had been preserved and were recently discovered in his mom's home. Having his father's handwritten documents made Brandon feel closer to him than ever. Brandon and his dad always enjoyed football together, and it was one of the primary pillars of their relationship. When his dad died, Brandon's love of football died with him. Since then, Brandon could only associate pain with his memory of playing football. However, now that Brandon had shared the story of his football career in great detail dating back to middle school with Patrick in the waiting room of the hospital, the memories once again evoked the euphoria Brandon and his dad shared over football. The idea of possibly playing again for Ohio State made Brandon very excited.

Brandon arrived at the field shortly before Dylan and his dad, Brad. He began setting up cones on the field in preparation for some agility drills. Brandon was really

CHAPTER 9

looking forward to seeing Jalen and witnessing the reunion of Jalen and Dylan. Brandon wasn't aware of Emma's and Patrick's plans to be additional surprise participants. Jalen, Emma and Patrick were hiding behind a grove of pine trees just beyond the end zone.

After Dylan had warmed up and started doing agility drills, Jalen ran onto the field and yelled, "Who is that young man? He looks like Ohio State material!"

Dylan immediately recognized his old friend, Jalen, and ran to midfield where he met him and gave him a hug. At that instant, Emma appeared on the field and shouted, "Save a hug for me, Dylan. I should have gotten one first because I've always been a better football player than Jalen!"

Dylan looked at Emma and giggled, then he promptly ran to her to give her a hug. Suddenly, another person came sprinting toward the group at full speed and yelling, "And I'm faster than Jalen and Brandon combined!" Patrick wasn't sure what that meant, but it was all he could think of to say in the moment.

Brandon yelled, "Patrick!", as he trotted to intercept his new friend and give him a hug. "What are you doing here?"

"I know how important these workouts with Dylan are to you, in part, because they honor your dad's memory, and I wanted to support you."

"That's great, Patrick. How's your dad doing?"

"He's getting stronger every day, and he may even get discharged from the hospital today."

"That's wonderful news. Obviously, you've already met Jalen. Let me introduce you to Dylan and his dad."

Dylan was elated to have so much participation and encouragement in his workout. Patrick, especially, enthusiastically praised him. He also had a keen ability to identify the fine details that would make a drill more effective. For instance, when it was time for Dylan to do thirty-yard sprints, Patrick suggested having Brandon and Jalen start ten yards behind Dylan, and Emma begin five yards in front of him. It made the sprints much more competitive and fun, and of course, reignited the usual spirited discourse from their playing days between Brandon and Jalen about which one was faster.

After they had completed the workout exactly as Brandon's dad had created it for Brandon over a decade ago, Patrick suggested that they have a touch football scrimmage with Emma and Dylan choosing the sides. Dylan's team included his dad and Brandon, and Emma was paired with Jalen and Patrick.

After about twenty minutes, the score was tied at two touchdowns each, and Patrick suggested that the team who scored next would win the game. It was Dylan's team's turn to be on offense. After three plays, they were unable to move the ball. In the huddle before their fourth and possibly final play, Brandon suggested that they try the halfback option pass. Dylan's eyes widened with excitement as he recalled witnessing Brandon's heroics with that play when he was a running back at Ohio State.

Brandon hiked the ball to Dylan's dad, and then he ran downfield for a pass. Brad passed the ball backwards to Dylan who was sweeping to the right. Jalen, who anticipated the play, was closing quickly on Dylan. Dylan cocked his arm to throw it downfield to Brandon. As he started to make the throw, Jalen jumped to block it. Dylan handily completed his pump fake and sidestepped the airborne

CHAPTER 9

Jalen without being touched and started sprinting downfield. As Patrick approached to make the "tackle", Dylan deftly cut to his left, leaving Patrick grasping at air. Dylan then outraced a chasing Emma to the end zone. All the competitors cheered wildly for Dylan and his brilliant touchdown.

Jalen was recalling a similar play five years ago at Ohio State when Brandon threw a touchdown pass to Jalen. Both Brandon and Jalen signed the ball and gave it to Dylan in the locker room after the game. Dylan was in the midst of treatment for leukemia at the time.

As Jalen approached Dylan, he said, "You're going to be signing a football for me one of these days if you keep playing like that."

Dylan, still joyfully aglow with scoring a touchdown among his football heroes, recognized the meaning behind Jalen's statement and said proudly, "I still sleep with that football every night." Jalen felt his heart melt and a tear came to his eye.

As Brandon was catching his breath after the last play, he felt the phone in his pocket vibrating. He glanced at the number coming across the screen, and smiled on the inside with recognition. He answered, "Good morning," and after a pause, "Yes, sir," and after another pause, "That's great news. I look forward to hearing more of the details soon. Thank you." Brandon put the phone back in his pocket and noticed that the others were looking at him curiously.

"Guess what, everyone... I'm returning to Ohio State to play football in the fall!"

Dylan and Patrick immediately began screaming and jumping up and down in celebration. Jalen noticed that

Emma's expression reflected her mixed reaction of surprise, curiosity and disappointment.

Chapter 10

ON THE OTHER SIDE of town, it was a quiet Saturday morning in a residential neighborhood constructed in the 1950's. The homes were built very close together, and about one in five of them was abandoned. Half of them had rickety chain-link fences caging the periphery of the tiny properties.

Antonio Alvarez and his girlfriend, Valeria, had just enjoyed a late breakfast and were playing with their two-year-old daughter, Sofia, in the front room of their rented home. They had recently moved to the neighborhood because Antonio's line of work necessitated frequent relocations. Sofia had reached the stage where she was proficient at walking, and her preference was to gleefully run whenever she could. At the moment, she was giggling as she alternately ran back and forth between her parents with their loving encouragement.

The blissful moment was shattered by the ominous sound of two semi-automatic rifles fired from a passing car at the front windows of Antonio's house. He instinctively grabbed Sofia and dove to the floor as he shouted at Valeria, "Get down, get down!" The onslaught lasted only a few seconds as the car sped away.

Antonio cautiously lifted his head and glanced at Sofia, who was lying beside him. She began screaming in terror. Antonio attempted to console her as he looked for Valeria on the other side of the room. She was lying face down and not moving. Antonio went to her quickly and gently rolled her onto her back. The front of her blouse was stained with blood, and she was non-responsive. Sofia began crying, "Mama, Mama!" Antonio quickly scooped Sofia into his arms and dialed 911 on his cell phone. When the operator answered, Antonio said urgently, "Please send an ambulance. There has been a shooting, and my girlfriend is hurt badly."

"What is your name, sir?"

"Lucas Delgado." Antonio was very accustomed to lying about his name.

"Your address, sir?"

"667 Franklin Street."

"I'll send an ambulance immediately."

"Please hurry," Antonio pleaded.

Antonio quickly put Sofia in her room and closed the door in spite of her vigorous protests. Fortunately, she had not yet learned how to open a door.

Antonio went to Valeria and quickly unbuttoned her blouse and saw two wounds in her chest, both of which were actively bleeding. He urgently grabbed two towels from the laundry basket and began applying pressure to her chest, as he spoke soothingly to Valeria while kneeling at her side. "Honey, wake up. Don't leave me. I love you. I'm so sorry. This is all my fault. Please don't die. Please!" Tears clouded his vision as he became aware of the sound of a siren a few blocks away.

CHAPTER 10

The ambulance and police cruisers arrived almost simultaneously. The EMTs immediately began working on Valeria under Antonio's desperate observance. He heard one of the EMTs say to his colleague, "I can't feel a pulse." The second EMT responded, "And her pupils are fixed and dilated."

In that moment, one of the police officers approached Antonio and asked, "Are you Lucas Delgado, the person who called 911 about the shooting?"

Antonio was completely distracted with Valeria, and it took him a moment to turn to the police officer who was talking to him. He responded, "What? Oh, yeah. I was the one who called."

As Antonio turned toward Officer Bolton, the policeman vaguely recognized Antonio. He said, "Would you excuse me one moment?"

Officer Bolton walked to his partner standing a few feet away and whispered to him, "This guy looks familiar to me. He says his name is Lucas Delgado, but he might be lying. Would you go out to the cruiser and scan the photos on the outstanding arrest warrants and see if he is listed?"

Antonio was engrossed in watching the EMTs working on Valeria, and he didn't notice Officer Bolton's partner studying his face before he went outside.

Officer Bolton stepped back to Antonio and said, "Can you tell me what happened, Mr. Delgado?"

"Valeria and I were playing with our daughter in this room when suddenly multiple shots from the street were fired through this window," stated Antonio as he pointed to the window.

"Is Valeria your wife?"

"She's my girlfriend."

"Where is your daughter?"

"She's in the bedroom back there," said Antonio, motioning toward the bedroom.

"Do you know why anyone would want to do this to you?" inquired Officer Bolton.

"I have no idea," Antonio lied.

Bolton's partner approached and said to Officer Bolton, "Can I speak with you privately for a moment?"

The two of them stepped several feet to one side, and Bolton's partner said in a hushed voice, "You were right. This guy is Antonio Alvarez, and we have been after him for a long time."

"The narcotics dealer?"

"One and the same."

"His really bad day just got worse."

Antonio had been watching the EMTs work on Valeria. In spite of resuscitative efforts, her EKG showed no activity, and he knew she was gone.

Officer Bolton approached him and said, "Antonio Alvarez?"

Without thinking, Antonio responded, "Yes?"

"You are under arrest." Officer Bolton proceeded to handcuff him and read him his Miranda rights.

"Before you take me, can I say goodbye to my daughter?"

Officer Bolton escorted Antonio to the bedroom, where Sofia was quietly weeping while lying on her side on the floor and sucking her thumb.

Antonio got down on his knees next to Sofia who stood up and hugged him for several minutes. Antonio whispered

CHAPTER 10

to her, "Mommy is hurt and is going to the hospital. I need to go too, but these nice people are going to take care of you."

"But I want to go with you, Daddy."

"I'm sorry, sweetie, but you can't. I'll see you again as soon as I can."

Sofia continued to cling to her father and cry quietly for several more minutes, until a female officer entered the room to take custody of Sofia. As Officer Bolton walked Antonio out of the room and toward the waiting police cruiser, he said, "C'mon, Diablo. It's time to go."

Diablo was the alias Antonio used with his illicit drug clientele, including a former addict named Brandon Campbell.

Chapter 11

AFTER THE CELEBRATION OF Brandon's announcement had subsided, everyone began gathering their belongings which were strewn along the sideline.

Emma approached Brandon and said evenly, "Can we discuss your decision to return to Ohio State to play football?"

Brandon recognized he was about to have a very serious conversation with Emma, and he responded, "Of course, Emma. I'll tell Jalen I need a few minutes before we meet for breakfast." He shouted, "Jalen, I'll meet you shortly at Panera."

Jalen responded, "Okay, see you in a few." Brandon then turned his full attention to Emma.

Emma began, "Brandon, I'm very happy for you, but I'm also confused and disappointed by your news. You know how badly I've been hurt by your behavior in our recent past. The part that was most painful for me was that you weren't forthcoming with me about the challenges you were facing, especially with your addictions. By not confiding in me, you eroded my trust in you. I've felt recently that our relationship has really been moving in the right direction, and I was beginning to hope that we could recapture what we once had. Your announcement today has shaken me,

CHAPTER 11

though. How could you pursue returning to Ohio State to play football without at least sharing your plans with me? Don't you think that your plan to move back to Columbus affects our relationship, or is that not important to you?" Emma was trying her best to keep her emotions under control, as tears began to stream down her face.

"Oh, Emma, I'm so sorry. This is not how I wanted you to find out, but I just got caught up in the moment with everyone standing around me when I got the call from Coach Anderson. Here's what happened. Last weekend, I spent those long nights with Patrick in the hospital, and I shared with him the story of my football career, as well as what happened to me after I left Ohio State. As I told him about the highlights of my playing days, especially the details of the state championship game, I again felt joy associated with football, rather than the pain of my dad's death.

Brandon continued, "As I drove back to Cincinnati on Wednesday with the box of my dad's workouts right beside me in the car, I began to feel my love of football seep back into my heart for the first time since Dad's accident. I allowed my mind to wander, and I began to fantasize about playing at Ohio State again. It was really no more than reminiscing about an enjoyable time in my life. I wasn't making any plans to pursue it. Then the very next day, Coach Anderson called out of the blue and asked me if I'd be interested in a coaching position that would involve mentoring some of the players. I introduced the idea of returning as a player instead. I thought he seemed open to the idea, but he needed to check with the NCAA on whether I was still eligible, and also with Coach Weaver on whether any scholarships were available. Honestly, I didn't expect to hear from him for several weeks, and I really thought it was a very long shot that all of the pieces would fall into place. My first thought after the call was that I needed to discuss all of this with you, but frankly, I was still trying to process it myself."

"One last thing, Emma, before you respond. You are, hands down, the most important aspect of my life. If you said, 'Brandon, I'd prefer that you not return to Ohio State', I would call Coach Anderson immediately and tell him I'm not coming."

Emma embraced Brandon and softly said, "Thank you, Brandon. That all makes me feel better." After a pause and while still embracing Brandon, she asked, "If you did return to Ohio State, how would that impact you and me?"

"As I mentioned, this has happened so fast that I haven't had any time to think about the details. I do know that I can hardly bear the thought of being separated from you. Would you consider trying to get a job at Nationwide Children's Hospital in Columbus?"

Emma leaned back in the embrace, looked into his eyes and said, "I love you, Brandon, and I want to be supportive of you. Nationwide has a very special place in my heart from my nursing school days. I'd love to go back there. Let me give it some thought. You'd better get going and not keep Jalen waiting any longer." Brandon and Emma kissed, then Brandon said, "I'll talk with you later," as he gathered his things and trotted to his car.

Emma, although partially relieved by Brandon's explanation, recognized that she still had some healing to do before she could trust Brandon completely.

CHAPTER 11

Brandon entered Panera and spotted Jalen at a table by the window. As Brandon approached, Jalen arose and the two former teammates and dear friends hugged. Brandon said, "Boy, it's great to see you, Jalen. I cannot tell you how much I've missed you."

"It's so good to see you again too, Brandon. I took the liberty of ordering some food for us. I hope a cinnamon crunch bagel with honey walnut cream cheese and hazelnut coffee are still your favorites?"

Brandon chuckled and said, "You have a good memory. Thank you. This looks great."

"I can't believe you're going to be playing football at our alma mater again! That sounds like an interesting development, but I'd rather hear from the beginning about your adventures since leaving Ohio State."

"I've been thinking about that. You know we're meeting with Mike Nelson at 1:00 today, and I'm going to share my story from the beginning. You're the only person who will be there who doesn't really know much about what happened to me. Mr. Nelson is very interested in witnessing your reactions to the various parts to help him write the article in the most impactful way. For that reason, it's best that we wait until this afternoon for me to share my sordid tale with you. By the way, Patrick and Sam Gilmore will also be there."

"I completely understand, Brandon. Are you able to tell me now how it came about that you're returning to Ohio State to play?"

"I sure can." Brandon recounted his extraordinary experiences of the past few days.

Jalen commented, "I see God's fingerprints all over that story. I take it that you were a bit surprised by Coach Anderson's call this morning?"

"I was surprised by how quickly he worked out the details with the NCAA and verified that he could offer me a scholarship, but I guess I shouldn't have been surprised, given that God is orchestrating it." Brandon paused thoughtfully for a moment. "Wait a minute, would you be interested in that coaching position? I remember how you mentored me, especially during my freshman year. You'd be a natural!"

"It's funny that you asked, because recently I've been thinking about a career change. I'd love to get into coaching, and that position sounds very intriguing. Do you see any reason why I shouldn't contact Coach Anderson and inquire about it?"

"None. The thought of you and me possibly being reunited at Ohio State is so exciting to me, Jalen. God is continuing to move in our lives."

"Amen. By the way, Emma seemed surprised and annoyed by your news this morning. Is everything okay?"

"It is now. She was upset that I hadn't discussed it with her before now, but I explained how innocently and quickly this all came about. Fortunately, she was understanding."

Emma had just arrived home after running several errands following Dylan's football practice when she received a phone call from Carol Hanrahan. Carol was one of the nurses on the oncology ward at Nationwide

CHAPTER 11

Children's Hospital in Columbus, and she was Emma's instructor in nursing school during that rotation. The two of them became friends and had remained in touch following Emma's graduation.

"Hi, Carol. What a nice surprise. It's good to hear from you. How are you?"

"I'm doing great. Before we talk about our personal lives, I'm also calling for a specific reason. The nursing manager position for the oncology ward at Nationwide has just been posted, and I can't think of anyone better than you for that job. Are you interested?"

Chapter 12

BRANDON AND HIS FRIENDS started arriving at the Graduate Hotel in Cincinnati shortly before 1:00. They were gathering in a small conference room Mike Nelson had reserved. Jalen, Mike and Sam were catching up in one corner of the room, as they hadn't seen each other since the funeral for Brandon's dad. Patrick and Brandon arrived together a few minutes later.

"Patrick, it was such a pleasant surprise to have you join us at Dylan's practice this morning," said Brandon.

"I really enjoyed being part of it. Next to Dylan scoring the touchdown at the end, the best part was your announcement that you're returning to Ohio State to play football. How long has that been in the works?"

"Just two days. Remember when I told you that sharing my story with you while we were together in the hospital lightened my burden of my dad's death?" Brandon then told Patrick about his unexpected call with Coach Anderson.

"I can't wait to see you terrorizing Ohio State's opponents again."

Brandon smiled and said, "I have a long way to go to get back into football shape, and I'm not sure I can ever get back to the same level again, but I'm sure gonna try. I noticed you

CHAPTER 12

were a natural coach with Dylan today. Would you consider overseeing my training much like my dad used to?"

"Are you kidding? I'd love to do that, but I really don't know much about football training. Would we use the same workouts that your dad created?"

"Exactly. My dad designed some specific workouts that we used in the spring and summer as I was recovering from my broken leg before my junior year. All we'll need to do is follow my dad's script."

"I can do that!" said Patrick excitedly.

Mike Nelson invited everyone to take a seat at the conference table, and he addressed the group, "Guys, thank you so much for coming. Although I've heard only bits and pieces of Brandon's story after leaving Ohio State, I believe it's a story with broad appeal. Brandon has agreed to share it with me so I can write it for possible publication in a national magazine. I know that Sam and Patrick have already heard Brandon's tale in its entirety and that Jalen is aware of virtually none of it. In a moment, I'm going to ask Brandon to tell his story from start to finish. What would be most valuable is to allow me to witness your reactions as the story unfolds and to ask clarifying questions when details are inconsistent with your knowledge of the events. Your input will be very helpful to me in shaping my writing of Brandon's account. Does that make sense?"

Jalen, Patrick and Sam all nodded affirmatively.

"The spotlight is all yours, Brandon," declared Mike.

Brandon began with the devastation of his father's accident just before the second game of his junior year. Because Brandon's love of football was so intrinsically connected to his dad, Brandon completely lost all interest in playing.

He initially took a leave of absence from school, which then extended into the spring semester. As summer rolled around, he remained apathetic about playing football or returning to school. His mom was beginning to encourage him to get on with his life. With the help of his friend, Jalen, Brandon landed a factory job in Cincinnati.

Brandon fell in with the wrong crowd, and drinking with them at a rundown bar after work became a fairly regular part of his routine. He felt himself get sucked into a downward spiral in which he was ashamed of what his life had become, and he continued to drink to diminish the shame. One day when he was particularly despondent, one of his friends gave him oxycodone to numb the emotional pain, and Brandon was quickly hooked. His use of oxycodone escalated, causing him financial problems. He was introduced to sports gambling by his friends, and he tried to use gambling to get out of debt. His performance at work deteriorated, and he lost his job at the factory. His financial debts quickly piled up, and his acts of petty theft accelerated into burglarizing houses to try to make ends meet. Eventually he was evicted from his apartment.

Brandon kept it together for a short while by working at a gas station and living in his car which he kept parked at a discount fitness center, where he could shower. He was also able to abstain from alcohol, narcotics and gambling for a brief time. Unfortunately, during a particularly weak moment, he contacted his dealer, and again started using opioids regularly. His personal hygiene and reliability deteriorated, and he was fired from the gas station.

At that point, he abandoned his SUV and began living on the street, scrounging for food wherever he could, including

CHAPTER 12

the dumpsters behind restaurants. When autumn and the onset of cold nights arrived, he entered a homeless shelter. Shortly after his admission, he got into a fight with another guest and broke his hand on the bedframe, necessitating going to the emergency department at the University of Cincinnati Medical Center, where he had a God-ordained meeting with his old friend and former high school teammate, medical student Sam Gilmore.

Sam had been encouraging Brandon's spiritual journey since high school. After learning about Brandon's troubled path since his father's death, Sam invited Brandon to a three-day Christian retreat. While attending the retreat about a month ago, Brandon accepted Jesus as the Lord and Savior of his life and was baptized.

Brandon shared how his life had completely turned around since the retreat, and that he was asked this morning to return to Ohio State and play football.

Mike and Sam simultaneously screamed, "What !?!?"

Brandon, Patrick and Jalen enjoyed their reaction, and Brandon quickly summarized his renewed passion for football and the conversations he'd had with Coach Anderson over the last two days.

During most of Brandon's recounting of his epic tale, Jalen sat completely engrossed and often slack-jawed. He occasionally groaned and shed more than a few tears because of his friend's struggles. Jalen was horrified by Brandon's alcohol, opioid and gambling addictions, as well as his stealing. He was moved with pity at his homelessness and joyously celebrated his redemption and baptism. Jalen was especially touched by the chance meeting of Brandon and Sam in the emergency department and recognized God's miracle in that moment.

At the conclusion of Brandon's storytelling and the feedback from all of the attendees, the group was exhausted after traveling the emotional journey with Brandon. Mike said, "Thank you Brandon, Jalen, Sam and Patrick for your help with this project. I will likely need to reach out to you some more, especially Brandon, but I certainly have enough to get started. Wow, I'm drained and hungry. Can I treat you all to dinner? One of my favorite Italian restaurants is just down the street."

They all enthusiastically agreed that it was the perfect antidote to an emotionally charged afternoon.

As they were exiting the conference room, Sam whispered in Brandon's ear, "I noticed that you didn't share the part about Joshua's accident and Daniel's adoption."

Brandon whispered back, "Those parts of the story impact more than just me, and the last thing I would want to do is reopen old wounds."

"Good call, Brandon."

Chapter 13

AS DINNER WAS CONCLUDING with Mike, Brandon and their friends, Brandon received a text from Emma, *Would you please give me a call when you have a chance?*

As the group was departing the restaurant, Brandon said goodnight to each of his friends, then called Emma from the car.

"Hi, Emma. How are you doing?"

"I'm good. What are you up to?"

"I spent the afternoon telling my story to Mike, Jalen, Sam and Patrick. Mike was pleased with it, and he thinks he has enough to start writing it. Jalen's reactions to hearing the story for the first time were invaluable for Mike. After our time together, we all went out to dinner. I've just gotten into my car outside of the restaurant."

"Would you mind dropping by my apartment on your way home? I have something I'd like to discuss with you."

"Of course, Emma. I'll see you in about twenty minutes."

As Brandon drove to Emma's place, he suspected she was still upset about the situation of him returning to OSU and how it unfolded without her knowledge. When he entered her apartment, Brandon began, "Emma, I just want to apologize to you again for not letting you know about my initial conversation with Coach Anderson immediately after it occurred."

"That's okay, Brandon. I forgive you, especially now that I know that you returning to Ohio State to play football is all part of God's plan."

"What do you mean?"

"Earlier today, I got a call from Carol Hanrahan. She's a nurse at Nationwide Children's Hospital and was my instructor there when I was in nursing school. She and I have remained in touch since I graduated. She called to see if I was interested in applying for the open nursing manager position on the oncology ward at Nationwide," Emma said, smiling.

"You're kidding, Emma," Brandon said excitedly. "That certainly seems more than coincidental."

"It has God's fingerprints all over it. I love my current job working at Cincinnati Children's Hospital. I love the nurses, the doctors and especially the patients, but recently I've been thinking about how tired I am of working nights. It really cuts into the time that you and I can spend together. Also, I've been thinking about how I feel ready to step into a leadership role, and Nationwide has a special place in my heart. One other thing which confirms that this is of God's doing. The reason why the position is open is because the current manager just announced her impending retirement, so the start date is not for another three months. That is just about the time when you'll be moving to Columbus to begin preseason practice and my lease expires on this apartment!"

"That's fantastic, Emma."

CHAPTER 13

"There's more though, Brandon. As I've thought about you and the opportunity for you to play football again at Ohio State, it seems so obvious that God wants you to use your extraordinary gifts to build his kingdom. I apologize to you for having such a self-centered reaction this morning when you revealed the news."

"No apology is necessary. It's pretty exciting that you and I are returning together to Columbus, the city of our college days."

"My job at Nationwide is not secured yet, but in my experience, God often removes obstacles when you're in harmony with his will."

"Speaking of God working his will in our lives, I think Jalen is going to contact Coach Anderson about that coaching position that he offered me."

"Wouldn't it be so fun if all three of us were reunited?" asked Emma gleefully.

Two days later, within the football complex at Ohio State, Coach Anderson received a call on his cell phone from Donna Blankenship, Head Coach Weaver's administrative assistant.

"Good morning, Donna," Coach Anderson answered.

"Hi, Rodney. Are you in the building?"

"Yes, I'm in my office."

"Coach Weaver would like to talk with you. Can you please come to his office?"

"Of course. I'm on my way."

As Rodney entered Coach Weaver's office, Coach Weaver said warmly, "Please close the door, Rodney. How was your weekend?"

"It was enjoyable. I spent Saturday doing some early spring cleanup around my yard. You know how it is. There's just no time once we begin spring practice."

"How well I know."

Rodney took a seat by Coach Weaver's desk. Coach Weaver began, "As you know, Curt Hansen has been interviewing for the head coaching job at Rutgers." Coach Hansen was the offensive coordinator at Ohio State. "Curt called me over the weekend to let me know that he's been offered the job, and he has accepted it. That isn't public knowledge yet, so please keep it to yourself. The reason I wanted to talk with you, Rodney, is that I'd like to promote you into Curt's job as our new offensive coordinator. Your performance has been outstanding, and the promotion is very well deserved. What do you say?"

Rodney's heart was beating wildly with the news he had been hoping to receive. "First, I'm really happy for Curt, and he'll be really missed around here. I'll congratulate him as soon as the time is right. As to your offer, I'm honored, and my answer is absolutely yes!"

"That's great, Rodney. It's really helpful that we can name Curt's replacement at the same time that the announcement is made about his departure. The last thing that we want is to make our players or recruits nervous about any perceived instability in our coaching staff. Also, I leave the decision to you as to who you'd like to replace you as the running backs coach. Any ideas?"

CHAPTER 13

"If Brandon Campbell wasn't returning as a player, he'd be at the top of my list. I'll need to give it some thought. Thank you, Herb. I really appreciate your confidence in me, and I won't let you down."

Later that afternoon, Coach Anderson's phone rang. He answered it distractedly without looking at the ID of the caller. "Hello, this is Rodney Anderson."

"Coach, it's Jalen Pittman. How are you?"

"Hi, Jalen. It's great to hear from you. I'm having a really great day."

"That's good. Speaking of having a great day, I happened to be with Brandon Campbell on Saturday morning when he got your call. He was so juiced about the chance to play for Ohio State again!"

"It will be really good to have him back again, but I'm concerned that he may have lost his edge after being away from football for all of these years."

"You know Brandon, Coach. When he puts his mind to it, he can train like no one I've ever seen. There were times when I was concerned that he was overtraining, and I tried to get him to let up some. You can rest assured he'll be ready to play." As Jalen was talking, Rodney was reminded of how Jalen had taken Brandon under his wing and coached, encouraged and mentored him, especially when Brandon was a freshman. Rodney suddenly was wondering if he was talking to his new running backs coach.

"The reason I'm calling, Coach," Jalen continued, "is that Brandon had mentioned to me on Saturday that you had offered him a coaching job. I was wondering if that job is still available, because I may be interested."

"I'm sorry to say, Jalen, that you can't have it," Coach Anderson teased as Jalen absorbed the weight of disappointment, "because I want you to take my job as running backs coach." Coach Anderson went on to explain how he had just been promoted to offensive coordinator that morning. Jalen was overjoyed, as he tried to comprehend all of the changes ahead and especially that he'd be reunited with Brandon Campbell.

Coach Anderson continued, "Let's set up some time later this week and discuss the details. One of the things I'll want to get you started on right away is building a relationship with Tristin Garner. He's our five-star recruit from Miami, and he's going to be a handful because of his ego."

"You know me, Coach. I love a challenge. I'm very excited to be working with you again, and I'm so grateful for the opportunity."

Later that afternoon, Coach Anderson phoned Tristin Garner because he wanted to notify him of the coaching changes before the news became public.

"Hi, Tristin. This is Coach Anderson. Do you have a minute?"

"Hey, Coach. Sure. What's up?"

"I want to let you know about some impending coaching changes before you hear it on ESPN. Coach Hansen, our offensive coordinator, took the head coaching job at Rutgers. I've been promoted to be the offensive coordinator, and I've hired Jalen Pittman to be the new running backs coach. I think you're really going to like him."

"Didn't he play about the same time as Brandon Campbell?"

CHAPTER 13

"That's right. Jalen was two years ahead of Brandon, and they were a dynamic pair when they played together. That reminds me, Brandon Campbell still has some eligibility left, and he is going to be rejoining our team."

"Are you kidding me, man? Isn't he old enough to be in a nursing home by now?"

"Brandon was possibly the most talented player to ever play for Ohio State."

Tristin cut him off, saying, "Until I get there. Thanks for letting me know about the changes, Coach, but they don't really matter. You see, I just do my thing. New coaches and different players don't affect me none, because I do what I do and nobody's gonna stop me."

Coach Anderson rolled his eyes on his end of the call and was becoming irritated, so he quickly ended the call rather curtly with, "I'll have Coach Pittman reach out to you to introduce himself once he gets on board."

Chapter 14

LATER THAT AFTERNOON, BRANDON called Patrick. "Hi Patrick. Do you have a few minutes to talk?" asked Brandon.

"Yes, I do. My next class is in about 30 minutes."

"How's your dad doing?"

"He continues to get better every day. He's understandably still weak, but he's walking around our house without assistance. We've noticed that he has some occasional memory lapses, which we were told to expect. Other than some pain from his broken ribs, he's had no other issues that we've seen."

"I'll continue to pray for him, Patrick. On another topic, I wanted to touch base with you on setting up some time for our workouts. We'll need to work around your spring class schedule, but I plan to train six days a week, including the workouts on Saturdays with Dylan. I hope you can join me on Saturday and then one additional day during the week. On the other days, I'll be lifting and doing cardio, so your help isn't needed as much then. On the days when I'm doing agility drills and other football-specific activities, that's when I can really use your assistance. In addition to Saturday, is there another day of the week that works well for you?"

CHAPTER 14

"Wednesday afternoons are wide open for me."

"That's perfect, Patrick. There's a little park close to my apartment where we can train. Let's plan to meet there at 3:00. I've also been looking around for a place where I can do some more intensive strength training."

"Have you thought about the football facility at UC? The head coach was a player at Ohio State about a decade ago. And I think he may have even begun his coaching career as a graduate assistant at Ohio State. He might be open to letting a Buckeye player use their facilities, especially one with your extraordinary circumstances. I think it may be worth a try."

"That's a great idea, Patrick. I knew you were going to be a huge help to me. I'm going to call Coach Anderson and see if he can pave the way for me with the UC coach. I'll see you on Wednesday, Patrick, and I'll text you the address of the park. I really appreciate you helping me in this way."

"It'll all be worth it if I can see you get back on that field some day in an Ohio State uniform!" exclaimed Patrick enthusiastically.

After their call, Brandon tried to envision what the coming days might look like. It was late March, and it would be five months until Ohio State's season opener at the end of August. He could hardly wait to get started. He then called Coach Anderson.

Coach said, "I'm so glad you called, because you were at the top of my list of people I wanted to reach out to today. I have some news I'd like to share with you. This morning, I was promoted to be the new offensive coordinator. The position became available when Coach Hansen was named as the head coach at Rutgers."

"Congratulations, Coach! You're so deserving of this role. I remember some of the innovative plays you designed for our offense. You're going to be very successful."

"Thanks. My chances of success went up significantly when you expressed your desire to return as a player. There's more I have to share with you. I asked Jalen Pittman to take my former role as running backs coach, and he has verbally accepted."

"Woohoo!!!" Brandon screamed at the top of his lungs.

Coach Anderson quickly moved his phone away from his ear and chuckled.

"That's fantastic news, Coach!" Brandon exclaimed exuberantly as he imagined what it would be like to be reunited with Jalen again.

"I thought you'd be pleased with that news, Brandon. But you called me, so what's on your mind?"

"I've begun to plan my training regimen to prepare for the season. I'm not yet ready to move to Columbus, and I don't have access to all the sophisticated equipment I need to get into peak fitness. I was wondering if you'd be willing to call the coach at UC to see if he would allow me to use their training facility for my workouts for a few months."

"Jeremy Bateman, the head coach at UC, is an old friend. Our playing careers at Ohio State overlapped a couple of years. I'm not sure what he'll say, but I'm happy to ask him."

"Thanks, Coach. I'm really excited about your news. Congratulations again!"

About twenty minutes later, Brandon received a call from Coach Anderson. "Hey, Brandon. I just talked with Coach Bateman, and he was amenable to you using the UC facilities. He is actually a fan of yours, and was disappointed

CHAPTER 14

in how your Ohio State career was cut short. He's excited to support your comeback. He'd like to meet with you in his office at 2:00 tomorrow to discuss the details."

"Thanks, Coach. That happened much quicker than I had hoped."

"You're welcome. Before you go, there's one more thing I'd like to discuss with you. One of our incoming recruits is a running back from Miami. His name is Tristin Garner, and he has a world of talent. When I recruited you, Brandon, I could see your dad's influence on you in your humility, your concern for your teammates and your awareness of how your actions affected the other members of our team. Tristin has never known his father, and I'm not sure that's the reason, but Tristin alienates nearly everyone around him because of his oversized ego. I'd love for you to take him under your wing much like Jalen did for you. I've also asked Jalen to start building a rapport with him."

"I'm honored that you confided in me, Coach, and I'll do the best I can to positively influence him."

"Thanks, Brandon. It's so good to have you back."

Besides Tristin Garner, another promising Ohio State recruit was Manny Garcia, a cornerback who was best known for his tight coverage of receivers and sure tackling in the open field. Manny was enjoying the early spring weather in Houston with his best friend, Mateo Morales.

"Are you excited about playing at Ohio State next year?" asked Mateo.

"Yes, but I'm also a bit nervous about it," confided Manny.

"You're the most confident dude I know. What do you have to be nervous about? All I ever hear is that you're one of the greatest high school cornerbacks ever to come out of Texas."

"No one in my family has ever gone to college, let alone played a sport. All I've ever known is Houston, and Ohio seems like a world away."

"That's nothing, man. You'll get used to college in no time."

"There's one other thing, Mateo, and you have to promise that you won't tell anyone."

"Sure, what is it?"

"You remember our third game of the season against Tech, our biggest rival, and they had that superstar receiver I knew I'd have to cover?"

"Of course I remember," said Mateo. "You killed it that night. You were making tackles all over the field and you had three interceptions, including the one that secured the victory."

"You also remember that my little brother has ADHD?"

"Sure, but what does that have to do with the Tech game?"

"My brother is on Adderall, and I heard that Adderall may improve athletic performance. I was really nervous about that Tech receiver before the game, so I stole one of my brother's Adderall pills and took it. I'm not really sure it helped me play better, but I did have a great game, so I continued to take it before every game the rest of the season. The pharmacy noticed that my brother's prescription was running out sooner than it should, so I started buying it on the street. Like I said, I'm not sure I need it to improve my performance, but if I do, I'll need to figure out

CHAPTER 14

where I can score some in Ohio. I'm also concerned about getting caught."

"Why don't you just stop using it?"

"The players in college are so much better than in high school, and I'm going to need every edge I can get. The truth is, man, my biggest fear is that I'm not going to be good enough and that I'm going to let down my family and friends."

Chapter 15

THE NEXT DAY, BRANDON met with Jeremy Bateman, the head football coach at the University of Cincinnati. Brandon entered his office, shook hands and said, "Hi, Coach Bateman. I'm Brandon Campbell."

"Hi, Brandon. It's a pleasure to meet you, especially since we're both part of the Ohio State football fraternity. I'm sorry about the hurdles you endured in your career with your injuries and particularly the sudden loss of your father. When Coach Anderson called me yesterday about you resuming your playing career at Ohio State, I was surprised but also very happy for you. What has made you decide to begin playing again after all these years?"

"After my dad died, I lost all of my passion for football. Recently, multiple events occurred simultaneously in my life, and my love of football has returned. I have recognized that God has given me some unique athletic gifts and I should be using them to bring glory to him."

"There is no better reason than that. I'll be praying for you, Brandon. Tell me how I can help you."

"Thank you for your prayers, Coach. If it wouldn't be too much trouble, I'd really appreciate having access to your football training facility for the next three months, so I can prepare for returning to Columbus for summer workouts

CHAPTER 15

with the team. Being able to use your specialized training equipment would really help me."

"That's not a problem. This time of the year, our team trains at various times during the day, but the busiest time is in the afternoon between 1:00 and 3:00. I'd appreciate it if you'd avoid those hours for using the strength equipment. In a few minutes, I'll take you on a tour of our facilities."

"Do you think there will be any issues with any of your players?"

"I don't think so, and if there are, just let me know. If anyone asks, just tell them who you are and that you have my support to help you revive your football career. I think most of our players will know who you are and will be honored to assist you with your comeback. Our team really embraces the notion that football is a brotherhood."

"There's an engineering student here at UC named Patrick Cutler. Sometimes, he may accompany me to help me with my workouts. Is that okay with you?"

"Absolutely, especially since he's a UC student."

"Also, can I have access to the Nippert Stadium field? There are some agility drills that I like to do, and the field would be the perfect place."

"That's not an issue. I'll get you a code to access our training facility and the stadium field."

"Coach, you've been so generous, and I'm really grateful. Could I get your help with one more favor?"

"Of course, what else can I do for you?"

"When I was walking to your office this afternoon, I noticed the track team practicing. Could you arrange an introduction to the track coach? When I was a freshman at Ohio State, I trained and competed with the track team during the indoor season, and it really improved my explosiveness. I wanted to see if the track coach would allow me to do some workouts with the sprinters."

"I remember when you did that your freshman year as well as the spectacular results you were having your sophomore year on the football field. I talked with Rodney Anderson about you at the time, and he was a big proponent of encouraging certain players to run track. We were considering doing the same thing with some of our running backs. I actually discussed the idea with George Parker, our track coach, and he was very supportive. Let's get him on the phone right now."

Coach Bateman called Coach Parker. "George, this is Jeremy. I have you on speaker phone right now, and Brandon Campbell is in my office."

"Brandon Campbell, as in the former Ohio State running back and track star?"

"That's the one," said Coach Bateman with a smile. "Brandon is trying to make a football comeback and resume playing at Ohio State, and he has a question for you."

"Hi, Coach," said Brandon. "I'm living in Cincinnati for several months before I move to Columbus and begin training with the football team. I'm going to use that time to get back into peak condition. Coach Bateman has graciously agreed to let me use the football facilities, and I was wondering if you would allow me to jump in with your sprinters when they're doing intervals?"

"Brandon, I suspect you don't know, that when you were in high school, you were the number one recruiting candidate on my list for our track team. I never actually contacted you because it was so clear your priority was to play

CHAPTER 15

football in college. I followed your brief track career at Ohio State, and it was no surprise to me how well you did. Also, your track coach at Ohio State shared with me after your season what a positive impact you had on the culture of the team. That's a long way of saying that you are welcome at our track practices anytime you'd like. Our practices begin at 3:00."

"Thank you, Coach. That sounds great. I'd like to take two weeks to get in a little bit better shape before I join you, but I'm really looking forward to meeting you."

"Me, too. Just ask for me when you get to the track. Bye, Brandon. See you around, Jeremy."

"Let's go on that tour now," said Coach Bateman.

When Brandon got home that afternoon, he immediately called Patrick. "Hi, Patrick, I took your advice and looked into the possibility of using the UC football facility for training." He then explained how he called Coach Anderson, who contacted Coach Bateman, who then phoned Coach Parker. Within twenty-four hours, he had access to the strength training facility and the Nippert Stadium field, as well as an open invitation to practice with the track team anytime he wished.

"I'm beginning to see how being a superstar opens doors all over the place," said Patrick, laughing.

"It's God who's opening the doors. I'm getting the sense that restarting my football career at Ohio State is in harmony with God's plans. Instead of meeting at the park by my apartment tomorrow for our workout, let's meet at Nippert."

"That's actually much more convenient for me," said Patrick, "because I'll be on campus anyway. I'll see you then."

That afternoon, Emma called Alissa Hendricks, the hiring manager for the position at Nationwide Children's Hospital.

"Hi, Alissa. My name is Emma Brooks. I'm currently a nurse on the oncology ward at Cincinnati Children's Hospital, and I'm also a friend of Carol Hanrahan. Carol suggested that I call you about the open manager position on the cancer ward."

"Hi, Emma. It's really nice to meet you. Carol said you'd be calling me. She also said that, of all the nursing students she taught over the years, none were as passionate about caring for children with cancer as you are. Carol shared as well that you were an extraordinary nursing student in many other favorable ways, and she thought you would be an excellent candidate for this role. Can you tell me why you are considering the transition from Cincinnati Children's to Nationwide?"

"Ever since nursing school, Nationwide Children's Hospital has had a special place in my heart. Since graduating from nursing school, I've been working the night shift at Cincinnati Children's, and daytime openings on the cancer unit don't occur very often. I'm also interested in being in a manager's position because I believe I have an aptitude for it. One final reason is that my boyfriend, who lives in Cincinnati, has decided to resume his football playing career at Ohio State."

CHAPTER 15

"I'm a lifelong Ohio State football fan. Do you mind sharing with me the name of your boyfriend?"

"Only if you promise to keep it confidential, because I don't think it's public information yet."

"Of course," said Alissa.

"It's Brandon Campbell."

"Brandon Campbell's coming back to play!" shrieked Alissa, her professionalism evaporating in an instant. She continued excitedly, "In all the years I've followed Ohio State football, none were as exciting as the years when Brandon was playing. I actually met him once. He used to come to the hospital regularly to visit one of our patients who had leukemia. He was there with Jalen Pittman. I remember how starstruck I was that day. I also remember Brandon giving that little boy a football that he used to throw a touchdown pass in a game. That young man was always holding that football during every moment he was in the hospital after that."

"I knew your name was familiar, Alissa. I was there when you met Brandon and Jalen that day."

"I apologize, Emma, all I could see was Brandon and Jalen, but especially Brandon." They both laughed, and Alissa continued, "But I do now vaguely remember a young lady being with them."

"That was me," said Emma, recalling how she always faded into the background whenever Brandon was around during his glory days as a football player. She resolved that she would need to prepare herself for that again.

"Emma, thank you for sharing that exciting news with me about Brandon, and I promise I will keep it confidential. Back to the position… Carol's recommendation of you carries a lot of weight, but we'll still need to go through an unbiased, thorough hiring process that considers all qualified applicants. At this point, though, I think you would make an excellent candidate, and I really encourage you to apply."

Chapter 16

THE FOLLOWING AFTERNOON, BRANDON and Patrick met on the Nippert Stadium field, right in the heart of the University of Cincinnati campus. As Brandon was putting on his shoes in preparation for stretching and warming up before the workout, Patrick asked, "Can I ask you a few questions before we begin?"

"Of course," replied Brandon, "but I can guess your first question. You want to know more about what your role is during these workouts."

"That's right," said Patrick, smiling. "How can I best help you?"

"It'll be much like Saturday when we were with Dylan. Even at that workout, you seemed to have a sense of what was needed. Part of it will be anticipating what I'm going to do next, and being ready for it so we can move through the training quickly and efficiently. That'll get easier for you as we do a few workouts together. I've chosen the workouts that my dad designed for the spring and early summer before my junior year at Ohio State. I was just coming back from a fracture in my lower leg at that time, so it should be a great template for gradually increasing the intensity of my workouts. Obviously, I'm not coming back from an injury, but it's a similar situation because I haven't trained seriously for several years."

"Is there anything you'd like me to look out for related to your running form?"

"Yeah. I need you to protect me from myself. I tend to go overboard with my training, and that will increase my risk of injury, especially with as long as I've been away. Please watch for any subtle changes in my running form, because it may mean that I'm favoring a certain part of my body and that might lead to an injury. You may notice a change even before I'm aware of it, because I'm so intent on powering through."

"Got it. Are there any other things you want me to watch out for and give you feedback on?"

"Yes, at times, we'll be working on certain training exercises, such as getting my knees high when I'm running. Also, sometimes I may ask you to take videos with my phone so I can study certain movements, like cutting to the right or left.

"Okay. Anything else?"

"Your encouragement is really important to me, but I want you also to be honest with me if you think I'm not giving as much effort as I should be. There's one more thing I want to share before we get started. When I did these workouts with my dad, my motivation was mostly about me. Of course, I wanted to do well to help Ohio State win games and to make my dad proud, but my primary motivation was for my own glory. I wanted to win the Heisman Trophy and eventually play in the NFL. I'm still very motivated, possibly even more so, but now my motivation is to

CHAPTER 16

bring glory to God. Would you pray for us before we begin our workout, Patrick?"

The first workout went smoothly, although it was of relatively low intensity. Brandon initially felt stiff and rusty, but as the workout progressed, he began to appreciate his gracefulness returning. He really enjoyed feeling his body performing again on a football field.

On Saturday, Patrick joined Brandon, Dylan and Dylan's dad for the workout at Bloomington High School. Unlike the previous two training sessions with Dylan, Brandon participated in all the drills with Dylan, and Patrick served as the coach. It was a dream come true for Dylan as he ran and did multiple agility drills with his hero. Dylan's focus and effort escalated significantly.

After a couple of weeks of lifting on his own and the training sessions with Patrick, Brandon felt adequately prepared to begin training with the UC track team. For the first several workouts, Brandon ran at about eighty percent of the speed of the track team sprinters. By the fourth workout, Brandon was able to keep up with them, and after a month, Brandon was pushing the pace, as he usually led the intervals.

In addition to his rigorous training schedule, Brandon closely adhered to an appropriate diet, eating fruits, vegetables and lean proteins, while avoiding sweets and high-fat foods. More than anything, though, he was diligent about his spiritual life. He spent at least an hour each day reading the Bible and praying. In addition, he and Patrick began a Bible study together on the book of Romans while using the study guide written by John MacArthur.

One day, Patrick said, "Brandon, I think your football training is really going well, and I can clearly see the results since we began. You're making great progress on the physical and spiritual parts of your preparation, but I wonder if we need to get ready mentally for football. I'm curious if you think watching some of your old game film might help re-engage your mind to responding to live action on the field."

"That's a great idea, Patrick! I'll call Coach Anderson. I'm sure he can help with that request."

Coach Anderson sent Brandon the videos of his previous Ohio State games. Brandon would spend long evenings reacquainting himself with the offensive terminology, the timing of the blockers, hitting the correct hole in the offensive line and accurately reading the defense. The most helpful times were when Patrick joined him in analyzing the film. Brandon found that he benefitted greatly when he ran the action in slow motion and taught Patrick how to break it down.

Over the course of the next several months, Brandon watched his body transform right before his eyes. It was a dramatic change from his stature during his days of living on the streets. He added about twenty-five pounds of muscle, cut his body fat percentage in half and regained his former strength, flexibility and explosiveness. He could hardly wait to get back on the field with his teammates.

Chapter 17

IT WAS MID-MAY AND about a month before Brandon was scheduled to report to Ohio State for the beginning of summer workouts in preparation for the upcoming football season. His relationship with Emma was continuing to heal, and they had both rediscovered a contented peace whenever they were together. Brandon so adored Emma, and he never took for granted any time they spent together.

Emma had undergone multiple interviews for the nursing position at Nationwide Children's Hospital over about six weeks, and Brandon was not surprised when she was offered the job. Brandon had never before felt that he was in so much harmony with God's will, and he had been certain that Emma getting the job was all part of God's plan. After Emma accepted the job, Brandon and Emma wasted no time securing apartments in Columbus. Their places were only a few miles apart, with Emma's being near the hospital and Brandon's being adjacent to the Ohio State campus.

That afternoon, Brandon received a call from Mike Nelson. "Hi, Mr. Nelson. How are you doing?"

"I'm great, Brandon. I'd like to give you a couple of updates. First, your mom is really engaged with the

Christian tutoring I've been providing her. She's quickly grasping the basic concepts, and she has a hunger to read the Bible even more than your dad did. It has been such a pleasure to watch her knowledge and her joy grow daily."

"That's so good to hear! She may have told you that she and I talk on the phone or FaceTime nearly every day. Your observations are similar to what I've seen and what she's shared with me. I'm so grateful for all that you've poured into both of my parents, Mr. Nelson!"

"It's been my pleasure, Brandon. The second thing I wanted to share with you is that I have finished writing the story about you. I really like how it turned out, but I'd like you to read it and provide any changes before I submit it to any magazines. I've begun shopping around the concept of the story to a number of publications, and the reception has been very favorable. Right now, the finalists appear to be *Time, GQ* and *Sports Illustrated*."

"That's great. Please email me the manuscript, and I'll make reviewing it my top priority."

"Sounds great, Brandon. Let me know your thoughts. I'll talk with you soon."

Later that evening, Brandon and Emma had dinner at the home of their friends, Sam and Grace Gilmore. Sam, Emma and Brandon were close friends in high school, and Brandon and Sam were teammates on the state championship football team their senior year. Sam and Grace met while attending Wheaton College, and they married the day before they graduated. The two couples had previously

CHAPTER 17

experienced challenging events together, and with God's help, they were pursuing rebuilding a healthy relationship.

As they sat down to a dinner of barbecue chicken breasts, brussels sprouts with pancetta, and garlic mashed potatoes, Emma said, "Grace, this dinner looks amazing. How did you learn to cook like this?"

"My mom is a really good cook, and I learned the basics from her. Sam is always very appreciative of anything I make, so it motivates me to continue to expand my skills in the kitchen. I learn from friends, and I read a lot about 'food as medicine'. I also occasionally watch cooking shows on TV, but that's difficult with two little ones constantly taking my attention."

As if on cue, one-year-old Daniel, who was seated in a high chair next to Grace, let out a joyous squeal as he threw a piece of chicken at Brandon. Brandon deftly plucked it out of midair with his left hand, tossed it up and caught it in his mouth. He playfully chewed it while grinning at Daniel. Sam intervened quickly before Daniel could hurl more chicken at his new playmate.

"You mentioned 'food as medicine', Grace. What did you mean by that?" asked Emma.

"There's a lot of scientific evidence about the beneficial effects of proper nutrition. Many foods can help reduce inflammation, boost immunity and promote healing. I have some books on the subject that I'd be happy to share with you, Emma."

"Thank you. Any useful knowledge I can pass on to my cancer patients and their families is valuable," said Emma.

"How is the story that Mike Nelson is writing about you coming along, Brandon?" inquired Sam.

"It's funny that you asked. Mr. Nelson called me today, and he has finished it. He sent it to me to review. He also has begun to present the concept of the story to several national magazines."

"This is the story about your challenges after your father died?" asked Grace.

"That's right," responded Brandon.

"Did Mr. Nelson include the parts about Joshua and Daniel?" Grace solicited hesitantly and fearfully. When Brandon had resorted to criminal activity to support his drug habit, he had unwittingly burglarized Sam and Grace's home. In the process, he had unknowingly kicked over a changing table in the dark, which accidentally took the life of Sam and Grace's firstborn son, Joshua, who had been left sleeping on the table. Both couples also had to navigate that Emma and Brandon were the biological parents of Daniel, who was adopted by Sam and Grace.

"No, I didn't even share those details of the story with Mr. Nelson," answered Brandon.

Emma quickly changed the subject and asked, "How are Daniel and Lauren doing?" Lauren was about eight-and-a-half months old and was contentedly sitting on her mom's lap at the dinner table. Emma was joyfully studying her son, Daniel, until she became aware that Grace was observing her closely. Emma had put Daniel up for adoption seventeen months earlier on the day he was born, and just three months ago, Emma, Brandon, Sam and Grace had learned simultaneously that Sam and Grace were the adoptive parents of Emma and Brandon's baby. Although Emma promised that she would never reveal to Daniel that she was his

CHAPTER 17

biological mother, she accurately sensed that Grace may still be insecure about Emma being around Daniel.

After Emma's question had hung in the air for an awkward moment, Sam interjected with, "The kids are both doing well. They are happy and healthy, and they genuinely seem to like being around each other." Sam started to say that Daniel seemed to have extraordinary balance, strength and coordination for a seventeen-month-old, but he decided wisely to keep that to himself.

Chapter 18

THE DAY FOLLOWING DINNER at the Gilmore's, Brandon set aside several hours to read Mike Nelson's account of Brandon's tragedy. As he read it, he found himself caught up in the story as if he were reliving it all over again. For the first time, Brandon fully appreciated God's grace as God guided him on the path that ultimately led to his redemption. Along the way, there were a number of miracles, including Brandon's meeting with Sam Gilmore in the emergency department. As Brandon read the story about his own life, he was moved to tears on multiple occasions because of God's goodness.

After reading it, Brandon immediately called Mike Nelson. "Hi, Mr. Nelson. I just finished reading your story."

"You mean *your* story, Brandon. What did you think?"

"It was very moving, even though I knew how it was going to end," chuckled Brandon. "You captured all the details accurately, and you portrayed the story in a way that was engaging, touching and tragic, yet hopeful."

"Are there any parts you are concerned will be embarrassing for you?"

"On the contrary, Mr. Nelson, it gives me the perfect platform to give glory to God for leading me out of the hell I was trapped in and completely changing my life."

CHAPTER 18

"Did you see any errors or anything you would change?"

"Not a thing. I think it's ready for print."

"It's funny you said that, Brandon, because I received a call from the editor of *Sports Illustrated* this morning. He's certain that this story is going to generate tremendous national attention, and he'd like to move forward with it quickly. He said that if we come to an agreement today, he can get it into the edition that comes out in two weeks. I had been leaning toward *Sports Illustrated* out of the three finalists, and I look at this as a sign to move forward with them. Is that okay with you?"

"You're the expert, and I completely trust whatever you think is best."

"Great. I'll call the *Sports Illustrated* editor right now and finalize the details. I suggest you contact anyone, such as Emma and Sam, who will be impacted by the story and give them a heads up that it will be published soon."

"The first call I make will be to Coach Anderson. I don't want him or Ohio State to be blindsided by this."

"Good idea, Brandon. You might ask him if the media inquiries can be funneled through the Ohio State media relations team, because you are going to be deluged with requests for interviews. Allowing Ohio State to manage that will likely be beneficial to both them and you."

"That's a terrific idea. Can I send Coach the version of the story that you shared with me?"

"Yes. This is the same one I'll submit to *Sports Illustrated*, although they may want to make some editorial changes."

"Thanks so much, Mr. Nelson. I'm excited about getting the story out in public and using it to glorify God."

Brandon immediately called Coach Anderson. "Hi, Coach, do you have a minute?"

"Hey, Brandon. I have fifteen, to be exact, before I need to attend a coaches meeting. What's up?"

"Do you remember when I was a freshman, and I joined the track team without asking your permission?"

"I sure do. What have you done now?"

"I want to avoid any more surprises like the one with the track situation. Mike Nelson is a sportswriter with the *Cleveland Plain Dealer* and has been a family friend dating back to when he and my dad were buddies in college. Mr. Nelson asked me a few months ago if I'd be willing to tell him my story after I left Ohio State for possible publication. I agreed, and he expects the article to be out in about two weeks."

"In the *Cleveland Plain Dealer*?"

"No." Brandon paused for dramatic effect. "*Sports Illustrated*."

"Really? I thought you worked in a factory after you recovered from your dad's death. Why would they want to write about that?"

"There was more to it than that."

"You want to tell me what happened?"

"Better yet, I know you're short on time, so I'll email you the story that Mr. Nelson is sending to *Sports Illustrated*. He said they may make some editorial changes, but it'll allow you to know what happened."

"Thank you, Brandon. I'll read it first chance I get, and I'll also forward it to our media relations folks. Although you weren't part of the football program at that time, it's still beneficial for media relations to be aware of what's coming."

CHAPTER 18

"I'm glad you mentioned them, Coach. Do you think they can help manage any interview requests that I get? Mr. Nelson suspects that there'll be a lot of interest."

"Yes, they will actually be grateful to influence the media attention this receives. I still don't understand the interest in a young man working in a factory, even if he was a former Ohio State football player."

"I just emailed the story to you, Coach. Like I said, there's a little more that happened than just me working in a factory."

Coach Anderson pulled up the story on his phone and read the first several paragraphs as he was walking down the hall to his meeting. He was already completely engrossed by the time he arrived. He shared the conversation he'd had with Brandon and forwarded the article to all of the football coaches in the meeting. As the nearly twenty coaches in the conference room began reading Brandon's story on their devices, the ninety-minute agenda of the meeting was replaced with the coaches being silently moved by reading Brandon's account. By the end of the meeting, every coach had the stark realization that there were some things that were much more important in life than football.

Later that afternoon, Antonio Alvarez, also known as Diablo professionally, was being released from jail in Cincinnati after being incarcerated for two months on drug-related charges. The police had been unable to build an adequate case against him and were finally forced to let him go. The most promising witnesses had either died of overdoses or had relocated elsewhere and couldn't be found.

While in jail, Antonio had done a great deal of soul searching. Witnessing Valeria, his longtime girlfriend and the love of his life, get murdered right before his eyes was too much to bear. His anguish was further compounded by losing custody of his daughter, at least temporarily, to foster care. Antonio was at his wit's end, but one thing he knew for certain. He was going to stop dealing in illegal drugs. Antonio was going to turn over a new leaf and start working in a legal occupation. He didn't yet know what that would be, but he did know that he was tired of the violence, the constant hiding from the police, the frequent need to relocate, and the harm to his customers as a drug dealer. If the occupational hazards weren't enough, the most compelling reason for changing jobs was to give Sofia a better life. One thing he realized during his time in jail was how deeply he loved Sofia.

Chapter 19

TWO WEEKS LATER, THE *Sports Illustrated* issue with Brandon on the cover hit the newsstands. The cover featured the iconic photo where Brandon was signaling a touchdown with his arms while being carted off the Ohio State field with a broken leg. He had been hit just as he released a long touchdown pass. The injury abruptly ended what had been a potential Heisman Trophy sophomore season for Brandon.

Other photos shown with the story included: the factory in Cincinnati where Brandon worked, the grungy bar where he would drink his days away, the homeless shelter where he briefly stayed, the church where the three-day retreat occurred and where Brandon was baptized, the site of his father's fatal accident, and Brandon working out with his dad when he was in middle school.

The publicity generated with the launch of the story was about ten times more than even Mike Nelson anticipated. The Ohio State media relations team estimated the volume of interview requests to be even greater than the week leading up to the Michigan contest, Ohio State's biggest rivalry game. It would've been impossible for Brandon to do all the interviews that were solicited, and he settled on Kirk Herbstreit with ESPN, Lesley Stahl on *60 Minutes*, Tom

Rinaldi with Fox Sports, and *The Pat McAfee Show*. Brandon attempted to use every interview as an opportunity to glorify God by talking about God's grace, power and deep love for us. His model for the interviews was Tyler Trent, the Purdue University student and superfan who succumbed to bone cancer but used his platform to discuss his faith with every public appearance and created a vibrant legacy. Every interviewer asked Brandon about the superstition of bad luck for any athlete whose picture appears on the cover of *Sports Illustrated*. Brandon's response was that he believes God is sovereign over everything and therefore he's convinced that there is no such thing as luck.

Even though Brandon participated in only four interviews, nearly every major talk show on radio and television, as well as many podcasts and blogs with a sports theme, covered the story. He went viral on social media for weeks. Although most of the fanfare was sympathetic to Brandon's plight and the majority of the nation embraced Brandon's return to college football, there were some detractors who thought the article was all about Brandon just seeking attention.

There was someone, however, who was personally struggling with Brandon's celebrity status. The favorable coverage of Brandon's story exposed some old wounds for Grace Gilmore. Although she had forgiven Brandon, with God's help, for the accidental death he caused to her son, Joshua, she resented the favorable publicity which portrayed him as some kind of hero. Although the death of Joshua wasn't covered in the story, Grace allowed her bitterness toward Brandon to quietly take root in her heart.

CHAPTER 19

About a week after the story launched, Brandon received a phone call one morning from a number that was vaguely familiar but wasn't identified on his phone. He answered, "This is Brandon."

"Hi, Brandon. This is Antonio Alvarez... but you know me as Diablo."

The memories of the fear, anxiety, hopelessness and guilt of Brandon's former opioid addiction suddenly surged through his mind and body, but they were instantly replaced by the peace of God. Brandon said with a chuckle, "If I had to pick from all the people I know who might call me this morning, one of the least likely people would be you. And how in the world did you get my new number, man?"

"Let's just say I have connections," quipped Antonio. "I get it that you're surprised to hear from me, Brandon, but I'm calling to apologize to you," he said contritely. "And to ask for your help. I read the story about you in *Sports Illustrated*, and I was so inspired by it. I want what you have, man. Would it be possible to meet somewhere so we could talk face-to-face?"

Brandon had a sense from the Holy Spirit that the conversation he was about to have with Antonio would be one of the most vital exchanges of Antonio's life. "I'm available right now," Brandon offered.

"Me, too," responded Antonio, surprised at Brandon's willingness to meet on the spot without more persuasion. "Where would you like to meet?"

"How about the French Café in Clifton? It's quiet this time of day, and there are some tables that will give us some privacy. I can be there in twenty minutes."

"I'll see you there, Brandon. Thanks for meeting me on such short notice."

Because the French Café was near Brandon's apartment, he arrived first and selected a secluded table. As he awaited Antonio's arrival, he was very curious about exactly what was on Antonio's mind, but Brandon felt certain that God was orchestrating this meeting.

When Antonio entered the restaurant and looked around, Brandon waved to him from his table in the back. As Antonio walked toward him, Brandon noticed the significant changes in Antonio. He had lost a noticeable amount weight, and his normally haughty bearing had been replaced by a completely defeated posture. His facial expression reflected profound sadness, regret and guilt.

As Antonio approached the table, Brandon said, "You look like someone who just lost his best friend."

As he sat down at the table, Antonio said, "Not only my best friend, but the love of my life." Antonio then shared with Brandon how a joyful morning with his family was shattered by a drive-by shooting. Within the course of about twenty minutes, his girlfriend was dead, his daughter was in the care of Child Protective Services, and Antonio had been arrested.

"Those two months in jail may have been the best thing that ever happened to me, Brandon. As I mourned Valeria's loss, I couldn't even attend her funeral, and I couldn't comfort my daughter, Sofia. I realized how much I love Sofia and that I want a better life for her. I recognized also how

CHAPTER 19

much I hate being a drug dealer and all that goes with it, including how my customers' lives were ravaged by their addictions. When I was released from jail about two weeks ago, I was ready to turn over a new leaf. I want to earn an honest living in a way that both Sofia and I can be proud of. For the last two weeks, I've known what I want, but I don't know where to begin. I feel lost, and I feel like there's a huge void in my life."

Antonio continued, "One of my cousins, who's a big Ohio State football fan, gave me the copy of *Sports Illustrated*—with you on the cover—to read. He was feeling sorry for me and thought reading about sports might cheer me up. When I started reading your story, I didn't realize at first that it was about you. I never knew that you played football at Ohio State, and I didn't recognize you on the cover. You were always a lot skinnier than the guy on the cover, and besides, when I saw you, it was always at night in the shadows. As I read the account of your life, I was so moved." Large tears welled up in Antonio's eyes, and he paused to compose himself.

"As I learned about your struggles, Brandon, I realized how much pain I caused you by supplying you with drugs. I am deeply sorry, and I ask you to forgive me."

"I forgive you, Antonio. I believe that the events of my life, as I was enduring my addictions, were used by God to pursue me. I ultimately found myself in such a deep, dark place that I recognized that the only way out was through God. At that desperate moment, in a hospital ER, God reunited me with one of my oldest and dearest friends, who had been trying to get me to give my life to Jesus for years. God made it so clear that even in my impaired state, I couldn't miss the signals in the emergency room that night."

Antonio commented, "When I said a moment ago about how much the article moved me, the part with the most impact was when you revealed your faith in Jesus. That's what I meant when I called you earlier and said that I want what you have."

"After your call today, the Holy Spirit gave me an inkling that I was about to have a life-changing conversation with you."

"I'm not sure what you're talking about, but before you explain it, I want to share one more revelation I had from your story. In your account, it was clear that you were devastated by your dad's fatal accident. It seemed to me that God was knocking on your door, but you refused to answer. You went deeper and deeper into despair. Like you, I've suddenly lost someone I loved very much. I believe that God is reaching for me as well, and I don't want to make the same mistake you did. I'm ready to seek him now and begin a new life. You obviously got to the same place, but I'd much rather avoid all the pain you endured along the way."

"Antonio, if the misery I went through eventually helps you to accept Jesus as the Lord and Savior of your life, it was worth every second."

"It's hard for me to understand," said Antonio, "how you would be willing to sacrifice your own well-being for me, someone who has hurt you repeatedly by fueling your addiction."

"In order for you to understand that reality, you must experience the depth and breadth of God's love for you. For years, several of my close friends were telling me

CHAPTER 19

about God's love for me. Even though I believed them, I didn't actually feel it in my heart until I went through a three-day retreat several months ago. I know that everybody can experience God in different ways, but that's when God clearly revealed himself to me. You mentioned earlier that you feel a void in your life. That's exactly how I felt, and I found that the only thing that could fill that void was to have God in my life. If you want to learn more about God's love, mercy, patience and forgiveness, the retreat is a great way to experience it. Fortunately, there's one that begins in about a week. What do you think?"

"It sounds interesting... can you tell me more?"

"The retreat begins on Thursday evening and lasts until Sunday evening. You spend the entire seventy-two hours in the church. There will be about thirty men who have previously attended the retreat as guests and who are now serving as the team who guides the current guests through the weekend. There are typically about thirty to forty guests. Over the course of the weekend, you will hear fifteen talks by various team members. The talks will teach you about God's grace and love, and you'll have an opportunity to discuss the talks afterwards with other guests and team members. In addition, there are multiple pleasant surprises throughout the weekend, including an abundance of fantastic food like you've never seen."

"Brandon, I can see how excited you are while talking about the retreat, and the *Sports Illustrated* story revealed how God has transformed your life. I know I'm at a crossroads where it's time for me to take a new direction, but I don't know how to make it happen. I trust you, which may sound odd given our pasts, and I believe that it was no accident that I was given your story to read. Sign me up!"

"That's great, Antonio! There are hundreds of people who've been praying for the guests at this upcoming retreat, including those who haven't even signed up yet. In addition to the retreat, I have another suggestion I'd like to offer to you. I meet weekly with a friend named Patrick Cutler, and we study the Bible together. Patrick is an engineering student, and he also helps me with my football training. He and his dad are both going to be guests at the upcoming retreat as well, so it would be great to have you know at least one person at your retreat. We meet tomorrow evening at 6:30, and we could spend the time teaching you some basics about Christianity. Are you interested?"

"Yes, I'd love to join you guys."

"Can I ask you a personal question?" inquired Brandon.

"Certainly."

"What's the status with your daughter, Sofia? Are you able to see her?"

Antonio sighed and said, "Not yet. My parole officer and Child Protective Services are evaluating the right time and place for me to see her. For now, she's still in foster care."

"It actually sounds like the perfect time for you to attend the retreat."

"I agree. Thank you so much for meeting with me today, and for your guidance. I'll see you tomorrow for the study with Patrick. I'm beginning to feel like there's light at the end of the tunnel."

"That's called hope, my friend," said Brandon warmly.

Chapter 20

AS BRANDON LEFT THE French Café, he phoned Sam Gilmore. "Hi, Sam. Do you have a few minutes to chat?"

"Hi, Brandon. I'm taking a lunch break, so your timing is perfect. How are you doing?"

"I'm great. I had the most unlikely encounter this morning and I wanted to share it with you. Do you remember the name Diablo?"

"Of course. He was your opioid dealer. He always sounded so sinister. Wait, did you have contact with him?!?"

"Yeah. He called me this morning, and we met at the French Café for several hours. He was recently released from jail after being incarcerated for two months. His long-term girlfriend was murdered right before he was arrested. The time in jail convinced him that he wants to take a completely different direction in life for the benefit of his little girl, but he doesn't know where to start. He was given a copy of the *Sports Illustrated* issue that contained my story. He began reading the story and didn't recognize it was about me at first. When he realized that it was me in the story, he was moved by the transformation that God brought about in my life. He basically called saying he wants what I have."

"That's incredible, Brandon! What happened next?"

"He talked about his grief over his girlfriend's death and how his love for his daughter began to change his heart while he was in jail. When he was released, he knew he wanted to leave the drug business and find an honest career. He didn't know where to begin, though, and he also sensed that there was a void in his life. When he read the *Sports Illustrated* story about me, he recognized that the void was the absence of God. He reached out to me to find out how to connect with God."

"What did you tell him?"

"That's the crazy part, Sam, and it's what made me want to call you right away. I invited him to the Christian retreat that begins next week, and he agreed to go. I also asked him to attend the Bible study session that Patrick and I do together tomorrow evening, and he's going to join us. I told him that we would spend tomorrow's time teaching him some basics about the Christian faith. I remembered that same point in my walk with Jesus when you taught me and Emma the basics many years ago when we were in high school. You did such a great job, Sam, and I was wondering if you would be able to join us tomorrow evening?"

"I'd be honored, Brandon. What a great example of how God pursues us no matter what we've done. Even a drug dealer. I'm looking forward to it."

"Amen. That's great that you can join us. I can't think of anyone else I'd rather have introduce Antonio to Jesus than you."

"Thanks. That's kind of you. Before we go, can I talk with you about one other thing?"

"Of course."

CHAPTER 20

"Ever since the *Sports Illustrated* article has come out, Grace has been struggling. It has reminded her again of Joshua's death, and she's reliving all the guilt she endured at that time. She also sees the national praise you've received for your courage in overcoming your addictions, and it's brought about some bitterness in Grace."

"Towards me?" Brandon asked softly.

"Yes," responded Sam.

"I'm so sorry for my part in all of this. I'll pray for her, Sam. Is there anything else I can do? Would it help if I talk with her?"

"Only God can heal her heart, so I don't think it would help for you to talk with her. I really appreciate your prayers. I just wanted you to be aware of what's going on."

The next evening, Brandon, Patrick, Antonio and Sam met at Brandon's apartment. Brandon introduced Antonio to Patrick and Sam, and he explained how Sam had taught him the basics of Christianity when they were in high school together.

Sam began, "Antonio, have you had any exposure to Christianity in your life?"

"Yes, when I was a child, my mother would take my siblings and me to church every Sunday. It was a Christian church, but I don't really remember much about it. I think it gave me just enough exposure to God to recognize that God was what was missing in my life when I read the story about Brandon's redemption."

"In my experience," Sam continued, "we often become aware of our need for God when we hit a low point. Our recognition of our need for God emerges when we realize we can no longer pull ourselves out of our dismal circumstances under our own strength."

"That's definitely true for me. I want God in my life. How do I find him?"

"He is already here with us in this room right now. In a moment, we're going to pray for God to enter your heart, but I'd like to make sure that you understand what that means first. After God created the world, as well as Adam and Eve, they disobeyed God in the Garden of Eden. As a result of Adam and Eve's sin, humans had an unharmonious relationship with God. However, God restored our relationship with him by sending his Son, Jesus, to Earth. Jesus led a sinless life and ultimately accepted the punishment for our sins by willingly undergoing death on a cross. By believing in Jesus and accepting him as the Lord and Savior of your life, you will be reconciled to God."

Tears began to well up in Antonio's eyes and he said, "I have done some really bad stuff in my life. That almost seems too good to be true."

"Are you sorry for your sins?" asked Sam.

"More than I can say," said Antonio as his tears began flowing freely. "When I was in jail, I kept thinking about all the evil things I'd done and all the people that I'd hurt. The sorrow and regret were unbearable, and still are, and you're saying that all of that will be forgiven if I accept Jesus. What exactly does that mean?"

Sam replied, "God's grace is a free gift through faith in Jesus. All of your sins—past, present and future—are

CHAPTER 20

forgiven through your faith in Jesus as the Son of God who died for your sins. Once you understand the magnitude of God's gift, you will begin to appreciate the depth of his love for us. You'll start to love him in return, and as an outpouring of your love, you'll want to do his will and serve others."

"I understand, Sam, and I'm ready to accept Jesus," declared Antonio.

Sam replied, "Repeat this prayer after me Antonio:

Dear Jesus, I know I am a sinner...
and I ask your forgiveness...
I believe that you died for my sins and rose from the dead...
I invite you to come into my heart and my life...
and I trust you as my Lord and Savior."

Antonio's tears of sorrow instantly became tears of joy, as he felt the weight of guilt and regret lifted from his shoulders. His three friends each embraced him tightly as the magnitude of this moment touched all of their hearts.

Chapter 21

A WEEK LATER, BRANDON DROVE his three guests, Antonio, Patrick and Patrick's dad, to the church for the start of the three-day retreat. Patrick's father, James, had completely recovered from the accident. The ordeal had heightened his appreciation of the preciousness of life, and he immediately accepted the invitation to the retreat. He was really looking forward to having some dedicated time to reflect on the goodness of God, but also to share the experience with Patrick.

Antonio was enjoying his new journey with God, and he was anticipating that the retreat would not only advance his knowledge of God's ways, but would also allow him to fully experience the depth and breadth of God's love for him. He was looking forward to making some new Christian friends, but he really missed Sofia. He still had not yet been able to see her since his release from jail, and his heart ached for her.

Patrick didn't know quite what to expect during the retreat, but he completely trusted Brandon, who relished the favorable impact the retreat had had on his life. Patrick had developed a close friendship with Brandon, and he respected and admired Brandon's deep faith in God.

CHAPTER 21

As the four men drove to the church, Brandon asked, "Did your trip from Cleveland to Cincinnati go smoothly today, James?"

"Yes, traffic was light, and I had no delays. I must admit, though, that my mind was reflecting frequently on the last time I traveled between Cincinnati and Cleveland, when I had the accident. By the way, I've never thanked you for taking such great care of Patrick in the aftermath of the accident."

"You're welcome, but I think it was all part of God's plan for Patrick and me to become friends. Besides, he has more than repaid me through all the assistance he's given me with my training."

"How's your conditioning coming along?" inquired James.

"Really well. I think I'm very close to being in peak shape, and I'm ready to begin summer workouts with the team next week."

"That begins next week?" asked Antonio.

"Yeah, I leave for Columbus on Monday, the day after the retreat ends."

Over the course of the weekend retreat, Patrick had the opportunity to get to know Antonio much better. Antonio shared with him many stories about the dark underbelly of drug trafficking, including turf wars, volatile relationships among dealers, supply issues, and intimidation through violence. By understanding Antonio's former life, Patrick had an even stronger appreciation for the significance of Antonio's recent transformation.

Patrick also spent a fair amount of time with his dad during the meals and breaks throughout the weekend. With the backdrop of James' recent near-fatal accident, both Patrick and James had similar responses to the weekend. They both experienced enormous gratitude for James' complete recovery from the accident, and they more fully understood God's power in orchestrating the healing.

Both James and Patrick became more thankful for the joy of living each day in God's presence, and they had a greater desire to serve God because of his gift in facilitating James' recovery. They also yearned to draw closer to God on a daily basis, especially through their prayer lives and in reading the Bible. Finally, James and Patrick recognized how much they cherished each other and their family.

While the retreat weekend was joyful, enlightening and gratifying for James and Patrick, it was an emotional roller coaster for Antonio. It was even more moving than witnessing the death of Valeria. Antonio learned that God loves him so much that he allowed his sinless Son to endure an agonizing death on a cross for the forgiveness of Antonio's sins.

As Antonio began to come to grips with the reality that all of his wrongdoings had been forgiven by God, he understood the immensity of God's love for him and the value of God's gift of grace. The tears for Antonio flowed early and often as he learned more and more about God's character. At times, Antonio cried quiet, steady tears of joy, and at other points in the weekend, his body was wracked with sobbing as he recognized how disappointed God must have been with him for his previous behaviors.

At one point in the weekend, Antonio was looking through the compartments in the bag he had brought from home for his razor so he could shave. The bag was the same one he had used in the past to make deliveries to

CHAPTER 21

his customers. As he was searching for his razor, he found a hypodermic needle that he carried in case any of his customers needed one. It was a stark, chilling reminder of his former life.

Later in the weekend, when the guests were given the opportunity to lay down personal events, actions, attitudes or emotions in order to give them up once and for all to the saving power of Jesus, Antonio placed the hypodermic needle there. This act was a powerfully cleansing moment for him. And, it was a profound example to all who witnessed it that no one is beyond the reach of the forgiveness of Jesus.

As the retreat progressed into the final day, Antonio experienced an overwhelming desire to get baptized, and he wanted to do it in front of the seventy men with whom he had shared the retreat weekend. When he was asked by the retreat team if there was anyone else he would like to witness his baptism, he said with a heavy sigh, "I'd love for my daughter, Sofia, to be here, but I know that isn't possible."

Fortunately, Brandon had attended a retreat weekend about four months ago and was baptized at the end of the weekend. He anticipated correctly that Antonio may also have a desire to get baptized and that he'd want Sofia to be there. Brandon had asked Antonio, without raising his suspicions, for the contact information of his parole officer about five days prior to the weekend, and Brandon had started working with him about the possibility of Sofia attending Antonio's baptism if it did occur over the weekend. The parole officer was very supportive of such a worthwhile effort and was able to get Child Protective

Services to agree. They also agreed to release Sofia to Antonio as soon as he had found acceptable housing.

The baptismal pool at the church was located in the front of the sanctuary on the left side. It was elevated about twelve feet above the sanctuary and was reached via a descending stairway from the second floor. The water was heated and about four feet deep which allowed for complete submersion. As Antonio descended the stairs into the water accompanied by the team member who would be baptizing him, he could hardly see because of the tears of joy that filled his eyes. He could hear the shouts of encouragement from his retreat brothers as he prepared to recite the baptismal pledge before being submerged.

Antonio could feel a rare combination of excitement and peace as he gave his verbal commitment to Jesus and was submerged. As he came up out of the water, he felt a joy unlike anything he'd ever experienced. He could hear the thunderous applause and shouting from the men in his retreat. As the water from the baptism cleared from his eyes and ears, he could discern a much higher-pitched voice among the clamor from the men. As the yelling from the men began to subside, he unmistakably could hear a small child's voice, which he immediately recognized, calling, "Daddy! Daddy!" He spotted Sofia behind the men and off to the left.

He yelled, "Sofia!", and he thought for a moment about jumping out of the baptismal pool to the ground below, but he realized that the twelve-foot drop probably wouldn't end well for him. He sprinted up the baptismal steps and then ran down a different staircase to the sanctuary floor, still soaking wet. Antonio raced to Sofia and lifted her into

CHAPTER 21

a tight embrace. He thought his heart would burst. After a full minute, he loosened his hug so he could see her face, and she said, "Daddy, can I go swimming with you?"

Accompanying Sofia was Brandon, as well as Sofia's case worker from Child Protective Services, Sofia's foster parents and Reverend Geller, the pastor of the host church for the retreat. Brandon said, "Congratulations on your baptism, Antonio. How do you feel?"

"Between the retreat, the baptism and seeing Sofia again, my joy is indescribable."

"I have some additional joyful news for you," Brandon continued. "Child Protective Services is ready to return Sofia to you as soon as you have an acceptable place to live. Before you say anything, Reverend Geller has a proposal for you."

Reverend Geller began, "I understand that you are at a transitional point in your life, Antonio, and we may be able to help each other. Our church recently lost a staff member who did maintenance and janitorial services for us. You're welcome to the job, either temporarily or permanently. It pays twenty dollars an hour. In addition, there's a fully-furnished house on the church campus, and no one is currently living there. You and Sofia are welcome to stay there for free as long as you are employed by the church. I'm also confident that we can find some volunteers who will gladly watch Sofia while you are working. I've heard about your situation, and I'd like to help you get back on your feet. You would also help us by filling a role on our staff on very short notice. What do you think?"

Antonio was still holding Sofia, who said, "Daddy, I'm so glad you're back. Promise you won't ever leave me again."

Sofia's words were spoken directly into Antonio's heart, and he immediately knew the answer to Reverend Geller's question.

Through even more tears, Antonio responded, "Thank you, Reverend, for your generous offer, and I gratefully accept!"

"That's great, Antonio. The closing ceremony for the retreat is going to start in a few minutes. Let's have you change into some dry clothes. Right after the closing festivities, I'll have one of the staff help you and Sofia get settled into the house."

Chapter 22

THE NEXT MORNING, BRANDON awoke thinking about the retreat and its impact on the lives of Patrick, James and especially Antonio. Shortly after he arose, he received a call from Jalen Pittman.

"Hi, Brandon. How's it going?"

"Hey, Jalen. I'm doing great. I sponsored three guests at the Christian retreat that concluded last night. As usual, God did some powerful things over the course of the weekend. How are you?"

"That's awesome. I'm doing really well. I'm looking forward to the start of summer practice tomorrow."

"Me, too, although I'm still adjusting to you being my coach," kidded Brandon.

"I know, right? That's part of the reason why I called. As you'll recall, Ohio State has a hotshot freshman running back named Tristin Garner. I've spent a lot of time on the phone getting to know him. He may possibly be the most arrogant person I've ever met in my life. Of course, he's aware that you're returning to the team, but he has absolutely no respect for you or your accomplishments on the football field. He knows that you and I were former teammates, and he's suspicious that I'll give you preferential treatment. I just want you to know that I must treat you just like any other player anytime we're on the field together."

"That's not a problem, Jalen. I've always felt that respect should be earned, and I definitely will need to re-establish myself at Ohio State, especially after having been away for nearly five years. You can also count on me being respectful of you, just like I would be with any other coach."

"Thanks, I knew I could depend on you. There's one other issue about Tristin that I want to discuss with you. He's insisting that he be given jersey number '21'."

"My old number."

"That's right, Brandon. Under normal circumstances, I'd be firm that the upperclassman retains his number until he graduates or leaves the program. Your situation is somewhat unique because it appeared that your Ohio State career was over. My concern is that this could be the sort of dispute that divides our team and destroys our chemistry. On the other hand, it kills me to see you get disrespected in this way."

"There's an easy solution to this. I'd like to assume the same humility that Jesus demonstrated and take a different jersey number. My preference would be number '23' if it's available, because that's the number that Dylan wears for his team."

"Thanks, Brandon. I knew you'd view this dilemma through a Christian perspective, and number '23' is available. There's one more thing... what time are you arriving in Columbus today?"

"I've already moved all my furniture to my Columbus apartment. I just need to pack up a few odds and ends, clean

CHAPTER 22

up my Cincinnati apartment, and drop off the keys. I should be in Columbus by early afternoon. Why?"

"That's great. What do you say to having dinner together tonight? I'd like you to meet my girlfriend, Jasmine. Can Emma join us as well?"

"That sounds like fun. Emma is available tonight. She moved into her new apartment in Columbus about a week ago and has started her new job, and we were already planning to have dinner together tonight. I'll check with her, but I suspect she'll be delighted that we'll be joining you and Jasmine."

"Good. I'll text you this afternoon with the details."

Later that morning, Manny Garcia was exploring a part of Columbus that was predominantly Hispanic. He had settled into his dorm room two days earlier. He was out of Adderall, and with practice beginning tomorrow, he was desperate to find a supplier in Columbus. He borrowed his roommate's car, and he was carefully scanning the streets as he drove through the neighborhood for any telltale signs of a dealer. He spotted a young man sitting on the front porch of a small, dilapidated house built a century ago. Manny drove around for about ten minutes and then cruised past the house again. The same person was still sitting on the porch, and a second man, wearing a tattered red Ohio State sweatshirt, was standing on the porch conversing with him.

Manny drove slowly past the house and again returned about fifteen minutes later. The guy sitting on the porch now had a different visitor who was again standing. Manny made another pass by the house and was fairly certain that he'd found a potential supplier. He parked his car around the corner about a block away and waited ten minutes before approaching the house on foot. The young man sitting on the porch was again alone.

As Manny approached, he felt like his heart was about to beat out of his chest. He tried his best to appear nonchalant. He called in Spanish from the sidewalk to the man on the porch, "Good morning. I'm new to Columbus, and I'm lost. I wonder if you could help me."

The man responded in Spanish, "What brings you to Columbus?"

"Football. I play for Ohio State."

"We don't see many football players around here. What are you looking for?"

"Uh... I want to buy some stuff. I need a little Adderall. Can you help me with that?"

"Maybe. What's your name?"

"Manny Garcia."

The young man, whose name was Pablo Ruiz, checked on his phone and was able to quickly verify that Ohio State had an incoming freshman player named Manny Garcia whose photo matched the young man standing in front of him. "You use Adderall to help your performance?" asked the man on the porch.

"Yeah."

"You know it's a banned performance enhancing drug, don't you?"

"Yeah."

CHAPTER 22

"What are you gonna say if you get caught by a drug screen?"

Manny nervously licked his lips and said, "I'll come up with some line about how I didn't know it was banned, and I have no idea how it got into my body."

"Just as long as you don't point any fingers at me, because if you do, there will be big trouble for you."

"I swear that won't happen."

"You just make sure that it doesn't. What size?"

"Fifteen milligrams."

"How many?"

"It's hard for me to get here because I don't have a car. Can you sell me thirty of them?"

"That'll be a thousand dollars."

Manny swallowed hard and said, "Look, all I have is five hundred dollars. We get paid NIL money for playing football, and we'll get paid in about a week." Manny was lying because he wasn't sure when the NIL funds would be distributed. Manny continued, "Can you please cut me a little slack, because I'll be a regular customer for you over the next four years?"

The man on the porch said, "My policy is to never extend credit, but you're catching me on a good day because I'm an Ohio State football fan. I'll take your five hundred dollars and give you until two weeks from today to pay me the other five hundred." The dealer lowered his voice and said gravely, "If you're even one day late, I'm going to come looking for you."

The two men exchanged the drugs, money and phone numbers, and Manny walked back to his car feeling very relieved.

Chapter 23

THAT EVENING, JALEN AND Jasmine met Brandon and Emma for dinner at a Mexican restaurant near the Ohio State campus. Brandon and Emma knew Jalen was quite smitten with Jasmine, and this was their first opportunity to meet her. They both instantly liked her. Jasmine had an energetic, engaging personality. She had a dazzling smile which she displayed frequently, and she had a lively sense of humor. Jasmine loved to laugh at her own jokes, and her laughter was infectious in a way that drew others to her. She had a self-assured manner that suggested an underlying confidence, but she was outwardly humble. Jasmine listened attentively and offered insightful perspective or asked thoughtful questions, giving others in the conversation her full attention. Her kind, endearing demeanor made Emma and Brandon feel as though they had been lifelong friends with her even though they had just met. It was no surprise that Jalen had fallen for her.

As they took their seats at the table, Emma asked Jasmine, "Have you relocated from Dallas to Columbus?"

"Yes, I got an apartment in Upper Arlington, not too far from Jalen's place."

"Did you grow up in Dallas?" inquired Brandon.

CHAPTER 23

"Yes, I've lived there all my life except for a couple of years when I did research at MD Anderson in Houston."

"How did you and Jalen meet?" asked Emma.

Jasmine and Jalen glanced at each other and smiled, and Jasmine said to Jalen while giggling, "Why don't you share your fabricated tale, then I'll tell Emma and Brandon what really happened."

"Let's let Brandon and Emma decide who's telling the truth," said Jalen as he winked at Emma and Brandon. "I liked to run through the park near my home in Dallas. There were a lot of people with their dogs, and sometimes I would get accosted by a dog. I began to carry dog treats in my pocket whenever I went running just in case I needed to tame a savage beast. One day, I was running through the park and went around a bend on the trail when I suddenly encountered Jasmine and her dog, Jessie, blocking the trail. Jessie immediately went into protective mode when she saw me, and I feared for my life. I barely managed to divert Jessie's attention with a dog treat so I could escape unharmed."

"Stop!" exclaimed Jasmine while laughing. "Let me tell you what really happened. Jessie is the most friendly, playful golden retriever that you're ever going to meet. She and I were laying on a blanket in the sun on a hill in the park, about forty feet removed from the running trail. Jalen came running along the trail when he spotted Jessie and me. He jumped off the trail, and ran up the hill through the grass to offer Jessie a treat. He had to wake her up from her nap to give it to her."

Emma and Brandon started laughing, and they both agreed that Jasmine's version of the story was the more likely one.

"So how long ago was it that Jessie introduced the two of you to each other?" asked Emma.

"It was about eight months ago, and we started dating shortly thereafter," said Jasmine. "When Jalen got the opportunity to return to Ohio State to coach, we both knew that we were already on a path to spending the rest of our lives together. Because I work virtually and can work from anywhere, we decided that it made sense for me to move to Columbus, too."

"What kind of work do you do?" inquired Brandon.

"I work for a consulting company and help to oversee cancer research. I have a PharmD degree, and my interest is in chemotherapy that treats primarily pediatric cancers."

"It sounds like our passions are aligned," exclaimed Emma excitedly. "I'm a nurse on the oncology ward at Nationwide Children's Hospital. I was drawn to caring for children with cancer ever since I was in nursing school."

"I sensed that we are kindred spirits, Emma. My company works closely with the pediatric oncologists at Ohio State. Tell me, is it difficult for you being on the front lines of treating children with cancer?"

"Some days are very difficult, especially when a patient and their family get the news that a particular treatment is not working or their cancer has recurred. Those rough days, fortunately, are balanced out by enough days where patients receive a favorable report about their disease. I really rely on my faith to help me manage the emotional roller coaster of caring for my patients and their families. Are you a person of faith, Jasmine?"

CHAPTER 23

"Yes, I'm a Christian. Like you, Emma, my faith is the foundation of my life. I haven't yet found a church I can embrace in Columbus. Do you have a recommendation?"

"I sure do. Let's plan to go together on Sunday morning, and I can introduce you to Pastor Apple. It's the same church I attended when I was a nursing student at Ohio State."

As Emma and Jasmine continued their dialogue about their respective faith journeys, Jalen said to Brandon, "Check out your gains, bro. It looks like you've put on a lot of muscle since I last saw you a couple of months ago."

"Thanks, man. I've been happy with how my body has responded to the training. Fortunately, I didn't have any injury setbacks, so I've been able to make steady progress. Both my speed and my strength are nearly back to my levels during my junior year at Ohio State. I'm really looking forward to starting practice tomorrow, but I know it'll take me a while to get acclimated to hitting again. How's the team looking this year?"

"Talent-wise, especially on offense, I think we are as good or better than we have ever been. It's the chemistry of the team that's a complete unknown. We lost a handful of our junior and senior leaders to the NFL and a few of our talented juniors and sophomores to the transfer portal. More than ever, we're going to be depending on freshmen to fill key holes. There are some players, such as Tristin Garner, whose self-centered attitude could have a very damaging impact on our team chemistry. I'm delighted that you're returning to our team Brandon. Normally, I'd expect you to have a very stabilizing effect on our team... but I'm just not sure how it'll go."

"What do you mean?" asked Brandon.

"It was interesting to see the various reactions to the *Sports Illustrated* article about you. Some of the players view you with awe as one of the legends of Ohio State football who is re-emerging from the past to join our team. They tend to view the hardships that you endured during your hiatus from Ohio State as only adding to your legendary status. Other players view you with sympathy or pity and are uncertain about what to expect from your performance on the field. Still others view you with disdain and disrespect. This category is mostly the freshmen, especially Tristin Garner and Manny Garcia, a defensive back."

"It sounds like I'm going to have to re-earn respect from my teammates," said Brandon with determination.

"Brandon, if you are even close to the level of player you were before, you can unite this team around you. There's no limit to what we can do, including a national championship."

"Sounds like we have some work to do. I can't wait to get started!"

"I'll tell you one thing, Brandon. You know how rabid Ohio State football fans are, but because of your return, I've never before seen them more excited than they are for the upcoming season. The stadium is going to explode the first time you touch the ball in our home opener!"

Chapter 24

ON A SULTRY MID-JUNE morning, Brandon awoke very early because he was so excited about the start of summer practice. After his father died, Brandon lost all his passion for playing football. Over the last several months, as he was training again, Brandon experienced a revitalized surge of desire to return to the field. He once again loved the sport of football, the camaraderie with his teammates, the physical and mental preparation, and the opportunity to secure a victory for the school he represented and loved. One additional motivation Brandon didn't previously have was the chance to glorify God through playing football. He often found himself silently praying between reps while training and joyfully appreciating God's presence in his life.

Brandon drove to the practice facility an hour before he was required to report. He wanted to savor being back in the fold of Ohio State football, and he also wanted to meet some of his teammates and to start forming bonds with them.

When Brandon entered the training facility, the first person he saw was Coach Anderson. Brandon embraced him heartily in a bear hug and said, "Coach, I can't tell you how grateful I am for the opportunity you've given me to play again."

"It's great to have you back, Brandon. Your promising football career ended prematurely, and this is our chance to take care of some unfinished business together. How has your conditioning been going?"

"I told Coach Pittman yesterday that I'm very close to my peak fitness. These upcoming workouts with the team over the summer will have me ready for the start of the season."

"Have you been doing any throwing?"

"Yes. I work on it a couple of days a week."

"Good. I'd definitely like to bring back the halfback option pass. That was such a powerful tool in our offense when you were here. Since you left, we just haven't had anyone with the unique gifts of running and throwing that you have."

"That's great, Coach. I was hoping you would use that play in our offense."

Coach Anderson moved closer to Brandon and lowered his voice. "Brandon, as excited as I am about having your football talent back on our team, I'm even more enthusiastic to see how your character and faith impact our players and coaches. I want to encourage you to use any opportunities to allow God's glory to shine through your words and actions."

"I appreciate you saying that, Coach, because that's exactly what I was praying for as I drove here this morning."

As Brandon entered the locker room, he immediately saw Tristin Garner with his back toward him. Even though Brandon had never met Tristin, he knew it was him because he was wearing number "21" on his practice jersey. Brandon approached him and said, "Hi, Tristin. I'm Brandon Campbell," and he extended his hand.

CHAPTER 24

Tristin turned around and sized up Brandon with a condescending expression on his face, then snarled, "Would you prefer I call you 'Sir' or 'Mr. Campbell', because you gotta be like forty?"

Brandon sensed immediately this was not good-natured kidding between teammates, but rather Tristin was mocking him. In a few seconds, Brandon would be certain of his impression. He responded with a smile, "No need for formality. You can call me whatever you like, but I prefer just 'Brandon'."

With a cruel, disdainful smirk, Tristin said, "Okay, I think I'll call you 'Pops'."

Brandon silently prayed for calmness and immediately felt the Holy Spirit's peace and guidance as he said amiably, "Number 21 looks good on you!"

"Certainly much better than it ever looked on you. I'm going to be taking it to new heights, all the way to the Heisman Trophy this year. I've already started writing my acceptance speech, so if you stay out of my way, I may even mention you in it."

Brandon had been warned about this young man's arrogance, but he wasn't prepared for this level of bravado. Determined to take the high road, Brandon replied, "I'll do what I can to help you." He noticed out of the corner of his eye as he walked away that Tristin and another freshman player, Manny Garcia, were laughing and high-fiving each other.

The first few days of practice were relatively easy as the coaches taught the players, especially the freshmen, the proper technique for every drill and stretching exercise.

Brandon noticed that Tristin never seemed to pay attention any time one of the coaches was speaking.

By the fourth day, the coaches began to ramp up the physical intensity of the practices. There was much more running overall, and the drills were done at 90% speed rather than 70%. Also, the coaches were much more precise and demanding that the appropriate technique was always used. Tristin seemed uninterested in accepting coaching input, as his only focus was to try to outperform Brandon on every drill.

As they started the fourth week, the players spent most of each practice with their position group, such as offensive linemen, running backs, linebackers and defensive backs. Brandon and Tristin were with the running backs group under Coach Pittman, who announced that at the end of the week, they would be doing a series of events, such as standing long jump, vertical leap, forty-yard dash and backwards weight throw, in order to assess their strength, conditioning and athleticism. Each event would be scored. The scores from the individual events would be totaled, and an overall winner would be declared. The results would then help to determine the order of the ranking of the running backs on the depth chart, with the winner having the edge for the top running back spot.

This was exactly what Tristin had been eagerly awaiting. He was so confident in his ability that he was certain that he'd win the competition and be publicly declared as the number one running back, a position he would never relinquish.

Brandon had several advantages over Tristin. At the age of twenty-four, his body was at the peak of athletic prowess.

CHAPTER 24

He had undergone this competition three times previously, during his freshman, sophomore and junior years. In his freshman year, he finished a close second, then won by a wide margin in both his sophomore and junior years. Finally, during the three months Brandon was training with Patrick, he practiced all the events specifically so he could be as well prepared as possible.

As the days leading up to the competition drew closer, Tristin relied on one of the tricks that had served him well up to this point in his athletic career – trash talking. Tristin found that he was very adept at disrupting the focus of his competitors by a maddening combination of brashness, rudeness, disrespect and threats. Tristin's favorite hot buttons to press with Brandon were his age and his previous addictions. Fortunately, Brandon's experience and faith served him well. During his football career, he had encountered so many trash talkers that he now rarely lost his focus. He also found that keeping God at the forefront of his consciousness helped him concentrate.

When the day of the competition arrived, Brandon could sense Tristin's uneasiness in spite of his cockiness. This was a new experience for him, and he was uncertain how he would perform relative to Brandon and the other more experienced running backs. Fortunately for him, the first event was the forty-yard dash, an event in which he had much skill and experience. Unfortunately for him, he was unaware that Brandon had run track for Ohio State and was among the top short sprinters in the Big Ten.

Coach Pittman had the players compete in pairs, and he arranged for Brandon and Tristin to be the final pair. That gave Tristin an extra ten minutes or so to needle Brandon relentlessly with comments such as, "Hey, Pops. You gonna use your walker in this race?" or "How about I give you a thirty-yard head start, and I'll still beat you by five yards." Brandon would laugh at the most humorous insults and commend Tristin on his cleverness. Tristin had never met a competitor who was not only unperturbed and amused by his insults, but also showed no inclination whatsoever to fire back. He found it very disconcerting.

When it came time for their race, Tristin could only think about how badly he was going to beat Brandon and how unmercifully he would rub it in his face afterwards. Tristin was completely focused when he took the starting line, and he was thinking only of blazing to the finish line when the starting gun fired. He ran with blinders on, not paying any attention to Brandon in the adjacent lane. Tristin ran a very respectable personal best of 4.41 seconds, while Brandon ran the race in an otherworldly time of 4.28 seconds.

At the finish line, Brandon warmly congratulated Tristin on his excellent race. Tristin's performance in the other events deteriorated from there. Brandon not only won the competition overall by a wide margin, but he also had the best score in every one of the individual events. Tristin finished in the middle of the pack in fourth place.

It didn't take long for Tristin to recover from the assault on his ego due to his disappointing performance. He rationalized that the multi-event competition was a poor substitute for what a running back really does – gaining yards and scoring touchdowns. Tristin was confident that once the team started practicing in pads in a couple of weeks, his superior ability would become very apparent to the other players and the coaches.

CHAPTER 24

On the following Monday after the competition, Coach Pittman began practice with the announcement that he wanted Brandon to spend the day practicing with the quarterbacks and wide receivers. Jalen had arranged this in advance to allow Brandon to prepare for the implementation of the halfback option pass into their offense. Not surprisingly, Tristin viewed the announcement as proof of his longstanding suspicion that Coach Pittman gave Brandon Campbell preferential treatment.

Like many freshmen, Manny Garcia was finding the transition from high school to college football more difficult than he had imagined. Ohio State was not just any football program but was usually in the top six teams in the country every year. One of the areas where Ohio State had sustained excellence was in the recruitment and development of defensive backs, the position which Manny played.

In spite of Manny's stardom in high school, he was having trouble keeping up with the other defensive backs, both physically and mentally. In order to try to compensate for his shortcomings, he had increased his dosage of Adderall. Although Manny hadn't yet recognized it, the higher dosage had actually hurt him more than it helped him. He was losing weight and sleeping poorly, and he was also more irritable and quick-tempered. He had alienated many of his teammates and coaches because of his bristly disposition both in the locker room and on the field.

His mood was further soured because he was using the Adderall at a faster rate and didn't have any money to purchase more, let alone to pay the balance on the first supply he received. Pablo Ruiz was now calling him multiple times a day for his money. Manny knew that he needed to have an uncomfortable conversation with Pablo where he would beg him for his patience until the NIL money came through from Ohio State, and also ask him to extend some additional credit to Manny for some more Adderall. Manny felt that it was best to talk to Pablo face-to-face, so he again borrowed his roommate's car, as well as two hundred dollars from him.

As Manny circled Pablo's block, he spotted him casually sitting on the same front porch where they met the first time. After he again parked the car about a block away, he walked to the house where Pablo was sitting. As Manny approached, Pablo spotted him and called out in Spanish, "I'm glad you came to see me. I was beginning to think that I was going to have to ask my friends to pay you a visit." The implication was not lost on Manny, as he began to fully grasp the level of danger of his situation.

Manny responded in Spanish, "Pablo, I'm sorry that I didn't return your calls, but I thought it was best that I talk with you face-to-face about my dilemma."

"I don't care about your problems. I just want my money."

"Look, when I saw you last time, I was told that the players would get some NIL money from Ohio State in a week. I've found out that we don't get paid until intensive practices start in two weeks." Manny's statement was based on hope and not on truth, as he really didn't know when he would receive the money.

He expanded his lie further by saying, "The Adderall really helps my performance. It looks like I'll be a starter

CHAPTER 24

this fall. That means I'll get an even bigger share of NIL money, so I can afford to pay you a premium for extending me the credit."

"So, what you're telling me is that you don't have my money today?" inquired Pablo menacingly.

Manny was using every ounce of his self-control to not show how frightened he was as he responded, "Not exactly. I have two hundred dollars as good faith money, but I really need another thirty Adderall's to help me keep my starting spot. I can pay you in two weeks."

Pablo's evil mind was focused on Manny like a black widow spider assesses a struggling fly in her web. "I'll tell you what I'll do. You still owe me three hundred dollars for the first round. In two weeks, that number becomes one thousand. I'll supply you with another thirty Adderall for three thousand dollars. So, in two weeks, you owe me four thousand dollars."

"Wait, that's not fair," exclaimed Manny. "You tripled the price!"

"I told you last time that I don't do business on credit. I'm making an exception for you because of your unique circumstances, but the price is higher because you failed to pay me on time the first time. You'd better not be late in two weeks, or my friends and I will be looking for you."

Manny believed that he had no other choice than to accept Pablo's terms. He handed him the two hundred dollars and accepted the Adderall. He had a very uneasy feeling as he walked back to the car.

Chapter 25

FOLLOWING THE MULTI-EVENTS COMPETITION among the running backs, the news of Brandon's performance quickly spread throughout the rest of the team. There were only a few of the current players who were on the team when Brandon last played for Ohio State five years ago. The rest of the team had only a vague awareness of the legend of Brandon's athletic prowess. The results of the running backs competition triggered the realization in his teammates that the mythical stories about Brandon's football heroics were actually true. The respect and admiration from Brandon's teammates were surging rapidly. As a result, Tristin's disdain for Brandon was also intensifying.

About ten days after the running backs had their multi-events competition, the football team began the core of its training camp. It was a chance for the offense to run plays under controlled conditions against the defense. It was the first time, since Tristin arrived at Ohio State, when there would be blocking and tackling in practice. He anticipated this would be his chance to shine. Tristin, however, experienced the same harsh reality as many other freshman college football players—including Brandon as a freshman—in that there was a huge difference between playing football at the high school level and at a Division I

CHAPTER 25

college. The players were bigger, stronger, faster, smarter and more experienced. Defensive players rarely missed a tackle. Everything unfolded so much quicker that most freshmen didn't react properly and became overwhelmed. For running backs, especially, the holes in the offensive line closed so fast that the ball carrier would often be tackled as soon as he reached the line.

Brandon, as a freshman, experienced the same frustration as Tristin. Jalen Pittman, who was a junior, tutored him by watching game film together and teaching him how to read the shifting of the offensive line. After a short while, Brandon learned to be patient when he received the handoff and to predict where the running lane was about to open. After watching Tristin getting increasingly frustrated with his first practice of running the ball against a live defense, Brandon quietly approached Coach Pittman on the sideline and whispered, "Tristin could benefit from the same teaching that you gave me when I was a freshman. Would you like me to take him under my wing?"

"Thanks, Brandon. I agree with you. Let me talk with him first, and I'll let you know how it goes."

Jalen, having been an elite player himself, understood that a coach sometimes had to light a fire under his players and sometimes he needed to take a gentler, consoling approach. He also had to discern which method was better for a given player at a particular moment. Jalen had all the right skills to be an excellent football coach.

After practice concluded, Coach Pittman called Tristin aside and said, "There's a lot to absorb in making the transition from high school to college football. I still remember how lost I felt during my freshman year. I eventually learned some very important lessons that were the keys to solving the challenges to becoming a successful college back. I'd like to teach you what I learned, and the best way is to study game film. What do you say we have our first lesson this evening in the film room?"

"Coach, thanks, but I got this. Nobody is as gifted as me, and I just need a little more time to make some adjustments, then I'll be running the ball all over this field."

Jalen was disappointed in his response, but not surprised. He also remembered how freshman players are especially careful not to reveal their vulnerabilities to their coaches. Jalen responded, "Let's see how tomorrow goes for you. Another option would be to have one of the upperclassmen give you some pointers."

The next day at practice was even worse for Tristin. He was convinced that the solution was to just try harder, but if anything, his results were even more unproductive. He tried to hit the holes in the offensive line quicker and with more force. Unfortunately, he would just run into the back of his offensive lineman or get tackled in the backfield by a defender who found a gap in the blocking scheme. To make matters worse, when Brandon was the running back, he would almost effortlessly make a large gain every time he carried the ball. Tristin tried to discern what he was doing differently than Brandon, but it was not apparent to him.

At a break in practice, Brandon pulled Tristin aside and said, "Hey man, I can see you're a really talented dude, but there are a few tricks to succeeding as a college running back. When I was a freshman, I was really struggling until one of the upperclassmen taught me how to read the developing holes in the offensive line more effectively. Once I

CHAPTER 25

understood it, everything got easier, and I started having some success. I'd be happy to pass that knowledge on to you."

"Look, Pops, we're both competing for the same thing—to be the starting running back in the season opener. I don't want you giving me crummy advice to try to mess me up. Why else would you be offering to help me?"

"It's not like that at all, Tristin. If every player is better, the whole team is better. I don't care who starts, I just want to win a Big Ten Championship and a National Championship."

"Yeah, right!" said Tristin with disgust.

"If you change your mind, I'm here for you," said Brandon cordially as he headed for the sideline.

Brandon heard a shrillness pierce the air, as Coach Anderson blew his whistle and called all the offensive players together at mid-field. "Guys, we're going to do a controlled scrimmage against the defense. We'll start with the ball on the thirty-yard line. The offense will have six plays to score a touchdown. If they do, they'll win the round. If they don't, the defense wins the round. We'll play three rounds. Whoever wins two of the three rounds will be excused from running sprints at the end of practice. Starters take the field, and backups stay ready to play."

The first play was a sweep around the left side for Brandon, resulting in an eight-yard gain. The next one was an off-tackle play where Brandon slithered through the narrowest of holes between the left tackle and tight end, then sidestepped the linebacker for a ten-yard gain. Brandon's astonishing athleticism was fully displayed on the third and final play of the round. It was a sweep to the right side, and Brandon used his explosive speed to get outside of the defensive end. As the cornerback closed to make the tackle,

Brandon faked to the outside with a jab step, then used a nifty jump cut to move inside without being touched by the cornerback. The safety hit Brandon at the five-yard line, but it had about the same impact as a fly striking a locomotive going sixty miles per hour. Brandon's touchdown gave the first round to the offense. The offensive players on the sideline cheered loudly, except for Tristin.

During the next round, Brandon was replaced by the second-string running back. The first play was a screen play to the back for two yards. The second play was an incomplete pass, and the third one was a draw play that lost four yards. Coach Pittman substituted Tristin Garner for the second-string running back for the next three plays, all of which were running plays for Tristin. On the first play, he carried the ball up the middle for no gain. The next one was a sweep around the right side, and it lost two yards. The final play of the second round was an off-tackle run on the left where Tristin was met in the backfield for a crushing four-yard loss. The defensive sideline celebrated loudly with winning the second round and causing the offense to lose a total of eight yards during the round.

For the tie-breaker round, Coach Pittman sent Brandon back in as the running back. The defense also made some substitutions, including the insertion of Manny Garcia at cornerback. In the defensive huddle, the players were pretty cocky after their success in the second round. Brock Maxwell, the All-American linebacker and defensive captain, said, "We can be almost certain that Campbell will be getting the ball. Everyone needs to close on him quickly and not let him get into the open field where he's most dangerous."

CHAPTER 25

On the first play, with the defense prepared to stop him, Brandon got the ball and swept to the left. The tight end effectively blocked the defensive end, allowing Brandon to get to the outside with Manny Garcia crouched to make the tackle as the safety was closing fast. Brandon lowered his shoulder in preparation to bowl over Manny, but at the last second he became partially upright and planted a stiff arm in Manny's chest that actually lifted his feet off the ground and knocked him into the approaching safety, removing him from the play as well. Brandon scampered untouched the remaining twenty-eight yards for the decisive touchdown. The offense cheered wildly. Even the defense applauded the spectacular nature of Brandon's touchdown, but that didn't stop them from good-naturedly ribbing Manny Garcia, calling him "Fly Boy."

Chapter 26

ALTHOUGH THE TEASING FROM his teammates after getting clobbered by Brandon was hurtful to Manny, it was the least of his problems. Today was the last day to pay Pablo Ruiz the four thousand dollars before the deadline. Manny had no doubt that Pablo would take action if he was late with the payment. Manny decided to talk with his defensive backs coach, Martin Brown, right after practice. As Manny left the practice field, he went directly to Coach Brown's office even before going to the locker room.

"Hi, Coach. Do you have a minute?"

Coached Brown looked up from his computer and smiled at Manny. "Tough practice, Garcia. Don't let that stiff arm or the other players' kidding bother you. Someday, you'll look back on this moment and think 'wow, I've come a long way since then'."

"Thanks for the encouragement, Coach, but I came to talk with you about something else."

"Sure, Manny. What's on your mind?"

"My parents are having some financial problems," Manny lied, "and I'd like to help them out. When can we expect to receive our NIL money?"

"Usually, it doesn't start getting paid out until classes begin with the fall semester, so it'll be another month."

CHAPTER 26

Manny felt his heart sink, but he didn't want Coach Brown to know how much trouble he was facing. He asked casually, "Is there any way that I can get an advance on the NIL money that's owed to me?"

"I'm sorry, but I don't think so, Manny. Calculating NIL allotments is a complicated financial exercise by the university, and I don't think that getting an advance is possible."

"Thanks, Coach. I appreciate your time." As Manny left Coach Brown's office on the way to the locker room, he anxiously considered his options. He thought about borrowing the money from his parents, but he knew they didn't have that much cash available. Besides, he didn't want to reveal to them his Adderall usage. He considered others to borrow from, including his teammates and friends back home, but he rejected the idea for the same reasons. He also thought about asking Pablo for an extension, but he already knew the answer, and the last thing he wanted to do was antagonize him. The best solution in Manny's mind was simply to lay low until he got the NIL money. He'd need to be careful to avoid going out alone, especially at night, until he had paid off Pablo.

When Manny got back to his locker, he noticed that he had a voicemail message from Pablo Ruiz. While sitting in his dressing stall in the noisy locker room, he listened to the message, "Garcia, today is the deadline for you to give me my money. You'd better be planning to bring it by tonight, or you won't like the consequences." His tone was menacing, and Manny felt a chill run down his spine. He immediately began planning how he would alter his daily routine to minimize the danger.

Around 11:00 that night, Pablo Ruiz placed a call to Hugo Lopez.

Hugo glanced at the caller ID on his phone and answered curtly in Spanish, "Yeah." His voice was deep and ominous like thunder.

Pablo, also speaking in Spanish, said, "Got a job for you if you're interested."

"Let's hear it."

"Name's Manny Garcia. He has stiffed me twice on paying his bill. Owes me four thousand bucks. The money was due today, and he didn't return my call."

"You want me to inflict some pain and tell him we need the money plus another thousand in interest in a week?"

"No, I want you to handle this one a little differently. This kid plays football for Ohio State. He's making a chump out of me, and I don't want anybody out there thinking I'm getting soft."

"The Louisville Slugger treatment, then?"

"Exactly. Don't kill him, but see that he needs to go to the hospital."

"Got it. I'll get right on it."

Within an hour, Hugo knew what Manny looked like and the residence hall where he lived. He also knew that football practice started at 6:00 AM. He discovered that the media had partial access to today's practice, so Hugo would need to be careful that his face wasn't inadvertently captured on camera. Hugo was very skilled at being inconspicuous. He made plans to keep an eye on Manny's dorm through the night and also avoid raising any suspicions from the campus police.

CHAPTER 26

Around 5:30 in the morning, Manny left his residence hall with five other young men who appeared to also be football players. They walked the short distance to the Woody Hayes Athletic Center. Hugo could easily discern how nervous Manny appeared, as he frequently and discreetly stole glimpses in every direction around him.

Hugo watched Manny and his teammates enter the Athletic Center, and he observed the chaos of the media moving in and out of the facility while preparing for their day of filming. He recognized that it was a perfect opportunity for him to gain access without being noticed. Hugo slipped into the building with several media staff who were carrying cameras and other equipment. No one spoke to him or noticed him.

Hugo lingered in the lobby momentarily, then he spotted three of the overnight cleaning staff down the hall. After completing their shift, they left their cleaning carts in the hallway as they slipped out a side door to enjoy breakfast together on the patio before going home.

Hugo casually approached their carts and noticed that one of them had left his uniform smock lying on the cart, and his ID swipe card was attached to it. Hugo quietly chuckled as he slipped the ID into his pocket, thinking that Mr. Sebastian Morales probably wouldn't mind if Hugo borrowed it. Ironically, Morales was going to be off for the next four days, and wouldn't need his ID until his return.

Chapter 27

THE OHIO STATE FOOTBALL team assembled at 6:00 AM in the auditorium of their training facility. The media was not present for the meeting, as Coach Weaver, the head coach, addressed the team. "Men, as you know, we have given the media access to our practice today. This is something we've never done before during our summer practices. About seven weeks ago, an article about Brandon Campbell's struggle was published in *Sports Illustrated*. We weren't sure how the story would be received by the general public, the media, and especially our recruits, but the feedback was mostly positive. Our recruits shared that the story gave them transparency into our football program in a way that highlighted our candor and trustworthiness. As a result of the impact of the *Sports Illustrated* story, we decided to experiment with giving the media access to our practice today to further raise our exposure before the season even begins."

Coach Weaver continued, "Historically, we were opposed to having the media at our practices because it had the potential to be a distraction for all of us, and also because we didn't want to provide an early scouting report to our opponents in the upcoming season. Obviously, we've

CHAPTER 27

had a change of heart and now think the benefits may outweigh the disadvantages."

"Before we take the field, I want to set a few expectations. First of all, watch your language. Think of how your parents would react if they saw you say something on the field that had to be edited out. Second, no showboating. I'd prefer that you conduct yourselves in your usual professional manner, as though the cameras weren't even present. Finally, let's practice hard out there like it's a game day."

"During this morning's session, we'll do some light drills and continue to refine both our offensive plays and our defensive sets. This afternoon, we'll spend some more time scrimmaging. We'll keep our plays basic so we don't give away any of our secrets. At the end of this afternoon's practice, some of you may be asked to participate in interviews with the media."

"Let's have a good practice today, men, and remember that you are representing The Ohio State University!" The auditorium was filled with enthusiastic cheers as the team began to make their way to the field.

The media's response to Ohio State's invitation to attend practice was even better than the coaches had hoped. In addition to all of the local network stations attending, there were representatives from multiple national print, radio and television organizations, including Kirk Herbstreit, Desmond Howard and Pat McAfee from ESPN's *College GameDay.*

The practice was fairly routine, with the players working on specific drills within their position groups for most of the morning. Even a casual observer, though, couldn't help noticing that the cameras were mostly tracking Brandon

Campbell wherever he was on the field. The recent *Sports Illustrated* story had launched him back into the national spotlight, and there was wide-ranging curiosity and speculation about whether he could perform anywhere close to his former stature.

About halfway through the practice, the team gathered at midfield for instructions prior to their scrimmage. The media had become energized at the prospect of witnessing some meaningful live action.

Coach Weaver addressed the players, "We're going to keep score again between the defense and the offense, but we'll use a different format than yesterday. The ball will begin on the twenty-five-yard line, seventy-five yards from the goal line, and the objective for the offense is to sustain long drives. The offense has three plays to get at least ten yards and earn a first down. If they do, they earn one point, and if they fail, the defense gets two points. Anytime the offense fails to get a first down, the ball is placed back on the twenty-five-yard line for their next possession. If the offense gets into the red zone, but doesn't score a touchdown, they get two points. If they score a touchdown, they get three points."

"If the defense gets a turnover, such as an interception or a fumble recovery, three points are awarded to them. We'll set the game clock at seven minutes, and it will run as it would in a normal game. Substitutions and time-outs can occur as they would in a regular game. We'll be using college referees who will be managing the game, including calling penalties. Once again, the winner is exempt from sprints at the end. In the event of a tie, no one is exempt."

CHAPTER 27

Manny Garcia was fourth on the depth chart at right cornerback, but because of injuries to the three players ahead of him, he would be on the starting defensive unit for the scrimmage. Although Manny was nervous about facing Brandon Campbell again, he was actually grateful to be on the field where he knew he was safe from Pablo Ruiz.

On the first play, Brandon carried the ball up the middle and gracefully and patiently danced and sliced for a twelve-yard gain. The media immediately began buzzing.

On the next play, Coach Anderson called the same one from yesterday that resulted in Brandon scoring a touchdown after lifting Manny Garcia off the ground with a stiff arm. Brandon received the pitch from the quarterback and rolled to his left. Manny immediately recognized the situation from the previous day, and he put himself in position to force Brandon to the inside, where the outside linebacker was closing fast to help him bring down Campbell. Manny was determined that he would at least slow down Brandon and also punish him for the embarrassment he suffered yesterday. As Brandon, Manny and the outside linebacker were about to collide at the same instant, Manny closed his eyes and launched himself at Brandon. Manny wrapped his arms around the player and drove him to the ground. When Manny opened his eyes, the outside linebacker was laying beneath him, and Brandon was flying down the sideline on his way to a touchdown without being touched. Brandon had pivoted away from Manny with lightning quickness and simultaneously avoided the tackle from the linebacker.

One of his defensive teammates approached Manny as he was getting to his feet and said, "Hey, Fly Boy, maybe they didn't teach you in high school that you're supposed to tackle the guy with the ball!" Manny's murderous rage—fueled by Adderall and the stress of the threats from Pablo Ruiz—was at a boiling point, and all he could think about was settling the score with Campbell.

The media, particularly those associated with television, were frantically contacting their producers to see how quickly they could air the video of Brandon's touchdown. Meanwhile, Coach Weaver, standing on the sideline for the offensive team, winked at Coach Anderson with a smile. This was exactly the type of excitement about his team that he was trying to generate through granting access to the media.

On the next three offensive series, Brandon's backups, including Tristin, played at the running back position. They were unable to secure a single first down. On the last play of the final offensive series, Tristin attempted to bull through the defenders for an extra yard, and he fumbled the ball. Fortunately, it was recovered by one of the offensive linemen.

The score was now 6-4, in favor of the defense. There were only fourteen seconds left on the clock. The ball was placed on the twenty-five-yard line for the final offensive series. The defense, sensing victory within their grasp, began to crow at their offensive teammates. Manny, however, had only one thing on his mind... vengeance on Brandon Campbell.

Coach Anderson huddled with the offense before they took the field. "We've got seventy-five yards to go in fourteen seconds, men. I think our best chance for a home run is to give the ball to Brandon. We're out of time-outs, so we have no way to stop the clock. If you get tackled inbounds,

CHAPTER 27

Brandon, the game is over. We'll run a play to the outside, and if it looks like you're going to get tackled, get out of bounds to stop the clock."

The first play was a sweep to the right. Brandon evaded multiple tacklers before stepping out of bounds after a forty-yard gain. There were only four seconds left, so this would be the last play. The offense could tie with another first down, or win if they could get the ball inside the twenty-yard line (which was fifteen yards away) or by scoring a touchdown.

Coach Anderson called for a screen pass to Brandon on the left, which was Manny's side of the field. When Brandon received the pass, he had four blockers who each successfully blocked a defensive player. As Brandon adeptly picked his way through the carnage, waiting for Brandon and his opportunity for revenge was Manny Garcia, who was still seething from his last two attempted tackles of Brandon yesterday and today. Manny thought, *I'm going to plant him so far in the bleachers that they'll never refer to me as Fly Boy again!*

As Manny prepared to bury his nemesis, Brandon made a sudden jab step to his right at the last possible second. The move surprised Manny and temporarily froze him, leaving him slightly off balance. Brandon hit Manny with a right straight arm to his chest that was so powerful that Manny tumbled six feet out of bounds, striking the table that held the Gatorade cooler. The table collapsed, and because the lid was not secured, Manny was drenched in Gatorade as he lay on the ground.

Meanwhile, Brandon raced down the sideline, adeptly avoiding the last defender in his path by cutting inside, and glided into the end zone just as time expired.

The offensive team raced onto the field toward the end zone in jubilant celebration, as if they had just won the national championship. The scene was captured by the cameras of multiple local and national sports news stations. The coverage of today's practice had the promise of igniting excitement about the upcoming college football season, and especially about Ohio State because of the return of Brandon Campbell.

As multiple cameras documented the end zone revelry, one remained focused on Manny Garcia. After being strewn amidst a toppled table, a cooler and its lid, as well as being completely drenched with Gatorade, he threw off the wreckage and sprang to his feet. He sprinted towards the end zone like a lion chasing a zebra. Brandon was high-fiving his teammates and had his back to the charging defensive back, when Manny blind-sided him by hitting him at full speed. The two players hit the ground with violent force, and Manny used the element of surprise to immediately pounce on his sprawled and stunned adversary.

Manny wrapped his hands around Brandon's neck and began choking him. Fortunately, Brandon's teammates immediately came to his rescue, and pulled Manny off him before he was seriously injured.

The celebration of Brandon's touchdown had suddenly become somber, and the entire incident was captured and broadcast widely on sports shows and social media sites throughout the country within an hour. The dark clouds gathering over Manny and Brandon were about to become much stormier.

Chapter 28

AFTER INCONSPICUOUSLY CASING THE Woody Hayes Athletic Center earlier that morning, Hugo Lopez went home to get some sleep, in preparation for tonight's stakeout of Manny Garcia. He wasn't sure yet if he would need the stolen ID or just how he was going to fulfill his job on Manny Garcia. He was still gathering intel on Manny's schedule and routines and covertly awaiting his opportunity.

As he was driving home, Hugo received a call from Pablo Ruiz. "Hey, man," Hugo answered in Spanish. "What's up?"

"I just wanted you to know that I've left a few more threatening messages with Manny Garcia. He's still ignoring me. I want him to be very, very frightened."

"It's working. I followed him on campus this morning, as he walked to football practice, and it was obvious how jumpy he was."

"Do you have a plan yet of how you'll get to him?"

"Not yet, but you can rest assured that I'll get him."

"You always do. I'll let you know if he calls me."

Later that afternoon, Hugo got another call from Pablo Ruiz. "Hugo, I'm watching ESPN, and there is some breaking news about Manny Garcia getting into a fight in practice today. I don't know if that affects your plans, but I wanted you to be aware."

"Thanks, man," said Hugo as he ended the call. As Hugo contemplated this new development, he concluded it was probably favorable for him. Manny would likely be even more prone to distraction, which would cause him to let down his guard. Hugo would head to campus immediately and try to pick up Manny's trail.

Hugo went to the football practice facility. After waiting outside for a few minutes, Hugo saw two people emerge from the facility who appeared to be football players. He casually approached them and said, "Hey, guys. I'm with the press, and I was hoping to talk with Manny Garcia. Do you know if he's still around?"

One of them responded, "Yeah, you and everybody else in the world wants to talk to Fly Boy. He left as soon as practice ended."

Manny Garcia had thrown his helmet and shoulder pads into his locker, grabbed his backpack and left the Athletic Center without even changing out of his football pants. He was so distracted that he was about halfway back to his residence hall before he remembered his imminent danger from Pablo Ruiz. He suddenly became much more wary, but arrived at his dorm safely. He immediately went to his room and was glad to have some quiet space to try to sort out the mess that he'd made of his life.

Just as he got to his room, Manny received a call from his mom. He answered while trying to sound nonchalant, "Hi, Mom. How are you?"

"Manny, your dad is here with me on speaker phone, and we are so worried about you. We saw on the news that you

CHAPTER 28

got into a fight at practice today. Are you alright?!?" she asked anxiously.

"Yeah, I'm fine. It was just one of those little scuffles that occur all the time in football."

"What caused it?" asked Manny's dad.

"He was making fun of me for being Hispanic," Manny lied.

"You just need to ignore that and turn the other cheek," advised Manny's dad.

"I know, Dad. You and Mom taught me well. I just got caught up in the heat of the moment."

"Are you sure you're okay?" asked Manny's mom.

"I'm sure, Mom. I need to go. Some of my teammates want to go to dinner now," Manny lied again.

Manny was so distraught about his situation that he remained in his dorm room all evening without any dinner. He couldn't sleep all night, and finally decided he'd go to the practice facility at 4:45 AM. He always had peace when working out, and he thought that doing some weightlifting would clear his mind. Manny also thought there wouldn't be any danger from Pablo Ruiz at such an early hour.

Brandon also had trouble sleeping that night. He was disturbed about what he could possibly have done that so enraged Manny Garcia. He didn't know Manny very well and had hardly interacted with him. He noticed that Manny would sometimes associate with Tristin Garner. After prayer and reflection, Brandon realized that Manny was upset because Brandon had humiliated him on the football field during the scrimmages. He had heard that some of the defensive players were ridiculing Manny about getting beaten. Brandon decided that he was going to go to practice early and try to reconcile with Manny before practice started. Prior to leaving for the Athletic Center, Brandon prayed that the Holy Spirit would give him the words to say to Manny and that Manny would be willing to forgive him and go forward peacefully as Ohio State football brothers.

As Manny walked across campus from his residence hall to the Athletic Center, Hugo followed him stealthily by staying in the shadows. He was convinced that Manny was unaware of being followed. Hugo was nearly certain that Manny was heading to the Athletic Center, and he could hardly believe his good fortune, as he clutched Sebastian Morales' key card/ID in his pocket.

Chapter 29

HUGO WATCHED UNDER THE shadow of a tree as Manny used his key card to enter the Athletic Center. Hugo slipped on a pair of gloves similar to the ones wide receivers use to help them catch the football. Next, he removed the Louisville Slugger baseball bat from his backpack. Hugo then reached in for the damp towel he always used to carefully wipe down the bat to remove all fingerprints. After meticulously cleaning the bat, he put the towel back into the backpack, slipped the backpack onto his back, and walked toward the Athletic Center with the bat in his left hand.

Hugo noticed that there were only a few cars in the parking lot as he cautiously approached the same door Manny had entered. When he held Morales' ID over the sensor, the light flashed green and the door audibly unlocked. Hugo quickly eased inside and started quietly toward the locker room, thankful that his reconnaissance yesterday had familiarized him with the building.

As Hugo entered the locker room, he spotted Manny getting dressed on one end of the bank of lockers, with his back to him. No one else was in the locker room. Hugo quickly and silently approached and said, "Manny Garcia, it's a pleasure to meet you."

Manny was startled and spun around quickly toward Hugo and uttered nervously, "Who are you?"

He said menacingly, "I'm a friend of Pablo Ruiz."

Manny simultaneously comprehended the words and saw the bat in Hugo's hand, but before he could react, Hugo forcefully jammed the end of the bat into Manny's abdomen. Manny cried out in pain as he fell backwards into his locker stall and onto the floor. Hugo swung viciously with the bat, first on Manny's thigh and then his rib cage. Manny had curled into a fetal position as he screamed in terror and agony.

Hugo stood over Manny, admiring the results of his work for a moment, then he said, "Sweet dreams, Manny," as he used the end of the bat to strike Manny's left temple. Manny immediately lost consciousness as he lay curled up on the floor on his right side. Hugo tossed the bat casually onto Manny's body and prepared to leave.

Just as he entered the Athletic Center, Brandon Campbell heard Manny's initial scream. He immediately started running toward the locker room. Hugo heard the approaching footsteps and quickly hid behind a row of lockers. He took the opportunity to slip out the door quickly, once the approaching person arrived and discovered Manny in his extremely injured state.

As Brandon entered the locker room, he promptly spotted Manny's crumpled body and rushed to his side. He was vaguely aware of someone exiting the locker room. Brandon didn't initially recognize that Manny had been beaten. As he knelt down at Manny's side, he absentmindedly picked up the baseball bat to lay it aside. Simultaneously, Bryce Stephenson, the OSU equipment manager, came into

CHAPTER 29

the locker room through a different door and saw Brandon crouched over Manny with the bat in his hand. Bryce had been in another part of the building and had not heard Manny's screams. Brandon looked up, and seeing Bryce, said, "Bryce, call 911 now! Manny's unconscious."

Bryce stepped out of earshot from Brandon and dialed 911. "There's a football player who's unconscious in the locker room at the Woody Hayes Athletic Center. Please send an ambulance right away." After hesitating for a second, Bryce added, "You'd better send the police, too. There may be foul play involved."

Meanwhile, Brandon tried unsuccessfully to awaken Manny, but he determined that Manny was still breathing and had a pulse. Bryce returned to Brandon and informed him that an ambulance was on the way. He then went to the entrance of the building to help direct the EMTs to the locker room. The five minutes before the ambulance arrived seemed like an eternity as Brandon tried to make sense of this tragedy.

When the ambulance arrived, Bryce led them to the locker room, where they sprang into action as Brandon shared with them his limited knowledge of how he found Manny. Bryce returned to the entrance to await the arrival of the police.

After the EMTs left with Manny, Brandon called Jalen Pittman. Jalen was about ready to head out the door on his way to the Athletic Center.

"Hey, Brandon. What's up?"

"Jalen, something terrible has happened. I came in early to the facility this morning. When I got here, Manny Garcia was lying unconscious by his locker with a baseball bat on top of him. No one else was here at first, but Bryce Stephenson came in right after me, and he called an ambulance. Manny's on his way to the hospital."

"What?!? Have you called any of the other coaches yet, Brandon?"

"No, you're the only person I've called."

"Sit tight. I'll be there in a few minutes, and I'll call Coach Weaver on my way."

Just then, two police officers arrived, and Bryce met them at the door. "Hi, I'm Bryce Stephenson, the equipment manager for the football team. I'm the one who called 911. Before I take you to the locker room, I'd like to tell you what I saw."

The first officer extended his hand and said, "My name is Officer Burns, and this is my partner, Officer Fisher. What can you tell us?"

Bryce began, "I arrived at the facility around 4:30 this morning, like usual. Nothing seemed out of the ordinary. I was working on the other side of the building, and came over here around 5:00. When I entered the locker room, I saw Brandon Campbell with a baseball bat in his hand, kneeling beside Manny Garcia who was lying on the floor unconscious."

The two officers exchanged glances.

Bryce continued, "I never heard anything that sounded like a scuffle, but I'm sure you're aware that Brandon and Manny got into a fight at practice yesterday."

"Did you see anyone else in the facility this morning besides Manny and Brandon?" inquired Officer Fisher.

"No one."

"Did Brandon Campbell say anything to you?"

CHAPTER 29

"He said that Manny was unconscious, and he told me to call 911."

"Anything else?" asked Fisher.

"No, that's everything. Manny has been taken to the hospital, but I'll take you to the locker room where he was found."

As the two police officers, accompanied by Bryce Stephenson, entered the locker room, Bryce showed them where Manny had been laying and also the baseball bat that was lying nearby. Brandon Campbell was sitting several feet away with his face in his hands. He felt so dazed and confused.

Burns whispered to Fisher, "Handle the bat carefully as evidence. Also, tape off this area as a crime scene and call the forensics team." Burns then approached Brandon Campbell.

"Hi, Mr. Campbell. I'm Officer Burns. Do you mind if I ask you a few questions?"

"Of course not, officer," as he took a deep breath to try to clear his mind.

"Bryce told me that you were kneeling over Manny this morning when he came into the locker room. Can you tell me what happened?"

"When I entered the building this morning at about 5:00, I heard someone screaming. It sounded like it was coming from the locker room, so I ran in here. When I got here, I found Manny sprawled on the floor and unconscious, right over there." Brandon was pointing to the spot.

"Was the bat where it is now?"

"No. It was laying on top of him, and I moved it to where it is now."

"Did you see anyone else in the locker room or on the premises besides Manny and Bryce?"

"No."

"Do you normally come to the Athletic Center this early?"

"No."

"What was different about today?"

"I was hoping to talk with Manny about the fight we had yesterday."

"I saw something about that on the news," said Burns. "What happened?"

"It was my fault," said Brandon.

By this time, most of the team and the coaches had arrived for practice, and the rumors about what had happened to Manny were swirling around the team.

Tristin Garner had been struggling all summer. Even though he was certain that he was by far the best running back on the team, his performance didn't show it. Tristin was dejected because, thanks to Brandon Campbell, he was going to get fewer and fewer chances to show his ability, let alone win the Heisman Trophy. This morning's events, however, had given him an idea of how he could get more playing time and supplant Brandon Campbell in the lineup.

Tristin found Officer Burns in the hallway outside the locker room. Tristin waited patiently while Burns finished a phone call.

Burns glanced at Tristin and said, "May I help you?"

"Are you one of the policemen investigating the situation with Manny Garcia?"

"Yes."

"I have some information that may help you. Can we go somewhere private to talk?"

CHAPTER 29

They found a conference room and closed the door.

"My name is Tristin Garner, and I play football for Ohio State."

"It's nice to meet you, Mr. Garner. I'm Officer Burns. What sort of information do you have?"

"As you may know, Brandon Campbell and Manny Garcia got into a fight in practice yesterday," began Tristin.

"I'm aware of that," said Officer Burns somewhat impatiently.

"After practice yesterday, I overheard Brandon Campbell say that he was going to arrange to meet Manny Garcia before practice this morning to settle the score," lied Tristin.

"Who else heard Campbell say that?" asked Burns.

"I'm not sure," said Tristin. "I was trying to look like I wasn't paying attention. There's something else, too."

"I spotted what looked like a baseball bat in Campbell's locker," Tristin lied again. "I didn't get a very good look at it because it seemed like he was trying to keep it hidden behind his clothes."

"Thank you for coming forward, Mr. Garner. That is very helpful. Is there anything else?"

Tristin completed the lying trifecta as he said, "It's not my nature to rat out one of my teammates, but I'm just thinking about poor Manny," he attempted to say convincingly.

Later that afternoon, Officer Burns contacted the emergency physician who examined Manny Garcia upon his arrival at the hospital.

"Hi, Dr. McClain. My name is Officer Burns, and I'm investigating the situation concerning the injuries sustained by Manny Garcia. We're still trying to determine if a crime occurred. I understand you examined Garcia this morning. What can you tell me about your findings?"

"He was unconscious, presumably due to blunt force trauma to his left temporal area. He also had evidence of blunt force trauma to his abdomen, left thigh, and the left side of his rib cage resulting in two fractured ribs."

"There was a baseball bat at the scene where he was found. Are his injuries consistent with possibly being caused by a bat?"

"Absolutely."

"How is he doing now?" asked Burns.

"He has been moved to the ICU, but last that I heard, he was still unconscious but stable."

"Is there anything else?"

"Just one thing. His blood tests showed Adderall in his system, and our records show no history of him using Adderall."

"Hmmm. I was just preparing to call his parents, and I'll see if they can shed any light on that. Thanks, Dr. McClain."

Officer Burns dialed the number of Manny Garcia's home in Texas. A female voice answered, and Burns asked, "Is this Mrs. Garcia?"

"Yes."

"Are you Manny Garcia's mother?"

"Yes, I am. Who's calling?" she asked hesitantly.

"Hi, Mrs. Garcia. I'm Officer Burns, and I'm with the Columbus Police Department in Columbus, Ohio. I believe that you're aware that Manny was injured on the Ohio State campus this morning, and we are investigating whether he was possibly assaulted."

CHAPTER 29

"Officer Burns, we heard from the hospital a few hours ago when he was in the emergency department, but do you have any update on Manny's condition? It's so hard to be halfway across the country from him at a time like this, and my husband and I can't get a flight to Columbus until tomorrow morning."

"I just got off the phone with one of the doctors at the hospital. He's now in the Intensive Care Unit. He's still unconscious, but he's stable."

"Oh, dear!" Mrs. Garcia murmured softly, trying to hold back her tears. "Thanks for the update, Officer Burns. Now, what can I do for you?"

"Do you know if Manny had any enemies at school?"

Mrs. Garcia thought for a brief moment and said, "No, everybody loves my Manny. Wait. He got into a fight with that boy on the team yesterday. Manny told us last night that it was because the boy was making fun of Manny for being Hispanic."

"Are you talking about the fight that was on TV?"

"Yes."

"One more question, Mrs. Garcia. The blood tests at the hospital showed that Manny had Adderall in his system. Do you know if Manny takes Adderall?"

"No, he doesn't. Manny's little brother takes it, but Manny has never taken it."

"Thank you, ma'am. We'll be in touch if we have any more news or questions. I'm sorry about your son's injuries, and we intend to get to the bottom of this."

Officer Burns then called the District Attorney and shared with him the evidence he had collected against

Brandon Campbell for the assault of Manny Garcia. The DA agreed that the evidence was adequate to justify an arrest.

Officer Burns looked at his watch and knew that he and Officer Fisher had just enough time to get to the Ohio State campus before the end of practice. He knew the campus would be chaotic because news of the assault of Manny Garcia had already reached the media, as well as social media. Speculation was rampant, given the highly publicized altercation yesterday between Brandon and Manny.

When Burns and Fisher arrived at the campus, they immediately proceeded to the practice football field, where they talked with Coach Weaver. While the team watched, the police officers placed Brandon in handcuffs and read him his Miranda rights. The national news was soon flooded with images of a handcuffed Brandon Campbell, still wearing his Ohio State practice uniform, being placed in the back seat of a police car. Within a few hours, it was confirmed that all the fingerprints found on the bat confiscated at the scene belonged to... Brandon Campbell.

Chapter 30

AS OFFICERS BURNS AND Fisher tried to drive away from the Athletic Center, their progress was hindered by the crush of reporters, photographers and videographers attempting to get additional images or information pertaining to Brandon's arrest. Fisher exclaimed to Burns, "What a circus!"

Brandon spoke up from the back seat, "I can't imagine what the two of you must endure from day-to-day."

Burns replied, "Every day is different, and we have no idea what we'll encounter on any given day. Honestly, that's what makes it fun and interesting. We often see human nature at its worst."

"How often do you face a really dangerous situation where your life is in jeopardy?" inquired Brandon.

"It's really sporadic," said Officer Fisher. "We may have three encounters like that in one day, and then go a couple of weeks before we have another occurrence."

"I know that police officers take a lot of abuse from the public, but I just want you to know how much I appreciate everything you do to keep us all safe."

"That's very kind of you, Mr. Campbell."

"Please, call me Brandon. Do you mind if I pray for you?"

"Of course we don't mind, but just so you know, this would be the first time someone sitting in the back seat of this car ever prayed for me," said Officer Burns with a chuckle.

Brandon bowed his head and closed his eyes and began, "Dear Father, thank you for people like Officers Burns and Fisher who have accepted positions to help keep the citizens of Columbus safe. Please protect them, Father, and guard their families from worrying about their safety. Please guide their decisions and their actions and help them to be just and compassionate as they carry out their duties. In Jesus' name I pray. Amen."

"Thank you, Brandon," said Hank Fisher while sensing a stirring in his heart. After a pause, he asked, "How does the team look this year?"

Brandon quickly became animated as he began describing all of the exceptionally talented players who comprised the Ohio State roster.

As they approached the police headquarters, Hank Fisher said, "Brandon, I know that this is highly irregular, but my six-year-old son's birthday is tomorrow. He's crazy about Ohio State football, and his favorite player is you. I bought him one of your jerseys at the campus bookstore earlier today, and it's in the trunk. Would you mind signing it?"

"I would be honored," Brandon replied.

Hank then said quickly to Officer Burns, who was driving, "Tim, quick, pull into this McDonald's parking lot just ahead. I suspect there will be another media circus at the police station, and I'd rather not have Brandon autographing my son's jersey showing up on ESPN."

CHAPTER 30

As the car rolled to a stop, Hank Fisher jumped out and retrieved the jersey and a Sharpie from the trunk. He got back into the cruiser and tossed them to Brandon in the back seat.

"Brandon, I can't tell you how much I appreciate this. There's something else I want to share with you, but I didn't want to say anything until you agreed to sign the jersey."

"What's that?" asked Brandon.

"My son has cancer, and his treatment is going poorly. The doctors are concerned that we may be running out of options."

"I'm so sorry, Officer Fisher. I'll be praying for him and your family. What's your son's name?"

"Ryan."

"I'll personalize my inscription to him, but there's just one problem. I can't write very well with my hands cuffed behind my back."

Officers Fisher and Burns smiled at each other, and Hank Fisher quickly unlocked and removed Brandon's handcuffs. "I don't think we need these anyway," he said as he reattached them to his belt.

After Brandon finished autographing Ryan's jersey, Hank Fisher laid it carefully in the trunk. As they pulled away from McDonald's to make the short jaunt to the police station and the awaiting media pandemonium, Brandon asked Hank, "Are you concerned that Ryan will become jaded when he finds out what his football hero has been accused of?"

"Like you, Brandon, I'm a Christian. In order to teach Ryan to trust God, I must show him that he can trust me and other adults in his life. I'm also teaching him that

God is fair and just, and that sometimes we need to wait patiently for God's plan to unfold. I believe that Ryan is going to experience what trusting in God feels like when you are exonerated. Because of the evidence against you, I had to do my duty and arrest you, even though I don't believe you're guilty."

"Thank you for your confidence in me. I believe that there are probably multiple reasons why God is putting me through this challenge, and one of them may be to build Ryan's faith in God."

Chapter 31

AS THE TWO OFFICERS and Brandon arrived at the police station, the number of media personnel had tripled over what they had encountered at the Athletic Center. As Brandon was escorted by the two police officers into the police station, past all the cameras and journalists, he felt peaceful because he knew he was innocent and also because he was aware that these events were all part of God's sovereign plan. Brandon was certain that God was using all of this, not only for Brandon's benefit, but also for the good of innumerable others who loved God.

After Brandon was fingerprinted, had his mugshot taken, and completed the remainder of the administrative process of being charged, he was given the opportunity to make a phone call. He knew without a doubt that his call would be to Emma. When Brandon had been enslaved by multiple addictions in his past, he was very careful about shielding his problems from Emma because he was frightened that he'd lose her. He was now certain that their faith-filled love of each other would not only withstand this current challenge, but also grow stronger through it.

Emma was in her office at Nationwide Children's Hospital when she received a call on her personal mobile phone. Normally, she would allow personal calls to go to voicemail when she was at work, but she decided to answer it when she saw the caller ID display the words 'Franklin County Correctional Facility'.

"Hello, this is Emma Brooks," she answered tentatively.

"Hi, Emma. It's me," said Brandon with as much positivity as he could muster.

"Brandon! Where are you? Are you okay?" Emma asked with a mixture of surprise and concern.

"I've been arrested for the assault on Manny Garcia. I'm fine. I know that it's all a big misunderstanding until they catch the person who actually did it. I'm also certain that this is part of God's plan. There's one other thing I want you to know, Emma. When I was given the opportunity to make one phone call, I instantly knew you were the person I wanted to call. I love you, Emma, and I'm never again going to hide the challenges in my life from you."

"I can't tell you how much that means to me, Brandon! I love you so much. What do you need? What can I do for you?"

"I know you're at work. The only thing I'd like you to do is to call my mom. It breaks my heart to think about my mom learning about this on the news."

"You've got it. I'll call her right now. Hang in there, Brandon. I'm praying for you."

As soon as Emma disconnected from her call with Brandon, she phoned Lydia. "Hi, Lydia. This is Emma."

"Hi, dear. What a pleasant surprise. How are you?"

"I'm doing well, thanks, but I'm actually calling about Brandon. He's been arrested. I just got off the phone with him, and he asked me to call you."

"Arrested?!? Does this have anything to do with that altercation in practice the other day? I saw it on the news."

CHAPTER 31

"Yes, it's related. The player, who attacked Brandon at practice yesterday, was assaulted in the locker room early this morning, and the police think that Brandon may have done it."

"Oh, my," whispered Lydia fearfully.

"Don't worry, Lydia. You and I both know he didn't do it. Brandon is fine, and he's certain that this is all part of God's plan. I'll keep you posted on any credible information I get from or about Brandon, and please don't pay attention to any unfavorable speculation you hear or read in the media."

"Okay. That's good advice. Poor Brandon. He's had one challenge after another since his dad died."

"I agree, Lydia, but now he has his faith to sustain him. He's depending on God to get him through this, and I think he's actually looking forward to seeing how God is going to use it."

"Thank you for your call, Emma. I'm so glad Brandon has you in his life."

As soon as Lydia finished her conversation with Emma, she called Mike Nelson. "Hi, Mike. Do you have a minute to talk?"

"I'm so glad you called, Lydia. I just saw the news on TV about Brandon's arrest. I was getting ready to call you, and I bet that's why you're calling me."

"You're right as usual," Lydia said as she reflected on how much her fondness for Mike had grown since he had been her spiritual mentor over the last several months. "Emma just called me with the news, and she said that Brandon is taking it all in stride. As his mother, naturally I'm worried. Emma shared with me some things that she intended to be a comfort to me, but honestly Mike, I'm not sure I understand, and I was hoping you could give me some insights."

"Of course. What did Emma say?"

"She said Brandon believes that this is all part of God's plan. Brandon is also depending on God to get him through this challenge, and he's looking forward to seeing how God is going to use it. Can you please explain that to me?"

"You probably remember when we discussed the verse in Romans where it says that God works all things for the good of those who love him. We have also talked about the verse in Proverbs which says 'trust in the Lord with all your heart and lean not on your own understanding'. We know that God is sovereign over all things that happen on Earth, and he uses all of those events for the good of those who love him, like Brandon. The good that God accomplishes may not always be apparent, and it may be different than what we expect. That's where faith comes in. We accept that God has our best interests at heart, and we trust him that his plan is better than our plan. Even though it appears that Brandon getting arrested is a bad thing, God will use it for favorable outcomes for not only Brandon, but also possibly for many others. That's what Brandon believes. Do you?"

"I'm trying, Mike, but it's hard when my heart is so anguished for my son."

"That's natural. I'll be praying that God gives you understanding and also peace about Brandon's situation. Let's keep our eyes open and see what God has in store for Brandon."

"Do you think Brandon assaulted his teammate?"

"No, I'm certain that he did not."

CHAPTER 31

"Thank you, Mike. You've given me great comfort. I'll see you tomorrow for our Bible lesson."

Within an hour of Brandon arriving at the police station, news of his arrest was widespread on television, radio talk shows and social media. The footage of Brandon giving Manny Garcia a stiff arm and causing him to tumble into the Gatorade table was being played repeatedly everywhere. Much of the speculation was that Brandon was taking performance-enhancing drugs that were fueling his extraordinary strength and also his apparently surly relationships with his teammates.

While her children napped, Grace Gilmore had spent an hour that afternoon reading and viewing as much as she could about Brandon's arrest. When her husband Sam arrived home later that evening after working at the hospital, Grace wasted no time sharing with him her anger about his old high school friend and football teammate.

"Did you hear that Brandon Campbell was all over the news this afternoon?" Grace asked Sam.

"Not really. The ER was really busy. I overheard some people talking about him, but I never caught what happened. Can you bring me up to speed?"

"He was arrested for beating up one of his teammates with a baseball bat!" Grace exclaimed heatedly.

"I don't believe Brandon did that. There must be another explanation."

"You're always so quick to take Brandon's side when he gets in trouble," Grace said angrily. "He tried to rob our house, and in the process, he killed our infant son. He's a drug addict, and yet that *Sports Illustrated* article portrayed him as some kind of hero. And now this!" Grace was shouting now, and beginning to cry.

Sam responded softly and calmly, "When Brandon tried to rob our house, he didn't know it was ours, and he was in the throes of a relentless opioid addiction. Joshua's death was entirely accidental, and Brandon was unaware at the time that he had caused it. He has recovered from his addiction, and he has dedicated his life to Jesus. I don't believe he did what he has been accused of today, and besides, it's not my place or your place to judge him. That is for God."

After a few moments, Grace composed herself, then said, "Once again, you're right, Sam. When I read that *Sports Illustrated* story about Brandon, it reawakened my own guilty feelings about my role in Joshua's death. I still struggle at times with my decision to leave him alone at home that night to quickly go buy diapers because we'd just run out."

"Don't let those thoughts get a foothold in your thinking, Grace. You know that God has forgiven you, just like he has forgiven Brandon. I imagine God is going to use Brandon's latest challenge, his arrest today, to reveal to us how he uses all the events in our lives to accomplish his divine plan. I can hardly wait to see how it all unfolds." Sam came to Grace and wrapped his arms around her in a long hug, rocking her gently back and forth.

A moment later, a much calmer Grace whispered in his ear with a smile in her voice, "Your faith continues to amaze me, my love."

Chapter 32

THE FOLLOWING AFTERNOON, JUAN Rodriguez was excited about playing soccer with his three friends who were visiting him from Columbus. Brothers Hector and Julian Gonzalez, along with Lucas Martinez, grew up in the same neighborhood in Columbus with Juan, and the four of them had remained close friends even though Juan had moved to Cincinnati about five years earlier. They were headed to a high school field near the campus of the University of Cincinnati to play pickup soccer with a group that Juan regularly joined.

After playing for about thirty minutes, Hector and an opposing player jumped simultaneously to head the ball. Unfortunately, their heads collided, and Hector sustained a laceration along his right eyebrow. Although the injury wasn't serious, Hector couldn't get it to stop bleeding, so the four friends went to the emergency room at the University of Cincinnati Medical Center.

Sam Gilmore, who was in his fourth year of medical school, was doing an emergency medicine rotation and was working that afternoon when the four soccer-playing friends arrived. Sam evaluated Hector and determined that he had no evidence of a concussion. By that time, the laceration had stopped bleeding. He felt that the cut required stitches, and his attending physician agreed. Sam numbed the area on Hector's face with a local anesthetic and prepared to begin suturing the laceration.

Hector's three friends were in the exam room with Sam and Hector, and they were speaking among themselves in Spanish. They were completely unaware that Sam had been a double major at Wheaton College in Applied Health Science and Spanish and that he was fluent in Spanish.

Julian said to Juan, "Did you hear about that Ohio State football player who got beat up in the locker room?"

"No, what happened?" asked Juan.

"The word on the street was that the assault was drug-related, but they've mistakenly arrested Brandon Campbell, Ohio State's star player," interjected Lucas with a malevolent chuckle.

Hearing Brandon's name, Sam's ears perked up, as he had been concentrating on the suturing.

"Hey, I used to work with a guy named Brandon Campbell at a factory a few years ago. He'd go out drinking after work with my friends and me sometimes. The rumor was that he had a drug problem and got fired. There's no way he could be the same dude," said Juan skeptically.

Julian said, as he started typing on his phone, "His mugshot's all over the internet. He apparently returned to Ohio State after being away for several years because of a drug habit he developed after his father died suddenly in a car accident. His story became famous after it was published in *Sports Illustrated* a few months ago. Here's a picture of him." Julian handed his phone to Juan.

As Juan looked at Brandon's image, his eyes grew wide and he exclaimed, "What?!? It is the same guy I used to

CHAPTER 32

work with! I can't believe it! He was so quiet and sad, and he didn't look like an athlete at all."

"The *Sports Illustrated* article portrayed that his turnaround came as a result of his faith in Jesus. We'll see how much his faith helps him now, because it looks like his playing career is over and he'll be locked up for a long time," added Lucas.

As soon as Sam finished treating Hector and released him, he found an empty conference room near the ER and called the Columbus police.

When the operator answered, Sam said, "Hi, my name is Sam Gilmore, and I have some information related to the Brandon Campbell case. May I speak to the officer who is leading the investigation?"

"One moment please, and I will connect you with Officer Fisher."

Officer Fisher answered, and Sam said, "Hi, Officer Fisher, my name is Sam Gilmore, and I have some information that may help you in the case regarding Brandon Campbell."

"What have you got?" asked Fisher with a touch of enthusiasm.

"I'm a fourth-year medical student at the University of Cincinnati, and I just saw a patient in the ER who was from Columbus. Three of his buddies were with him. While I was treating the patient, his buddies were talking to each other in Spanish. They were unaware that I'm fluent in Spanish and could understand every word. They said that the word on the street was that the assault on Manny Garcia was drug-related and that Brandon Campbell mistakenly is taking the fall."

"Did they say why they believe that to be true?"

"No, they really didn't give any other details. I don't know if that might give you another lead to pursue, but I wanted to make sure I shared it with you."

"Thanks, Sam. It sounds like it's hearsay and will probably be a dead end, but I'll certainly check it out. Do you have any contact info?"

"Yes." Sam gave Officer Fisher the contact information from Hector's chart. Sam was unaware that Hector had falsified his name as Alejandro Perez because he knew he was unable to pay the bill. "Just to be transparent, Brandon Campbell is a close friend of mine."

"Thank you, Sam. I'll give Mr. Perez a call."

Chapter 33

AFTER BRANDON'S PHONE CALL with Emma, he was taken to his cell. As Brandon entered his cell, the door behind him was closed and locked with an echoing clang. Brandon's cellmate sat on the edge of his bunk, leaning forward with his elbows on his knees and his face buried in his hands. He appeared very forlorn and didn't even look up when Brandon entered.

Brandon immediately approached him, extended his hand and said, "Hi, I'm Brandon Campbell."

Brandon's cellmate seemed to emerge from his deep thoughts and became aware of Brandon for the first time. He shook hands with Brandon and said, "I'm Carlos Flores."

"You seemed to be deep in thought when I came in, like you have the weight of the world on your shoulders," Brandon observed.

With a mirthless laugh, Carlos said, "I was just thinking about how badly I've screwed up my life."

"If you don't mind me asking, what have you done?" asked Brandon with concern.

Carlos glanced at Brandon, and sensing that his compassion was genuine, said, "There's not enough time to go into all the details because I'm supposed to be getting out this afternoon. Let's just say that I've made one bad decision after another, mostly through dealing drugs, and I've really let down the people that I love. I'm ready to turn my life around."

"You remind me of my friend, Antonio. He was in a similar spot as you a few months ago, and he's emerged from the ashes of his broken life. He's a new man."

"What did he do?"

"He recognized that he couldn't change under his own strength. He needed help, so he committed his life to Jesus as his Lord and Savior."

"I just got goosebumps on my arms when you said that. I was taught about Jesus as a child, but I haven't been anywhere near a church for decades. Tell me more about your friend."

"Antonio had been a drug dealer in Cincinnati for years. In fact, he was my supplier of opioids a few years ago. He hit bottom when he was arrested for dealing drugs literally minutes after his long-time girlfriend was murdered in a drive-by shooting. His girlfriend was also the mother of his toddler daughter. His life was shattered in the blink of an eye. During the time he was incarcerated, he realized in the depths of his anguish that he was ready to start a new life. After he was released, he had heard that I had redeemed my broken life through the power of Jesus, so he contacted me. Not long after, he was baptized and reunited with his daughter. God has been blessing him abundantly as he has embarked on his new life."

"I'd really like to talk to him when I get out. I have a lot of questions, and he sounds like he could give me some answers from his own experience."

CHAPTER 33

A guard approached their cell door and said, "Gather your things, Flores. You're getting released."

Brandon said to the guard, "Sir, can I have a piece of paper and a pen? I'd like to give Carlos the phone number of someone who can help him fix his life."

The guard would normally have quickly dismissed such a request, but something compelled him to honor it this time. He returned with a pen and paper and handed them through the bars to Brandon. Brandon didn't normally memorize his friends' phone numbers. But on this occasion, Antonio Alvarez's phone number immediately came to his mind, and he wrote it down with the name 'Antonio' and handed it to Carlos.

As Carlos finished gathering his few belongings and prepared to exit the cell, he said to Brandon, "How long are you going to be in here, Brandon?"

"I don't know. That's up to God, but it shouldn't be too long, because I'm innocent," replied Brandon while smiling.

As Carlos exited the cell, he thought, *Yeah, right. That's what they all say.* Carlos couldn't help wondering though, about who Brandon was and what he was all about.

A few hours after Sam had talked with Officer Fisher, he was finishing up his shift in the ER and preparing to go home when his phone buzzed. It was a number he didn't recognize. "Hello, this is Sam Gilmore."

"Hi, Sam. This is Officer Fisher from the Columbus Police Department. I'm calling to let you know that the phone number and address you gave me were both fictitious, and

I suspect that the name was not his real name either. When you told me your lead had possible drug-related connections, I was excited because it could have given us another motive and lined up with some findings on the victim. Can you think of any other details that would allow us to track down your patient or his companions?"

"Nothing else comes to mind, but I'll let you know if I think of anything. Sorry I wasted your time, Officer Fisher."

"No problem. That's the nature of these investigations. Thanks for your time."

As Sam was driving home, he was trying to recall any other details about Hector and his friends that would assist the police in finding them. As he began to become convinced that finding Hector was a lost cause, he expanded his thinking to other ways he might help the investigation and clear Brandon's name. Suddenly, as if a light bulb had turned on in his brain, he thought of Antonio Alvarez. If the assault on Manny was drug-related, Antonio may have some contacts to the drug scene in Columbus. It was worth a try.

When Sam got home, he kissed Grace, Daniel and Lauren, and excused himself momentarily to make an important phone call.

Antonio Alvarez answered on the first ring. "Hi, Sam. How are you doing, brother?"

"I'm good, Antonio, but I'm worried about Brandon. Are you aware of what's happened to him in Columbus?"

"It would be hard not to know about it. It's all over the news."

"Antonio, I have reason to believe the assault on Manny Garcia may have been drug-related." Sam quickly shared with Antonio the conversation he overheard with Hector's

CHAPTER 33

friends and the discussions he'd had with Officer Fisher. "If there are any rumors in the Columbus drug community about who really assaulted Manny Garcia, I'm wondering if you have any acquaintances from your former life who are part of that scene, and who could give you the scuttlebutt?"

"I sure do. I know just the guy. His name is Carlos Flores. I'd do anything for Brandon. I'll call Carlos right now, and I'll let you know what I find out, Sam."

As soon as Antonio disconnected the call with Sam, he looked in the contacts on his phone for Carlos's number. As he was searching for it, his phone began buzzing and the caller ID showed it to be Carlos Flores. Antonio felt goose flesh throughout his body. Carlos experienced the identical sensation in the same instant as he dialed the number Brandon had just given him for 'Antonio', as his phone showed that he was calling his longtime acquaintance, Antonio Alvarez.

"Carlos? Hey, dude, this is weird," answered Antonio. "I was just looking up your number to call you when your call came through. It's probably been three or four years since we last talked."

"Hey Antonio. It's about to get weirder," laughed Carlos. "I just got sprung from jail earlier today. Right before I was released, I got a new cellmate who told me about his friend, named Antonio, from Cincinnati who turned his life around after finding Jesus. He only gave me Antonio's first name and his phone number, and man, was I surprised when your name popped up after I dialed the number."

"Let me guess," said Antonio. "Your cellmate was Brandon Campbell."

"That's right!" exclaimed Carlos.

"Wow, this has so clearly been orchestrated by God. By now, you probably won't be surprised to learn that the reason I was calling you is because of Brandon Campbell."

"Who is this guy?" asked Carlos, who was bewildered about Brandon's identity.

"How long have you been in jail, man?"

"About three days, but what does that matter?" asked a confused Carlos.

"You'd have to be living under a rock or incarcerated to not know who Brandon Campbell is, because he's been all over the news. He is a star football player for Ohio State. A couple of days ago, he got into a fight during practice with one of his teammates. Early the next morning, that player was beaten to a pulp with a baseball bat in the locker room, and the police think Brandon Campbell did it."

"Whoa! He sure didn't look or act like someone who would do that," mused Carlos.

"That's because he didn't. He's a standup guy. And that's why I'm calling you," said Antonio. "There's reason to believe the assault was drug-related, according to some rumors I have heard third hand. Have you heard any noise from your colleagues?"

Carlos responded, "I haven't been in touch with any of my pharmaceutical co-workers since I got out of the hoosegow. In fact, the reason I'm calling you is because I shared with Brandon that I'm ready to turn my life around, and he suggested I call you to learn about your journey with Jesus."

"I'd be happy to tell you my story, but first, I think it'd be worthwhile for you to perform your last official act in

CHAPTER 33

your profession before you retire, and see if you can find out anything about the assault on Manny Garcia."

"You've got it. I'll call you back as soon as I have something," said Carlos.

Chapter 34

IN LESS THAN TEN minutes after completing their previous call, Antonio's phone was buzzing with an incoming call from Carlos.

"That was fast!" answered Antonio.

"I know a guy who's well-connected, and if anyone would know what's going on, he would."

"What did he say?"

"The guy who beat up Manny Garcia is Hugo Lopez. He makes a nice living doing the dirty work for multiple dealers around Columbus. He often gets involved when a customer is tardy in paying their bills. Hugo uses a baseball bat to enhance his power of persuasion, and recently, he has started leaving the bat at the scene after he has roughed up his victim. He apparently does it for several reasons. He sees it as a form of advertising to remind dealers to use his services. He's extremely arrogant, and it's his way of taunting the police that they'll never figure out who he is and how to catch him. Finally, he's from the Dominican Republic and loves baseball, so he views the bat as paying homage to his heritage."

"That's very encouraging news for Brandon, but how compelling is the case against this Hugo guy?"

CHAPTER 34

"That's the thing, Antonio. No one other than his victims has ever actually seen Lopez use a bat to assault someone. His victims are too terrified of him to identify him, and besides, they're guilty of their own crimes. At this point, it seems that the evidence is only hearsay."

"Thanks, Carlos. Even though this info may be of limited use, I think I'll pass it on to my friend who's trying to help Brandon Campbell. On a different topic, I have some time tomorrow morning to share my story of redemption with you. Are you free then?"

"Yes, I'm looking forward to learning about your journey and beginning my own."

Antonio immediately called Sam. "Hey, Sam. I've got some news for you," Antonio began.

"That didn't take you long, Antonio!"

"Brandon saved my life, and I would do anything for him. Here's what I learned. The word on the street is that the person who beat up Manny Garcia is named Hugo Lopez. He serves as the muscle for multiple dealers to help persuade their customers whose payments are overdue. Recently, he has started leaving a baseball bat at the scene of the assault as his calling card."

"It sounds like he may be the guy the police want instead of Brandon."

"It does, but the problem is that the evidence is all hearsay. There are no credible witnesses, and the Hispanic drug community is notoriously tight-lipped. It's unlikely they'll cooperate with the police."

"Even though it may be a dead end, I think I'll still pass the information on to the police," said Sam. "Do you have any additional details to identify this Hugo Lopez?"

"Only that he's originally from the Dominican Republic."

"Thanks, my friend. I'm sure Brandon will really appreciate what you've done to try and help," concluded Sam.

Sam called Officer Fisher right away. "Hi, Officer Fisher. This is Sam Gilmore again."

"Hi, Sam. What can I do for you?"

"I have another possible lead for you. Let me begin by telling you how I acquired this information. You probably remember that the companions of my ER patient were talking about the rumors in the drug community in Columbus. I have a friend who's a reformed drug dealer, and I asked him if he'd reach out to his former contacts and ask them about the circulating rumors. He learned that there is a guy, named Hugo Lopez, who works for drug dealers to rough up their customers who owe money. He uses a baseball bat, and recently, he has apparently started leaving his bat at the scene of the assault as his signature."

"That certainly sounds promising, Sam. Do you have any witnesses or other identifying information about Mr. Lopez?"

"Only that he's from the Dominican Republic. Is this enough information to allow you to investigate this guy?"

"It's going to be close. If we pursue a search warrant, it would need to be granted by Judge Cutler, the judge presiding over Brandon's case. He feels strongly about preventing innocent people from having their rights violated by the police, but he's also fair and reasonable. We'd need to show some evidence that Hugo Lopez is a danger to the public in order to convince him."

As Hank Fisher was finishing his call with Sam, Tim Burns approached his desk and said, "I have the report on

CHAPTER 34

the key cards that were used on the morning of Garcia's assault. Between the hours of midnight and 5:30 AM, the following individuals entered the Athletic Center in this order: Bryce Stephenson, Manny Garcia, Sebastian Morales and Brandon Campbell."

"Who's Sebastian Morales?" asked Fisher.

"He works on the housekeeping team at the Athletic Center. Here's the interesting thing—he has been on vacation in Florida for the past several days. His supervisor confirmed with him that he has not loaned his key card to anyone. With Morales' permission, he checked Morales' locker and found that his ID wasn't clipped to his uniform and was apparently stolen or lost."

"Hmmm, that's another interesting wrinkle," said Fisher and he proceeded to share with Burns what he'd learned from Sam about Hugo Lopez. "Tim, would you see if we have any record of criminal activity on Hugo Lopez? Would you also see if there have been any assaults in the last twelve months where a baseball bat was left at the scene?"

After Sam's conversation with Officer Fisher, his mind was spinning for any additional ways he could possibly clear Brandon's name. The only idea that came to mind was a long shot, and he called Patrick Cutler.

Patrick answered on the first ring and said, "Hey, Sam. How are you?"

"Other than being really concerned about Brandon, I'm doing well. How about you?"

"The whole thing is killing me. I'm certain that Brandon is innocent. I'd do anything to help him, but I just don't know what that could be," lamented Patrick.

"That's exactly why I called you, because there may be something you can do. By any chance, are you related to Judge Cutler in Columbus?"

"Yeah, he's my uncle. My dad's brother. Why do you ask?"

"He's the judge who will be deciding whether to grant the Columbus police a search warrant for another possible suspect in the case." Sam quickly summarized what he knew about Hugo Lopez and the potential difficulty in obtaining a search warrant of his home.

"Would you be willing to call your uncle and tell him why you're so convinced that Brandon is innocent?"

"Of course I will, Sam. This whole thing is frustrating because I don't know what to do to clear Brandon's name. Until now."

Patrick called his uncle's mobile number right away but didn't expect to reach him immediately. On the second ring, Judge Joseph Cutler answered, "Well, hello, Patrick. How are you?"

"I'm doing well, Uncle Joe. I wasn't expecting to connect with you so quickly."

"Ever since your dad's accident, I've recognized how precious my family is to me. How's your dad doing?"

"He's great! He seems to have recovered completely. He and I recently spent three days together participating in a Christian retreat. It was the most amazing experience in my life, and indirectly, it's the reason I'm calling you."

"This sounds interesting. I'm all ears, Patrick."

"Uncle Joe, let me start by saying that I'm not trying to interfere with any of your court cases, but I have some information that will connect some dots for you and possibly help you with your ruling. You probably recall that when

CHAPTER 34

my dad and I were in the accident, a young man stopped to help. He drove me to the hospital where my dad was taken, and he stayed with me all night in the waiting room while my dad was recovering."

"I do remember. Wasn't he a former Ohio State football player?"

"Yes, his name is Brandon Campbell."

"The same person arrested related to the assault on his teammate?"

"Same one. Brandon and I have become close friends since the accident. I've helped him with his workouts as he prepared to return to college football. He and I are in a weekly Bible study together, and I assist him in coaching a young boy who's a cancer survivor. Brandon was the one who sponsored my dad and me in the Christian retreat. The bottom line is, I know Brandon well. I also know his heart, and his heart is for Jesus. I'm telling you, Uncle Joe, there is absolutely no way Brandon assaulted his teammate. I know the police have recently developed a different lead in the case, and they're going to be coming to you in the next day or so seeking a search warrant on the new suspect. Please strongly consider granting that warrant."

"Patrick, the merits of the search warrant request must stand on their own, but I really appreciate what you've shared with me. I also love what you told me about the retreat. I'd like to learn more and potentially attend it someday. I need to go, as I'm due in court in about ten minutes. Thank you for calling, Patrick."

Chapter 35

THE FOLLOWING MORNING, EMMA was making rounds on the oncology floor with the attending physician, the pediatric oncology fellow, residents and medical students. Because of her multiple responsibilities, Emma wasn't able to participate in rounds with them every day, but she did it whenever she could. It helped her to stay abreast of all the new treatments in pediatric oncology, and it gave her the opportunity to support the medical team and her patients in an exceptional manner which was the essence of Emma's makeup.

The team stopped in the hallway in front of room 306, and as was customary, one of the medical students presented the history and physical exam findings on the patient who had been admitted the previous evening.

"The patient is a six-year-old Caucasian male with a history of neuroblastoma. He was admitted for fever of uncertain etiology. His past medical history is significant for neuroblastoma, diagnosed four years ago. He has been treated with surgery, chemo and radiation. A CT scan last week showed a new tumor in his lung. He has exhausted all of the conventional treatment protocols, as well as several clinical trials. His oncologist, Dr. Andrews, believes there's nothing left to offer him."

CHAPTER 35

Those last words overwhelmed Emma, and she struggled to focus on the rest of the medical student's presentation. Even though Emma had cared for many children who'd succumbed to cancer, the emotional toll was always difficult for her. Intellectually, she trusted God and his all-knowing character. He would ultimately use everything for good, but seeing a child's life cut short still always saddened her.

The presentation and brief discussion concluded in the hallway, and the medical team entered the patient's room. As the attending physician talked with the patient and his parents, Emma noticed that the patient was wearing an Ohio State jersey, and it was Brandon's number. As she studied it more closely, she noticed that Brandon had inscribed it. She clearly recognized his handwriting and his signature, but she wasn't close enough to read the inscription.

As the medical team finished their discussion with the little boy and his parents and exited the room to continue their rounds, Emma lingered behind. Greeting the young, angelic-looking patient, she said, "Hi, my name is Emma Brooks."

The boy responded with a weary smile, "I'm Ryan Fisher."

"It's nice to meet you, Ryan." Then turning to Ryan's parents, she said, "I'm the nursing manager on the oncology floor here."

"We're Ryan's parents. I'm Hank and this is my wife, Pam. It's a pleasure to meet you, Emma," said Hank Fisher. Despite their polite greeting, he and his wife looked devastated.

Emma turned back to Ryan and cheerfully said, "I see you have on Brandon Campbell's jersey."

Ryan's face lit up, and he said as if he didn't have a care in the world, "He gave it to me for my birthday. He's a friend of my dad's."

Emma looked at Mr. Fisher and said with a smile, "Brandon and I are very good friends. How do you know each other?"

Emma watched Hank glance momentarily at his son and then appear even more dejected, if that was even possible, and said in a hushed tone, "I was his arresting officer, and he graciously signed Ryan's jersey as I was (another glance at Ryan) transporting him to the police station."

"That sounds like Brandon," Emma said with a warm grin.

"The thing is, I'm the investigating officer, and I know in my heart that he's innocent. It's such a challenge, on top of everything else (another glance at Ryan), to strive to catch who's really responsible."

"I, along with many others, appreciate what you're doing and are praying for you."

"Thank you, Emma. Brandon said he would be praying for me, too," said Hank as his eyes filled with tears.

"Could I ask you both a question about Ryan?" Emma inquired of Ryan's parents, as she looked at Ryan, who was completely engrossed in something on his iPad.

"Of course," said Mrs. Fisher.

"I understand that Dr. Andrews feels that Ryan has exhausted all of his options and there's nothing further to offer him to treat this new lung tumor. Is that accurate?"

Mrs. Fisher responded, "That's true. Dr. Andrews told us he's going to search for any additional clinical trials that Ryan could be eligible for, but he's not very optimistic."

CHAPTER 35

Emma replied, "I have a friend who's very involved with clinical trials for children's cancer. She may be aware of some cutting-edge trial that's still under the radar of the oncology world at large. With your permission, I'll ask her if she's aware of any trials for which Ryan may be a candidate. If she is, I'll share it with Dr. Andrews."

"Absolutely, you have our permission," said Mrs. Fisher with guarded hope.

"We have nothing to lose at this point," said Hank solemnly.

As soon as Emma left Ryan's room, she headed to her office, where she called Jasmine.

"Hi, Emma. What a pleasant surprise. How are you doing with everything that's going on with Brandon?"

"Actually, I'm doing well, because God is constantly reminding me of his presence, like just now. The son of Brandon's arresting and investigating officer was admitted to my unit last night. He's six years old and was diagnosed with neuroblastoma four years ago." Emma explained the situation to Jasmine. "I'm calling to see if you could search for any experimental clinical trials that he might be a candidate for. His parents are open to the idea."

"Of course, I will. What's his name?"

"It's Ryan Fisher."

"I'll come by the hospital later and review his chart and old medical records to obtain his full clinical history, and then I'll see if there are any appropriate trials available to him."

"If you find anything, Jasmine, the first thing we'll need to do is discuss it with Dr. Andrews."

"Sure thing, Emma. I'm going to get to work on this. I'll see you at church on Sunday. And, I'll be praying for Brandon."

Chapter 36

LATER THAT AFTERNOON, OFFICER Fisher joined Officer Burns in Judge Cutler's courtroom to request the search warrant for the property of Hugo Lopez. Judge Cutler carefully read the affidavit and asked several clarifying questions. He then agreed to issue the search warrant.

As the two officers left the courthouse, Tim said to Hank, "That went smoother than I thought it would. I didn't even need to use my two aces in the hole."

"What do you mean?" asked Hank.

"Although Hugo Lopez hasn't ever been arrested, he has been on the outskirts as a person of interest in multiple criminal investigations. Also, within the last three months, there have been two other assaults where a baseball bat was left at the scene. They're both still unsolved."

"Interesting. It sounds like it's time to pay Mr. Lopez a visit."

As Officer Fisher and Burns pulled up to the address they had on file for Hugo Lopez, it wasn't what either of them expected. The home was in a well-kept, charming middle-class neighborhood. Lopez' house had a beautiful lawn

CHAPTER 36

which had been recently mowed. The shrubs were trimmed, and the beds were mulched and free of weeds. Tasteful ornamental pots filled with colorful flowers enhanced the front porch. His car, a late model silver Honda Accord, was parked in the driveway.

"This is a bit more upscale than what I was anticipating," said Officer Burns as they walked up to the front door.

"If you look around, everything is neat and tidy, and there's nothing that draws one's attention. Maybe that's just the effect Lopez wants to portray, given his line of work."

Fisher rang the doorbell, and it was answered by a powerfully built man with a shaved head. He appeared to be about five-feet, ten inches, and in his late thirties.

Lopez greeted them in a self-assured, friendly manner with, "Good afternoon, officers. How may I help you?" Both Tim and Hank were not fooled by his smile and recognized a very bad temper simmering just below the surface of his genial façade.

"Are you Hugo Lopez?" asked Officer Fisher.

"Yes, I am."

"We have a search warrant for your premises," said Fisher as he showed Lopez the warrant.

For a brief moment, a dark cloud passed over Hugo's eyes, then his friendly, over-confident manner returned. "You're welcome to thoroughly search my entire property, gentlemen."

As Fisher and Burns searched the house, they found nothing suspicious. Lopez seemed to get cockier as the unsuccessful hunt continued. They had one final bedroom to explore. It appeared to be a guest room and was decorated relatively sparsely except for a bed, nightstand, lamp and dresser. When they opened the closet door, there were eight wooden Louisville Slugger baseball bats standing in the corner. They appeared brand new and were identical to each other. Lopez saw the two officers glance at each other, but he was already convinced that he was infinitely smarter than these two incompetent morons.

Fisher asked, "What are all the bats for?"

Lopez was proud of how quickly he could think on his feet, and he lied, "I'm an assistant coach for my cousin's baseball team."

"These bats don't look like they've ever touched a baseball," said Burns.

"I just bought them. I'm in charge of the bats, and most of our other bats got broken during the season." *This is child's play*, thought Lopez.

"I would've thought there would be more variety in the size and shape of the bats for your team," stated Fisher inquiringly.

"All the kids are the same age and about the same stature, so they all use the same size bat," said Lopez smoothly as he thought, *You two are no match for me!*

As the two officers and Lopez walked toward the front door, Burns said, "We'd also like to search your car. Is it locked?"

"Yes, but I have the key in my pocket, and I'll unlock it for you."

"By the way, what's your cousin's name?" asked Fisher.

"Huh?"

"Your cousin. The one whose baseball team you help coach. What's his name?"

CHAPTER 36

Hugo's arrogance was growing by the second, and in the blink of an eye, he decided to toy with these two guys and stated, "Sebastian Morales."

As the officers searched Lopez' car, they found it to be much like his house—neat, orderly and devoid of any significant evidence. When they opened the trunk, the only thing there was a backpack. Hugo smiled to himself, because he carefully cleaned out his backpack after every job, including the one on Manny Garcia. Fisher and Lopez watched while Tim Burns unzipped and searched every empty compartment of the backpack. As he reached into a small side pocket, Burns touched an object that felt like a credit card. What he withdrew was a key card to the Athletic Center for Sebastian Morales. He held it up to Lopez and asked, "What is this doing in your backpack?"

Lopez instantly recognized his error while maintaining his poker face to the officers. He had forgotten that he put Morales' ID in that side pocket, because he normally didn't put anything there. Thinking quickly, he couldn't believe his good fortune in saying that his cousin is Sebastian Morales, but they were getting into dangerous territory. He would need to go into hiding as soon as they left.

"That belongs to my cousin. He borrowed my backpack recently and must have left his ID in it when he returned the backpack to me."

Officers Burns and Fisher looked at each other, and there was a barely perceptible nod between them. Hank Fisher turned to Lopez and said, "Hugo Lopez, you're under arrest for the assault of Manny Garcia."

Chapter 37

WHEN OFFICERS FISHER AND Burns arrived at the police station, Fisher handled the administrative duties of booking Lopez while Burns worked through his contacts at the university to reach out to Sebastian Morales. Morales was relieved that his key card had been recovered, and he confirmed that he didn't coach a baseball team and didn't know anyone by the name of Hugo Lopez.

At the same time, Jasmine Owens was on the oncology ward at Nationwide Children's Hospital, and she had just completed a thorough review of Ryan Fisher's extensive medical records. Jasmine maintained a personal library of active clinical trials on pediatric patients with various types of cancers. Her library included both trials that were known to the oncological community, as well as some small-scale studies that were limited in scope and already closed to additional patients. Jasmine's contacts at MD Anderson Cancer Center allowed her to stay abreast of the limited, obscure pediatric cancer trials.

As Jasmine searched her library, she saw only one clinical trial for which Ryan may be eligible. The study, being

CHAPTER 37

done on patients with neuroblastoma, used a breakthrough technique called immunotherapy. The particular agent being studied had dramatic results in other types of childhood cancers, and there was reason to believe that it may be effective for neuroblastoma. The trial was being done on a small number of subjects who had recurrence of their neuroblastoma after being treated with multiple other therapies. Ryan met all of the criteria for inclusion in the study, but there was just one problem. The investigators had already recruited their targeted number of patients.

Fortunately, the Principal Investigator, Sheryl Bevins, was a former colleague of Jasmine's at MD Anderson, and it was worth calling her to see if there was any chance of enrolling Ryan in the study. Jasmine phoned her immediately. "Hi, Sheryl. This is Jasmine Owens."

"Hi, Jasmine, it's so good to hear your voice. How are you?"

"I'm doing really well. I've gotten settled in Ohio nicely, but there are still some things I really miss about Texas, especially the barbecue."

Sheryl laughed. "I'm sure you do. Tell you what, the next time you get back here, let's plan on getting some barbecue together."

"It's a date," said Jasmine with a smile in her voice. "The reason I'm calling you, Sheryl, is that I noticed you're the PI on the neuroblastoma trial using the new immunotherapy agent. I have a patient here in Columbus who seems to qualify, but it appears that your study is now closed to additional subjects. Is that accurate?"

"Your call couldn't have come at a better time, Jasmine. The study was filled, and we were just preparing to begin, when we got word yesterday that one of the patients developed appendicitis and needed an appendectomy, which eliminated him from the study. We were just having a discussion about whether to try to recruit another patient or to proceed with the trial. Our preference would be to add another patient, but the criteria are pretty narrow, and it could take months before we find one. I'll email you an application which includes all the pertinent information required to enroll your patient. We'll need the completed application within forty-eight hours. Once I get it, I can give you an answer pretty quickly on whether your patient qualifies."

"Thank you, Sheryl. I'll return it to you this afternoon, as soon as I touch base with Dr. Andrews, the patient's oncologist."

Right after Jasmine finished her call with Sheryl, she phoned Emma.

"Hi, Emma, I'm on your ward, and I just finished reviewing Ryan Fisher's records. He appears to qualify for a trial using one of the new immunotherapy agents, but the trial was closed. I called the Principal Investigator, who happens to be one of my friends at MD Anderson. As it so happened, one of their study patients had to drop out yesterday, and a slot has reopened. I'd like to submit an application for Ryan to be enrolled in the study, but let's discuss it with Dr. Andrews first."

"I agree, Jasmine. I saw him making rounds on the floor a few minutes ago. I'm down the hall from you in my office. I'll meet you at the nurse's station, and we can go together to try to find Dr. Andrews."

Emma arrived at the nurse's station a few minutes later, and they walked together down the hallway of the oncology

CHAPTER 37

unit, peeking into patients' rooms looking for Dr. Andrews. Ironically, they found him in the room of Ryan Fisher and waited in the hallway for him to finish.

When Dr. Andrews emerged from Ryan's room, he saw Emma and smiled brightly. "Hi, Emma."

"Hi, Dr. Andrews. How's Ryan doing?"

"It appears that the source of his fever is due to strep throat, which is a relief. He's on the right antibiotics, but he still has a fever. Because of his fragile status, I'd like to leave him in the hospital until his fever is gone just to make sure there isn't something else going on. I just wish I had another option to offer him for his cancer," said Dr. Andrews forlornly.

"That's what we wanted to talk with you about. Dr. Andrews, this is a friend of mine, Jasmine Owens."

"It's nice to meet you, Jasmine," said Dr. Andrews as he shook hands with Jasmine.

Emma continued, "Jasmine is a PharmD. She trained at MD Anderson with a specialty in pediatric oncology. One of her areas of expertise is the clinical trials that are occurring around the world. I asked her to review Ryan's medical records and see if she could find any studies he might be eligible for." Emma looked at Jasmine, who continued the presentation to Dr. Andrews. Jasmine succinctly summarized the details of the neuroblastoma study being led through MD Anderson.

Jasmine added, "My information showed the study to be closed because they had their desired number of participants, but because I personally know the PI, I called her. It so happens that one of their patients dropped out yesterday, so now they have another opening."

"I love when we get to witness the providence of God," said Dr. Andrews as his eyes moistened. "Let's go in right now and talk to Mrs. Fisher about this possible opportunity."

As Emma, Jasmine and Dr. Andrews entered the room, Ryan was sound asleep in his bed. Dr. Andrews quickly and in a hushed tone updated Ryan's mom about the new clinical trial opportunity. After he finished, she said with tears in her eyes, "It sounds like an answered prayer. Please proceed with seeing if Ryan is eligible."

Back at the police station, Hank Fisher said to Tim Burns, "The only thing that doesn't add up in this case is the testimony of Tristin Garner. I think we should have another conversation with him, and if we hurry, we can catch him before practice begins."

"Let's get moving, partner," replied Burns.

As the two officers walked into the Athletic Center, the team was dressing in preparation for practice. They found Coach Weaver and asked him to facilitate a conversation with Tristin. The officers were taken to an empty conference room, and a few minutes later, Tristin Garner, wearing his practice uniform, warily entered the room.

"Hi, Tristin," said Officer Fisher. "Please have a seat." Both officers noted that he appeared very ill at ease.

Officer Burns said, "Since you talked with me the other day about what you saw and heard pertaining to Brandon Campbell, have you had any additional recollections or clarity in your memory of the events leading up to Manny Garcia's assault?"

CHAPTER 37

Tristin shifted uneasily in his chair and said, "Not really."

Officer Burns took out his notebook, and reading his notes, he said, "You stated, 'I spotted what looked like a baseball bat in Campbell's locker'. How certain are you that it was a baseball bat?"

"Kind of certain, but I didn't get a great look at it."

"Let's see," Burns said as he looked at his notes. "You also said you overheard Campbell say he was going to meet with Garcia before practice 'to settle the score'. Could you possibly have misunderstood what he said?"

"It's possible, but not very likely," said Tristin hesitantly.

The two officers glanced at each other, then Hank Fisher said, "Look, Tristin. There has been some new evidence that has arisen in this case, and it casts doubt on your testimony. If you're misrepresenting the truth for some reason, you could be in a lot of trouble."

Tristin exploded, "I lied! I lied so I could get more playing time. It's all lies. I didn't overhear Brandon Campbell, and I didn't see a bat in his locker." Tristin looked relieved to have come clean.

"You may go now," said Hank Fisher quietly.

As Fisher and Burns were driving back to the police station following their conversation with Tristin Garner, Fisher got a call from his wife.

"Hi, honey. How's Ryan doing?" inquired Hank.

"He took a nap earlier this afternoon, and he's playing on his iPad now. He still has a low-grade fever, but I think he's feeling better. Hey, I have some encouraging news, do you have a minute?"

"Yes, of course. Tim and I are driving back to the station now. And when you're finished, I have some good news, too."

Mrs. Fisher explained all the details about the trial drug opportunity to Hank. She shared how Dr. Andrews and Jasmine had submitted an application for Ryan. "You may remember Emma Brooks, the nurse manager who we met this morning and who is also Brandon Campbell's friend? She just came into our room and said that Ryan's application qualifies him for the trial, and he can begin tomorrow! Isn't that great news? It feels like God's hand is definitely in all of this."

Hank's eyes began tearing, and he said with a shaky voice, "This is the first time I've had hope, short of a miracle, since we got that CT scan result last week."

"Our prayers, and those of so many others, have been answered, Hank," she said with joy. "Now... what's your good news?"

"Please keep this quiet, hon, because it hasn't been announced publicly yet, but the evidence against Brandon Campbell has crumbled, and we'll be releasing him this afternoon. Also, we believe we have arrested the guy who really did assault Manny Garcia."

"That's great, Hank, and it must be a load off your mind."

"Between that and what you've shared, I feel like a new man!"

Chapter 38

WHEN OFFICERS FISHER AND Burns arrived at Police Headquarters, they immediately went to the jail and asked if they could personally escort Brandon through the process of his release. As they approached Brandon's cell, he was sitting on the edge of his bunk reading the Bible. He looked up and greeted Hank and Tim with a warm smile and said, "Hey you guys. It's good to see you."

Hank Fisher said, "Hi, Brandon. This isn't a social visit. We're here to release you, because you're free to go."

As the jailer unlocked Brandon's cell door, Brandon asked, "What's changed?"

"Basically, two things," responded Fisher. "We've arrested the person who we believe is actually responsible for the assault on Manny Garcia. The other change is that the key witness against you has admitted that he was lying."

"May I ask who that is?"

"It's Tristin Garner."

"That's understandable," said Brandon. "I'm sure he was only trying to get more playing time. He must have been ready to explode with guilt over his lies."

"I think that's a fair assessment," said Burns. "He fell apart after just a few questions. We're considering charging him with obstruction of justice."

"Please don't do that, Officer Burns. Tristin grew up without his father in his life, and his priorities are misguided. He just needs to mature, and being on the football team will help him. Pressing charges will only set him back. I think I'll go to the Athletic Center right away, so I can talk with him after practice."

"I'll tell you what," said Fisher, "we'll honor your recommendation on not charging Garner. Would you like us to give you a ride to the Athletic Center?"

Brandon said with a warm smile, "Thank you, that would be great."

Brandon picked up his personal belongings and changed back into his practice uniform, which was what he was wearing when he was arrested. Brandon and the two officers climbed into the squad car and headed to the Athletic Center. On the way, Hank Fisher said, "Brandon, I want to thank you again for signing the jersey for my son's birthday. He was so excited when he opened it, and he put it on immediately. In fact, right after his birthday, he got sick and was admitted to the hospital. He has worn your jersey every day in the hospital."

Brandon said kindly, "I'm so glad he's enjoying it. I've been praying for him ever since you told me about his cancer. Is his hospitalization related to the cancer?" asked Brandon.

"No, he had a fever due to strep throat. It's much better now, and your prayers have been answered. His caregivers have found a promising clinical trial, and he has been successfully enrolled. He'll remain in the hospital, and he'll start on the new chemotherapy tomorrow if his fever is gone. This seems like a miracle because we thought we were out of options."

CHAPTER 38

As they pulled up to the Athletic Center, Brandon said, "That's great news! I'll continue to pray for Ryan and your family, Officer Fisher. Thanks for the ride, you guys."

As Brandon entered the locker room, practice had just concluded, and team members were straggling in. A few surprised teammates greeted Brandon enthusiastically. He made his way to the corner of the room where Tristin Garner was sitting sullenly in front of his locker, still fully dressed in his uniform. As Brandon approached, he pulled up a chair next to Tristin and sat down. Tristin looked up with an expression that was a mix of shame, humiliation and embarrassment.

Before Brandon could speak, Tristin said, "I owe you an apology, Brandon. I lied to the police about you, and I believe I was responsible for you getting arrested. It was so selfish on my part. I hurt the team, and I especially hurt you. I am so, so sorry."

"I forgive you, Tristin, and I understand why you did it. Being a freshman is tough, and you look for every opportunity to get an edge. I get it. You made a mistake, and I have no hard feelings."

"I look back, and you've been so kind to me. You have constantly tried to help me, but I've been too proud to accept your guidance. Thank you for being so gracious."

Brandon arose, shook hands with Tristin and left the locker room. He returned a few minutes later holding a football and a Sharpie. By now, the entire team was there, and the environment was boisterous. Brandon, standing in the center of the locker room, whistled loudly and then shouted, "Guys, listen up!" The chatter quickly dissipated, although there were many surprised and happy expressions as numerous team members recognized for the first time that Brandon had rejoined them.

Brandon began, "I've been released from jail, and my name has been cleared. I had nothing to do with the assault on Manny. It's understandable that I'd be a suspect, given our altercation on the field the day before he was assaulted, and the fact that I apparently found him right after he was beaten up. Plus, Tristin Garner gave the police some misleading information that further raised the suspicions of the police about me. I want all of you to know that Tristin has apologized to me and I've forgiven him, and I ask all of you to do the same. Also, the police have arrested the man they believe hurt Manny. I'm planning to visit Manny in the hospital tomorrow right after our practice. I'd welcome any of you who'd like to join me." There was respectful applause and shouts of "Count me in", "I'll be there", and "It's great to have you back, Brandon!"

As the applause died down, Brandon held up the football and the Sharpie, and said, "One last thing, guys. Would you please all sign this football for me? There's a little boy who's the son of one of the officers who arrested me. He's fighting for his life with cancer, and he's going to start on a new kind of chemotherapy tomorrow. He's a huge Ohio State football fan, and a signed ball from all of us will really lift his spirits. I'll take it to him at the hospital this evening." The cheers were robust as the team expressed their excitement and appreciation that Brandon, their leader both on and off the field, had returned to the fold.

CHAPTER 38

Emma, Jasmine, Jalen and Brandon met in the lobby of Nationwide Children's Hospital early that evening and went up to Ryan Fisher's room, where Ryan's parents were visiting with him. As the four of them walked into the room together, Ryan already knew Emma and Jasmine, and he was eyeing Jalen and Brandon curiously. Jalen stepped up to his bedside first and said, "Hi, Ryan. I'm Jalen Pittman. I'm one of the Ohio State coaches, and I used to play on the same team with Brandon Campbell."

Then Brandon, with the signed football under his arm, stepped beside Jalen and said, "Hi, Ryan, and I'm Brandon Campbell." He then winked at Hank Fisher and without missing a beat, he exclaimed, "Wait, you're wearing my jersey! I've been looking for that. I need it back. Without my jersey, I won't have anything to keep my shoulder pads from falling off!"

Ryan giggled and said, "This jersey's mine. You're just going to have to get another one."

"Well, if you're not going to give me my jersey back, I guess you'll just have to take this football which matches the jersey," said Brandon as he handed Ryan the football.

Ryan's eyes widened with delight as he studied it. "Is it signed by the whole team?"

"It sure is, Ryan, because our whole team wants you to get better so you and your parents can come and cheer for us at our first game," said Brandon as he handed Ryan three tickets. He glanced at Ryan's parents who both had tears streaming down their faces at seeing the most joy in their little boy since he was diagnosed with cancer four years ago.

Later that evening, Sam and Grace were watching the evening news after putting Daniel and Lauren to bed. As they watched the coverage of Brandon being released from jail after being completely cleared of the charges, Grace said to Sam with a tear in her eye, "I'm so ashamed for judging Brandon. From now on, I'll leave the judging to Jesus and instead focus on extending grace to others, like God did for me."

Chapter 39

AS BRANDON WAS WALKING into the Athletic Center the next morning for football practice, he received a call from Officer Fisher.

"Good morning, Brandon. This is Hank Fisher."

"Hey, Officer Fisher. I sure enjoyed the time with Ryan last evening."

"That's part of the reason I'm calling. I can't thank you enough for visiting Ryan. The joy you brought him was priceless to his mom and me. Thank you!"

"It was my pleasure," said Brandon sincerely.

"I also wanted you to know that Manny Garcia regained consciousness last night, and this morning he confirmed from photographs that Hugo Lopez was his assailant."

"Thanks for the great news. A bunch of the guys from the football team and I are going to visit Manny in the hospital after practice this morning."

"I have no doubt that Manny and his family will be delighted to see all of you, but there are a couple of things you should know prior to your visit. Before he was assaulted, Manny had told his parents that the scuffle between you and Manny in practice the other day was because you were making racist taunts towards him for being Hispanic. The other thing is that Manny was using Adderall from the black market to help his performance on the football field. He was assaulted because he wasn't paying his drug bills to his dealer. Manny has come clean and apologized to his parents on both the racist lie about you and the Adderall issue. I wouldn't be surprised if he tries to make amends with you as well."

"The pieces of the story are all beginning to fall into place, aren't they? Thank you for the heads up, Officer Fisher."

After practice, the players showered and changed, then walked the short distance to the Ohio State Medical Center, which was on campus. Nearly all of the players and coaches participated in the parade to visit Manny. When the team arrived, the nurses put Manny in a large, reclining mobile chair and wheeled him to a waiting area that was large enough to accommodate the entire football team and Manny's family.

The reunion was energetic and celebratory, while also being respectful of the setting. Groups of four or five teammates took turns talking with Manny and encouraging him in his recovery. The final person to come to Manny's side was Brandon, as the rest of the team became quiet and witnessed their interaction. Up to this point, Manny had been joyful and had relished the attention from his teammates. When he saw Brandon at his side, his expression transformed from blissful to anguished.

Manny raised his voice and said, "I have something to say to Brandon, and I'd like all of you to hear it. I owe him a huge apology, and I feel you all deserve an explanation."

CHAPTER 39

Manny took a deep breath, and continued, "While lying in the hospital, I've had some time to think and reflect on how and why I ended up in this situation. My parents are devout Christians, and they always encouraged me in my faith. I regularly went to church with them until I got to high school, when I started having success playing football. At that point, I stopped going to church because I thought I didn't need God. In my mind, I figured I could handle my life very well on my own. About that time, I began stealing my brother's Adderall to help my performance on game nights."

"When I got to Ohio State, I started getting Adderall illegally from a dealer and began using it every day. I got into trouble when I couldn't pay the money that I owed my dealer. He was threatening me, and I was scared. My physical attack of Brandon during practice was fueled by a combination of my pride, the effects of the Adderall and the pressure from the dealer. Brandon did nothing to deserve my outrage, and he certainly was NOT making racist remarks about me, like I dishonestly told my parents."

"I'm aware that Brandon was just released from jail after being falsely accused of assaulting me. It has occurred to me that Brandon took the punishment for my mistakes even though he was completely innocent, just like Jesus was crucified for the forgiveness of my sins. I never fully understood that concept until I recognized the parallel to Brandon's involvement in my mess."

"With all of you as my witnesses, I want to tell Brandon how sorry I am for the hardship that I caused him." Turning to Brandon, he said, "I am deeply sorry, Brandon. Will you please forgive me?"

Brandon nodded affirmatively and said quietly, "Yes, of course. I forgive you, Manny."

With his eyes glistening, Manny turned his eyes from Brandon to the coaches and teammates standing around him. "As I mentioned, these recent events in my life and Brandon's role in them have convinced me that I need Jesus in my life." Turning again to Brandon, he said, "Brandon, as soon as I get released from the hospital, would you please baptize me as I make my public commitment to Jesus as the Lord and Savior of my life?" Brandon tearfully nodded affirmatively once again, as Manny looked around the room and exclaimed loudly, "And all of you are invited!"

The jubilant roar in the waiting room reverberated throughout three floors of the hospital. An eternal touchdown had just been scored, and no one was more moved than Manny's parents who cried unabashedly as they witnessed their prayer for the last four years get answered.

After leaving the hospital, Brandon called Emma at work. "Hi, Emma. I can't wait to tell you about the most amazing thing that happened when the team visited Manny Garcia at the hospital."

"I've got about three minutes until I have to run to a meeting with several of my nurses, but I'd love to hear about it if you can make it quick."

"I've got a better idea. Seeing you last night when we visited Ryan Fisher made me realize how long it's been since we spent a leisurely evening together. What would you say to dinner tonight at Jeff Ruby's Steakhouse?"

"That sounds wonderful, Brandon!"

CHAPTER 39

"I need to be transparent, Emma. I have an ulterior motive. The food in jail was not very good. The whole time I was in there, I dreamed about a good steak."

Emma giggled, "That's understandable. Under the circumstances, I don't mind being second fiddle."

"You'll never be second fiddle. I'll see you tonight."

As Emma and Brandon settled into their cozy booth at Jeff Ruby's Steakhouse, Brandon asked, "How's your job going?"

"I love it. Yesterday, when I got Jasmine involved in researching treatment alternatives for little Ryan Fisher, is a perfect example of why I feel so empowered to help our patients, and at the same time, embolden my staff to take initiative."

"I'm so proud of you, Emma, and I really hope Ryan responds to his latest chemotherapy."

"Me, too. Now, I want to hear more about what you mentioned over the phone about you and the team visiting Manny in the hospital."

"It was incredible." Brandon shared the details of the visit with Manny and the uproar that occurred when Manny declared his faith in Christ. "I have this feeling, Emma, that the upcoming season is going to be about much more than football. It feels like the Holy Spirit is already moving hearts." Brandon went on to share with Emma about Tristin's contrite apology. Brandon concluded with, "We're going to need to find a place to perform Manny's baptism. Do you think Pastor Apple would allow us to do it at his church?" The church was the one that Brandon and Emma, as well as Jalen and Jasmine, attended. Brandon and Emma had gone to Pastor Apple's church during Brandon's first stint at Ohio State as well.

Emma replied, "I have no doubt that Pastor Apple will be delighted to host the baptism. Let's ask him on Sunday."

After finishing their fabulous dinner, Brandon suggested they go for a walk around the Ohio State campus. It was one of their favorite places, and they had so many memories of engaging conversations on the beautiful, spacious campus where they first fell in love. When they arrived on campus, they began their walk at the Oval, which was in the center of the university grounds.

Holding hands as they strolled, Emma said, "Brandon, I haven't told you yet how impressed I am with the gracious way you handled your incarceration. When you called me right after you were arrested, you were so calm, and it was clear that you were putting your trust completely in God. Over the past four months, you've transformed as your faith has matured."

They stopped on the edge of Mirror Lake, and Emma turned to face Brandon while holding both of his hands. "I'm ready, Brandon."

"For dessert?" asked Brandon with a dopey grin.

"No, silly," Emma giggled. "I'm finally ready to pick up where we left off before your dad's accident. I'd like to begin planning our lives together."

Brandon pulled her into his arms and kissed her passionately. "Those are words I've waited a long time to hear you say," Brandon whispered between kisses. "What convinced you?"

CHAPTER 39

"Nothing, really. I just find ex-cons to be sexy," Emma said as she giggled. She pulled back from the kiss, looked deeply into Brandon's eyes, and said softly, "I love you, Brandon."

"I love you, too, Emma, and I always will."

Chapter 40

THE NEXT DAY, AFTER practice, Jalen pulled Brandon aside privately.

"Brandon, since Manny proclaimed his faith in Jesus at the hospital yesterday in front of the entire team, the other coaches and I have received multiple questions from the players about Jesus, Christianity, and what it means to be saved. I've never sensed the Holy Spirit moving among a group of individuals like I have with this team. It's clear to me that God has big plans for this team and that God will be glorified in the process. What do you think about the two of us organizing a voluntary team meeting for the players and coaches and teaching everyone who's interested about the basics of Jesus, Christianity and baptism? We can do it before Manny's baptism so everyone who attends will have a better understanding of the significance of Manny's commitment."

"I love the idea, Jalen. Emma and I were planning to ask Pastor Apple on Sunday if we could use his church for the baptism. I'll bet he'd allow us to use it for a team meeting about Jesus as well. He might even be willing to do the teaching for us. I'll give him a call right after I shower."

Brandon called Pastor Apple a short while later, and as he expected, Pastor Apple was excited about hosting

CHAPTER 40

Manny's baptism as well as a preparatory meeting for the team. They agreed to have the meeting in the early afternoon in two days, which was a day off for the team. Leading up to the meeting with Pastor Apple, Brandon overheard many conversations about faith among his teammates. When a particular issue was being debated, his teammates often asked him to settle the disagreement with the truth from the Bible.

Brandon was uncertain how he'd become an authority on Bible knowledge in the eyes of his teammates, so he asked Jalen for his insights.

"Brandon, I agree with you that your teammates really respect and admire you as a Christian, and I believe there are multiple reasons. First, you're the oldest player on our team, which naturally entitles you to a certain level of respect. Also, every member of the team read the article about you in *Sports Illustrated*, and they learned how you credited Jesus with completely transforming your life. Finally, and most importantly, they've witnessed how graciously you've conducted yourself with the events of the last few days."

Jalen continued, "You publicly forgave Tristin after his lie landed you in jail. As soon as you got out of jail, you organized and led a hospital visit of Manny, who savagely attacked you in practice. And, oh yeah, you took a signed football to the hospitalized son of the policeman who arrested you. There's an old adage, 'actions speak louder than words'. Well, your actions are screaming proof of your transformed heart through Jesus. This team won't hesitate to follow you into battle on a football field, as well as anywhere else you care to lead them. You are being watched

INSPIRING GLORY

by your teammates, Brandon, so be sure you lead them through God's strength and direction."

"Thank you, Jalen. I just remembered why I was drawn to you during my freshman year. There's just something different about you."

"Thanks, Brandon, but it's what's different about you that's drawing your teammates to you. I can sense the power of the Holy Spirit in you like no other time in my life."

On the day of the meeting at church—not surprisingly—nearly the entire team, including players and coaches, attended. Pastor Apple explained the basics of the Christian faith and the central role played by Jesus through his crucifixion and resurrection. He encouraged questions, as he addressed the group, in order to make the time more like a discussion rather than a lecture. They had allotted one hour for the session, but the discussion was still lively after two-and-a-half hours. It probably would have gone for another several hours had Pastor Apple not had other responsibilities that required his attention.

One week later, Manny Garcia was baptized by Brandon at Pastor Apple's church in front of the entire football team. When Manny stood up after being submerged in the water, the uproar from the team was louder than if Ohio State had just scored a touchdown in the game against Michigan.

CHAPTER 40

Immediately after Manny was baptized, Pastor Apple stepped in front of the group and talked about the significance of Manny's expression of faith. He then encouraged any of the other attendees who wished to profess Jesus as their Lord and Savior to consider getting baptized today. Ninety minutes later, thirty-two players and coaches had committed their lives to Jesus and gotten baptized. Tristin Garner was one of them.

After the team's baptisms had concluded, all the players dried off, changed out of wet gowns and back into dry clothes, and returned to their seats. Many heads were still damp from the cleansing water. It was a sight to see.

Pastor Apple once again stepped in front of them. "Gentlemen, we have one additional baptism this afternoon. This one is unique because the individual is not directly part of your team, and I'd like to share the story with you." Brandon was unaware of what was coming. He heard the sound of moving water in the elevated baptismal tank above the audience, and he looked up to see his mom and Mike Nelson entering the baptistry.

Pastor Apple continued, "A number of years ago, Brandon Campbell tragically lost his dad in an auto accident during his junior year of college. Brandon and his dad had a very close relationship, and the thing they enjoyed sharing the most together was Brandon's football career. It was only a few months ago, after an unread letter from Brandon's dad was discovered, that Brandon and his mom learned that Mr. Campbell had accepted Christ and was baptized less than a week before his death. The revelation piqued the interest of Brandon's mom."

INSPIRING GLORY

Pastor Apple's presentation was interrupted by a sob, and the team saw Brandon dissolve into a pool of tears as he sat among them.

Pastor Apple continued, "Brandon's mom, Lydia, has been taught about Jesus by her friend, Mike Nelson, who will now baptize her as an outward sign of her inward decision to follow Jesus."

As Brandon's mom emerged from the baptismal water, the team celebrated as much for Brandon as for her. For many of them, it was the first time they had knowingly witnessed God using tragic circumstances for the good of those who love him.

Later that day, Brandon called Jenny Hubbard, Dylan's mom.

"Hi, Brandon. It's so good to hear from you," answered Jenny. "We were so relieved to hear that you were released from jail and that your name has been cleared."

"Thank you, Jenny. Has my ordeal shaken Dylan's confidence and respect of me?"

"Just the opposite. You have always taught Dylan to anticipate adversity both on the football field and in life. Through insights from his dad and from Patrick, he sees how you have handled your situation with grace and determination. If possible, Dylan actually respects you even more."

"That's such a relief. Are Dylan and Brad also available to talk on the phone now?"

"Yes, they are. They're in the hearth room watching TV."

CHAPTER 40

"Great. Would you put me on speaker? There's something I'd like to discuss with your family."

"Of course. Give me a minute to move to the other room." After about thirty seconds, Jenny said, "Okay, Brandon, you're on speaker, and we're all here."

"Hi, Dylan. Hi, Brad," said Brandon enthusiastically.

"Hi Brandon!" they both shouted joyfully in unison.

"How's your football training going with your dad and Patrick, Dylan?"

"It's going great! I'm getting faster and faster. In fact, I'm pretty sure I could beat you in the 40-yard dash," said Dylan with a giggle.

"Let's plan to race the next time we're together. I actually called you, Dylan, to ask you and your parents for a favor. There's a little boy I met recently who has cancer. His name is Ryan. He's six years old, about the same age you were when we first met. He's had his cancer for four years, and it has recently returned. He needs a friend like you, Dylan, who can help him remain determined to get through the tough days of chemotherapy."

Dylan interjected, "And I can also teach him to trust Jesus to help him through."

Brandon smiled and said, "That's right. Because you've gone through what he's enduring, you can really encourage him and help lift his spirits. Here's what I have in mind. I've arranged to get seven tickets together to all of our home games... three for you and your parents, three for the little boy and his parents, and one for Patrick. Would you be willing to sit with Ryan at the football games and be his friend?"

Before Brandon had finished his question, he heard a deafening celebration through the phone. Jenny took the phone off of speaker and said, "Brandon, I've taken you off of speaker. The ruckus that you hear is Dylan dancing around the room with his dad. You can take that as a 'yes'."

"That's great. I'll be in touch with you later with more details."

Brandon then immediately called Patrick. The two close friends had a joyous reunion, as they hadn't talked for several weeks. Brandon shared the plan of inviting Patrick, Dylan and Ryan to all the home games. Patrick described for Brandon all the progress Dylan was making in their workouts. Brandon then told Patrick the details about his eventful last week with media day, the scuffle with Manny Garcia, Manny's assault, Brandon's incarceration, and finally his release from jail. Patrick was already familiar with much of the story. Patrick, however, was moved to tears of joy when Brandon relayed the story of the team baptisms, as well as the baptism of Brandon's mom.

Chapter 41

IT WAS MID-AUGUST, ONE month following the team baptisms, and two weeks before the season opener for the Ohio State football team. The coaching staff was beginning their daily early morning meeting before engaging with the players. One of the changes they'd made since the baptisms was that they now always began their meetings with a prayer. As was often the case, Jalen Pittman led the prayer that morning.

"Dear Father, we praise you for your creation, for your strength and mercy, and we thank you for loving us. Thank you also for your protection of our players, and your guidance of our team and coaches as we prepare for the upcoming season. We ask you, Father, to please allow us to witness your impact and influence on our team today and that it may stir our hearts to love you more deeply and to desire to do your will more fervently. In Jesus' name, we pray. Amen."

"Thank you, Jalen," said Coach Weaver. "It's interesting that you prayed that God would reveal to us today the specific ways he's influencing and impacting our team. This morning, I happened to be thinking about all the subtle and not-so-subtle ways our team has changed over the past month, since so many of them gave their lives to Christ and were baptized. Before we talk about the details of today's practice, let's share our observations about God's influence on our team."

Coach Anderson said, "I've noticed less bravado and boasting, yet our team has a quiet confidence. It also seems like our players have shifted their focus away from individual goals and toward team objectives."

"Our practices have been crisper. There's more focus and heightened camaraderie among the players," interjected Coach Swanson.

"You can walk into the locker room and immediately notice that any salty language is virtually gone," exclaimed Coach Perkins.

"I've noticed how much more gratitude and respect there is now for the team managers and trainers," remarked Jalen Pittman.

"I see more honesty and accountability," added Coach Jackson, "and an improved work ethic."

"The thing that has stood out to me is the enhanced willingness to help each other. Between practices, our film room is packed with the more experienced players using game film to mentor the newer players. I've never seen anything like it, and I attribute it to God's influence," said Coach Weaver. "Thank you for sharing your observations, everyone. Let's get back to preparing for today."

After Brandon's release from jail, Grace had completely forgiven him for causing the accidental death of her son, Joshua. Although Grace continued to grieve the

CHAPTER 41

loss of Joshua, she reveled in her family life comprised of her and Sam's adopted son, Daniel, and their daughter Lauren. Daniel's biological parents were Emma Brooks and Brandon Campbell. Grace loved both Brandon and Emma, and she was glad they were in her and Sam's life, but she continued to fear that someday, somehow, her relationship with her sweet Daniel would be forever altered if Emma had a change of heart which would lead to Daniel discovering the truth.

Grace decided that the best way to deal with her lingering anxiety was to confront it forthrightly. She invited Emma to lunch. As she was preparing to leave her house to meet Emma, she spontaneously decided to take twenty-month-old Daniel with her and to leave Lauren at home with her nanny.

As Grace was driving the short distance to the restaurant, she kept replaying in her mind the expression on Emma's face as she observed Daniel at their last dinner together in the Gilmore's home. Grace interpreted the look as a combination of longing, pride and sadness, and she knew that it was Emma's unexpressed feelings about Daniel that made Grace so uneasy. Her hope was that she could spend some of her time with Emma today exploring how Emma felt about giving Daniel up for adoption.

Grace and Daniel arrived at the trendy bistro first, and the two of them were seated. When Emma arrived, Grace arose to embrace her warmly. Emma heartily returned the hug and sat down. She smiled at Daniel, who was seated in a booster seat next to Grace in the booth. "Hi, Daniel, how are you, buddy?" she cooed.

"Thanks for inviting me, Grace. It's good to see you. How are you and Sam doing?"

"We're doing well. Sam has started his final year of medical school and has begun to apply to residency programs."

"That's great. Has he decided what field he wants to pursue?"

"He seems most interested in emergency medicine, but he'll probably apply to a few internal medicine programs as well."

"Both of those fields sound exciting. Have you two decided where he'd like to do his residency?" Emma inquired.

"Right now, we'd prefer to stay in the Midwest to be near our families, but he'll be better equipped to rank his preferences after he goes through the interview process."

"How are you doing with all of this, Grace? I imagine it's difficult for you with Sam working long hours and you working and taking care of two young children."

"Thanks for asking, Emma. Most days I'm managing really well, but sometimes I'm exhausted by the end of the day, especially if one or both of the kids are sick."

A waiter approached to take their orders. Emma made her selection first. Grace lingered on several choices before making a decision. As she looked up from her menu and gave the waiter her order, she glanced at Emma, who had that familiar facial expression as she studied Daniel.

"I'm so glad you brought Daniel with you today," Emma said without taking her eyes off of him.

"What do you think about when you look at Daniel?" Grace asked earnestly.

"I just admire how beautiful he is."

"Do you have any regrets?"

CHAPTER 41

"You mean about putting him up for adoption?" Emma asked.

Grace gently nodded affirmatively as she searched Emma's eyes for whatever they might give away about Emma's true feelings.

"No. It just wasn't the right time in my life to take care of a baby. Brandon and I were estranged at that time, and it didn't look like we would ever get back together. Plus, I was dedicated to my career and taking care of all my kids with cancer."

"Do you ever allow your mind to imagine what it would be like if the circumstances had been different and you hadn't put Daniel up for adoption?" Grace didn't even recognize it, but she was holding her breath.

Suddenly, Emma realized what was really behind Grace's question. Emma sensed that Grace was trying to discern if Emma may ever try to undermine Grace's relationship with Daniel in the future. Emma looked warmly at Grace with a smile. "Please understand, Grace, that I can see how happy your family is and how much Lauren and Daniel love each other. I would never, ever do anything to jeopardize your beautiful family, and I'm so grateful and delighted that it was you and Sam who adopted him." She paused thoughtfully.

"Daniel will forever have a special place in my heart, and I hope that you'll always allow me to watch him grow up from afar."

Grace subconsciously exhaled with relief. "Thank you, Emma. I can't tell you how much peace you've given me just now. And yes, you'll always be able to watch Daniel grow up, but I'd prefer that it be from nearby rather than from afar!"

They enjoyed conversation throughout the rest of their lunch, and afterwards Emma and Grace shared a warm hug.

As Grace drove home after having lunch with Emma, her heart was filled with peace after her open conversation with Emma, and Emma's sincere expressions of her heart.

As she left the restaurant, Emma thought joyfully about how much she was looking forward to having a family with Brandon someday.

Chapter 42

TWO DAYS AFTER EMMA had lunch with Grace, she had a date with Brandon at The Refectory, widely considered the most romantic restaurant in Columbus. It held a special place in their hearts because, at this very restaurant years ago, they both realized for the first time that they wanted their relationship to be more than just a friendship. Emma had been looking forward to this evening with great anticipation as she reflected on the memories of the last time she and Brandon had dined there and experienced the most spectacular meal either of them had ever eaten.

As they drove up to The Refectory, Emma said reflectively, "How long has it been since the last time we were here?"

"I was thinking about that, too. It was the fall of my freshman year, so it's been almost seven years."

"Wow, that was a while ago. One of the many things I remember about the last time we were here was asking you how you could afford this place."

Brandon chuckled and said, "I hope your memories of when we were last here are more breathtaking than how I scraped up the cash to pay the check. Just in case you were wondering, I'm doing fine in that department with the combination of my scholarship, impending NIL money and my mom's intermittent cash gifts."

Emma smiled at Brandon and said dreamily, "Oh, I remember much more than that about our magical evening, trust me. And I'm glad to see how God is blessing you financially."

As Brandon and Emma, holding hands, walked up to the front door of the restaurant, Emma said, "I wonder if Constantine still works here? Do you remember him?"

Constantine was their waiter seven years ago, and in addition to the fabulous food, he was a big part of what made their dining experience so special. "Of course, I remember him, especially how you flirted with him all evening," teased Brandon.

Emma giggled and exclaimed, "I think your memory is getting foggy from too many hits on the football field."

As they entered the restaurant, they heard a shout from the maître d' stand, "Brandon! Emma! Welcome!"

They looked, and it was none other than Constantine. Emma said excitedly, "We were just talking about you, Constantine, and wondering if you still worked here." Emma didn't notice Brandon and Constantine stealing a knowing glance with each other. "I can't believe you still remember us after all these years."

"I could never forget the most beautiful young lady I've ever met, and it happened to be especially memorable because she was with one of my all-time favorite Ohio State football players."

Emma blushed. "I see you're as charming as ever, Constantine. Is there any chance you can wait on our table tonight?" asked Emma.

CHAPTER 42

"That charm, that you so kindly noted, Emma, has gotten me promoted to maître d', but I'll see what I can do for you."

Brandon and Emma were seated, and about a minute later Constantine stepped up to the table and said, "Can I tell you about tonight's specials?"

"Wait," exclaimed Emma, "are you going to be taking care of us after all?"

"Yes, I couldn't pass up this opportunity to share in this special evening with the two of you. I've arranged for one of the other staff members to cover my maître d' responsibilities."

Emma and Brandon took full advantage of Constantine's vast knowledge of the menu and how each offering was prepared. They also leaned heavily on his preferences, because they knew he wouldn't steer them wrong. After thoughtfully placing their order with Constantine, Brandon and Emma settled in to enjoy their evening with each other.

As they both sipped Perrier with lime wedges and savored an appetizer of calamari, Brandon asked, "Has there been any news on how Ryan Fisher is responding to his new chemotherapy?"

"Yes," exclaimed Emma excitedly, "it slipped my mind to tell you. His CT results came back today, and the tumor in his lung has shrunk significantly."

"That's great news! It's also really cool that your collaboration with Jasmine initiated those encouraging results."

"That's just been the beginning. Since Jasmine and I worked together on Ryan's case, I've involved her in about a half dozen other patients' care. Because of her knowledge of the pipeline of chemotherapy drugs and the clinical trials involving them, she's been a tremendous asset. She has really gained the respect of our oncologists. On a personal note, we've become really close friends, and I think she and Jalen are getting serious."

Brandon said with a grin, "Yeah, Jalen seems to be crushing on her pretty hard."

After a moment of comfortable silence, Emma asked, "Have you talked with your mom recently? How is she doing since her baptism?"

"I talked with her yesterday," said Brandon, "and she's so joyful, like never before. This may be a bad analogy, given the recent events of my life, but it's as if she's been released from jail. She's finally living freely under God's grace."

"That's wonderful. Speaking of living freely under God's grace," interjected Emma, "I had lunch with Grace a couple of days ago. She confided in me that when you were released from jail, she finally has been able to forgive you completely for what happened to Joshua. There's been something else, though, that's been haunting her. She's been worried that I'll regret having put Daniel up for adoption, and will someday do something to sabotage her relationship with him. Fortunately, I was able to successfully assure her that I'd never do anything to disrupt Daniel's beautiful family situation with Sam, Lauren and her." After pausing for a moment, Emma said somewhat hesitantly, "Being with Daniel and Grace the other day got me thinking about children in our future. I know we've already agreed that we both want to have children after we're married, but I'm beginning to think that I'd like to start our family shortly after we get married. What do you think, Brandon?"

Suddenly, there was a flurry of activity as several servers surrounded their table, clearing the dishes from

CHAPTER 42

their appetizers, replacing their silverware, serving their entrees and refilling their water glasses. Emma's question became lost in the shuffle as they both became distracted by the cascade of various delectable flavors in the entrees.

As they were both finishing their sumptuous dishes, Emma added with a giggle, "Do you think it would be frowned upon if I licked my plate?"

Brandon laughed and said, "Surely not by the chef. He'd view it as the highest compliment." His expression then became more earnest, and he leaned forward, locking his eyes on hers and began, "Emma, just before our food arrived, you asked me for my thoughts about the timing of having children. Ironically, ever since the last time we were here seven years ago, I've thought constantly about my future life with you. If it were up to me, I'd love to start our family right after we're married, too."

Emma's eyes filled with tears of joy as she said quietly, "I'm so happy to hear you say that, Brandon." Brandon used Emma's temporary visual impairment to give Constantine, who was standing about ten feet behind Emma, a brief, meaningful nod.

A moment later, Constantine approached their table and handed them both dessert menus. He then placed a small box in front of each of them, and said, "While you are considering your choices for dessert, you can prepare your sweet tooth with the finest Swiss chocolate in the world."

After they studied their dessert menus for a few minutes, Emma laid hers aside and said, "I think I know what I'd like."

"What did you decide on?" asked Brandon.

"Mango sorbet, and we can share it if you'd like," said Emma as she reached for her box of Swiss chocolate.

"I spoke with your dad this week," Brandon said casually as Emma looked up from opening the lid on her chocolate.

"Was he asking you about getting him some football tickets again?" asked Emma as she looked down at her now open box, containing the most beautiful diamond ring she'd ever seen.

Emma's eyes widened and she gasped with joyous surprise as Brandon arose from his chair while saying, "No, I was seeking your dad's blessing for me to propose to you." Brandon got down on one knee and took Emma's hand as he looked into her soul and said, "Emma Brooks, you are the love of my life. Will you marry me?"

Emma, overwhelmed with elation and delighted laughter, exclaimed, "Yes! Yes, I will marry you, Brandon!" They embraced tightly as both of them were overcome with joyful tears. Brandon took the ring out of the box and slipped it on Emma's finger. This was something they'd both longed for with their whole hearts for a long time, and as they laughed and cried together, they marveled at God's goodness in restoring their relationship, their love, and their hope for a beautiful future together.

Chapter 43

AS MUCH AS BRANDON enjoyed the excitement of Christmas morning as a child, it was no comparison to the thrill of the Ohio State football team's season opener in Columbus. The day was going to be warm and sunny, and Brandon could hardly wait to get on the field with his teammates. After his long hiatus from the game he loved, he never thought he'd experience another season opener as a player ever again. He intended to cherish every moment of the season, regardless of how it unfolded.

The preseason polls had Ohio State ranked eighth, which was unusually low by their standards. Although their incoming recruiting class was among the best in the nation, they still had question marks at several key positions. Also, the consensus among sports journalists was that Brandon Campbell was going to be more of a distraction than a contributor, given his lengthy time away from the game. This summer's events with the scuffle in practice and Brandon's subsequent arrest seemed to confirm the journalists' predictions.

The college football world outside of the Ohio State locker room, however, was unaware of the galvanizing effect on the team through Brandon and the Holy Spirit. The team had witnessed Brandon's faith in God and his grace in forgiving Tristin and Manny this past summer. They also saw his performance on the field every day in practice and knew that his speed, strength, elusiveness and vision were elite. In short, the team was prepared to play their hearts out, inspired by Brandon's leadership.

In addition to the team, diehard Ohio State fans supported Brandon passionately. They still remembered his heroics during his first three years of being a Buckeye. They viewed his struggles with his dad's tragic accident, his multiple addictions, and his recent incarceration as they would a wounded war hero. It made them embrace him even more and long for his success on the field. Brandon frequently received adoration from Ohio State fans when he was out in public around Columbus or on campus. Part of his motivation was to not disappoint the fans who supported him. But most of all, Brandon's desire was to inspire others and to bring glory to God.

Brandon was especially excited about this game because Ryan Fisher and his parents, Dylan Hubbard and his parents, Emma, Patrick Cutler, Brandon's mom and Mike Nelson would all be sitting together. It would be the first time Dylan and Ryan, the two boys who had battled cancer, would meet, and Brandon believed they would be really good for each other. Brandon had also arranged that all of his guests, as well as Jalen, Jasmine, Tristin and Manny would have dinner together at Angelo's Italian Restaurant after all of their home games.

Brandon had met Angelo at an Ohio State alumni function held at Angelo's restaurant. The two of them immediately connected, and Angelo jumped at the chance to host

CHAPTER 43

Brandon and his guests in the large private dining room at his restaurant after home games.

Brandon's relationship with both Tristin and Manny had grown closer and closer as the season approached. Manny had been cleared to return to practice only about two weeks earlier. Brandon, Manny, Tristin and Jalen spent a lot of extra time in the film room. Brandon and Jalen were able to tutor the two freshmen in the strategy behind various offensive and defensive schemes. As a result, they both had become much more adept at recognizing game plans and reacting to them accordingly. Tristin, especially, was beginning to make substantial improvements in practice, and Brandon was really looking forward to seeing how he performed in a game.

As the Ohio State team gathered in the tunnel, prior to making their grand entrance onto the field before the start of the game, Brandon found Manny and Tristin and advised them to take in every detail of what they were about to experience but not to be overwhelmed by it. The three teammates interlocked their arms, with Brandon in the middle, and ran onto the field together amongst the rest of the team. The image of Brandon, Tristin and Manny locking arms was captured by the television coverage, but at the time, no one recognized that it would be a metaphor for Ohio State's season.

After the kickoff, Ohio State's defense was on the field first. It was unlikely that Manny would get in today's game because of all the practice he'd missed. Brandon helped teach him how to look for certain formations that would suggest what the other team's offense was likely going to run. Brandon's message to him was to use every opportunity, even when not on the field, to learn more, to prepare himself, and to support his teammates. Likewise, Brandon taught Tristin to stay ready even when Ohio State's defense was on the field, because a turnover could happen at any time and he needed to be prepared.

Ohio State's defense stopped their opponent after one first down. After a punt, Brandon and the rest of the offense trotted onto the field. Brandon was oblivious when a roar erupted from the Ohio State fans when he stepped on the field.

On the first play from scrimmage for Ohio State, it was a handoff to Brandon. The right offensive tackle opened a huge hole which Brandon barreled through in an instant. The crowd exploded as they realized that Brandon had a sliver of daylight. As the linebacker came from Brandon's left for the tackle, Brandon stiff-armed him into the ground. The crowd roared louder as it appeared that Brandon may be able to streak to the end zone on one of his long gallops, but at the last instant, the cornerback dove fully extended at Brandon's feet and got just enough of the top of his foot to trip him up and bring him down. When Brandon got back to the huddle, he congratulated the right tackle for creating such a big hole and vowed to the rest of the offense that he wouldn't waste another similar opportunity.

The next play was another handoff to Brandon. When he surveyed the line as he received the handoff, he couldn't believe his eyes. The offensive linemen had so decimated their counterparts on the defensive line that it appeared that a bomb had exploded. Brandon had multiple routes he could take, but he felt like he had some unfinished business from the previous play, so he again ran through the right

CHAPTER 43

side of the line. The same cornerback who tripped him on the last play tried to tackle Brandon by diving in front of his legs. Brandon nimbly jumped over him and raced sixty-four yards untouched for the touchdown. When Brandon reached the end zone, the stadium was so loud that it was shaking. Brandon held the football over his head in his left hand and pointed to the area in the stadium where Ryan and Dylan were seated with his right hand. Dylan shouted over the tumult at Ryan, who was standing next to him, "He's pointing at us!" Ryan looked on in awe as his parents wept with joy.

As Brandon was trotting back to the sideline, he was thinking that this would be a good game for Tristin to get some experience. Tristin had steadily improved over the course of the summer and eventually had worked his way up to the second-string running back. When Brandon got to the sideline, he shared his thoughts with Coach Pittman and suggested they run some of their two-back formations so Brandon could be on the field at the same time as Tristin and show him the ropes. Coach Pittman, as well as Coach Anderson, agreed with Brandon's suggestion, as they both had developed great respect for Brandon's insights, especially when it came to reading the psyches of his teammates. Brandon went to find Tristin to prepare him for his first opportunity to play in an Ohio State game.

When Ohio State got the ball back on offense, their first play was one where Brandon and Tristin were lined up side-by-side in the backfield with Brandon on the left. The play was designed to be a sweep around the left by Tristin, with Brandon leading the way. Brandon's responsibility was to block the defensive end on that side. When the snap occurred, Brandon exploded out of his stance and blocked the defensive end into next week. Tristin gained six yards on the play, and Brandon could tell that Tristin's jitters were calmed.

On the next play, Brandon was a decoy and moved to the far left of the backfield pre-snap. Tristin got the handoff and tried to run through the right side of the offensive line for a minimal gain. On the third down play, Tristin was looking for his running lane before getting the ball, and he fumbled it. Their opponent recovered the fumble and ultimately scored a field goal on their ensuing possession. Brandon immediately reassured Tristin that mistakes are just part of the learning process to becoming an elite back.

After the kickoff to Ohio State, their first offensive play was a screen pass to Brandon on the right side. Brandon became a one-man wrecking crew as he broke several tackles, nimbly evaded three other defenders and outran the rest on his way to a seventy-five-yard touchdown romp. The celebrating Ohio State fans were reawakened, and once again, Brandon stood in the end zone and pointed to the area of the stadium where Ryan and Dylan were hysterically celebrating.

Shortly before halftime, Ohio State got another offensive possession with seventy-two yards to the goal line. Their first play was a short pass to their wide receiver along the left sideline. As always, Brandon hustled to the area looking for a blocking opportunity. As Brandon approached, the wide receiver fumbled as he was being tackled. Brandon scooped up the fumble but was immediately surrounded by three defenders. Brandon saw no way to avoid being tackled, when he heard his name being called by Tristin

CHAPTER 43

who was approaching at full speed down the sideline. Brandon alertly lateraled the ball backwards to Tristin as he raced untouched to the goal line. Brandon was the first player to arrive and join in Tristin's celebration.

The second half was more of the same as Ohio State racked up a decisive victory. Although Brandon didn't play at all in the fourth quarter, he scored two more touchdowns in the second half, for a total of four touchdowns and well over two-hundred yards rushing for the game. The media highlights, however, were of Brandon entering the stadium arm-in-arm with Tristin and Manny before the game, and Brandon and Tristin celebrating together after Tristin's touchdown. Those were the highlights of the game for Brandon as well.

Chapter 44

DINNER THAT EVENING AT Angelo's was an energetic, festive celebration. The room was set up with one long table placed in the center of the room with seating on both sides. The table was generously decorated with votive candles, greenery and flowers. A buffet on one end of the room included: lasagna, spaghetti with meatballs, chicken alfredo, linguini with crab, shrimp and scallops, salad and warm Italian bread. The setup in the room allowed the fifteen dinner guests the ability to either sit at the table, or move about the room visiting with the other guests. Angelo had outdone himself in creating an atmosphere of casual elegance.

Brandon spent the majority of the evening seated at the table between Ryan and Dylan, with his new fiancée Emma across from him. Both boys had a small mountain of spaghetti piled in front of them, with an equally impressive amount of tomato sauce on their faces, especially Ryan. Brandon asked the boys, "What did you think of the game?"

Both Ryan and Dylan began talking excitedly at the same time. Brandon was unable to have a meaningful conversation with either of them, as he waited patiently, smiled and winked at Emma. Finally, as they both paused to catch

CHAPTER 44

a breath, Brandon said, "Ryan, did you and Dylan become friends today?"

"We sure did. We had so much fun at the game. Dylan loves Ohio State football as much as me."

"Dylan, did you tell Ryan that you've also had cancer, like him?"

"Yeah, we talked about it a little bit, but we were too busy watching you score touchdowns!"

"Hey, Brandon," Ryan interjected, "were you pointing at us after you scored those touchdowns today?"

"I sure was. I was pointing at you to make sure you were both having a good time. Were you?"

The two boys immediately sprang again into their excited, independent monologues about their experiences at the game. Brandon looked at Emma with a sparkle in his eye, and the two of them broke into laughter.

Manny and Tristin were seated with Coach Pittman and Jasmine, adjacent to Brandon and the boys. They were reveling in the camaraderie, great food and the aftermath of experiencing their first Ohio State football game. Although both Manny and Tristin were sharing their own excited impressions of the game with each other, they also observed Brandon and his interactions with his young guests. They were starting to understand how a Christian's heart is revealed in his actions, and also the meaning of a servant leader.

During dinner, Patrick came up behind Brandon and whispered in his ear, "Did you know that Dylan's first football game is at 1:00 tomorrow?"

"No, I didn't know that."

"Is there any chance you could come to Cincinnati and surprise him?"

Brandon thought for a moment, then said "Yes, I can... and I have another idea, too." Brandon arose from the table and had a quick whispered conversation with Emma, then a second one with Ryan's parents.

As Brandon returned to his seat, Jalen approached Brandon with a small duffel bag and handed it to him. Brandon moved to the head of the long, elegant table and said, "Good evening, everyone. May I have your attention please? Thank you all for coming this evening and celebrating our victory in Ohio State's season opener. We have one very important piece of business before we get to the even more crucial matter of dessert. I have the honor of announcing the winner of the award for the loudest fan at the game today. Our judges have concluded that we have a tie, and they've also decided that each winner will receive one of the footballs used to score the first two touchdowns of the season. Without further ado, our winners are Ryan Fisher and Dylan Hubbard!"

Brandon had inscribed a personal message on each of the balls he presented to both Dylan and Ryan, and he handed each of them their football, amidst loud shouting and applause from the other guests. The most enthusiastic responses were from Ryan's parents. Ryan was overwhelmed with joy in receiving the special football, and Dylan immediately showed him how to carry it and take care of it. He also shared with Ryan the story of how Brandon had presented him with the game ball in the Ohio State locker room and how Dylan carried it with him everywhere for years. The ball was still proudly on display in

CHAPTER 44

Dylan's bedroom. Brandon and Jalen smiled at each other as they overheard Dylan's retelling of the story.

Right after the early church service the next morning, Emma and Brandon went to the Fisher's house to pick up Ryan. Ryan was wearing his Brandon Campbell Ohio State jersey and carrying his special football as he said goodbye to his parents. He climbed into the car with Brandon and Emma for the trip to Cincinnati to surprise Dylan and join his fan section at his first football game of the season.

When Brandon, Emma and Ryan arrived at the field, they joined Patrick and Dylan's parents in the bleachers. The game hadn't started yet, and they could see Dylan on the field, surrounded by the players and coaches of both teams, as he proudly showed them the football that he had been awarded yesterday by his friend Brandon Campbell. There were more than a few doubtful glances exchanged among the group. As the teams went to their respective sidelines for the start of the game, Dylan looked up into the bleachers to wave to his parents and Patrick. He spotted Brandon, Emma and Ryan for the first time and began jumping up and down with excitement and pointing to where Brandon was sitting for the benefit of his teammates. Dylan was also determined to show Brandon how good he had become because of the workouts with his dad and Patrick.

At Dylan's age, it wasn't uncommon for one or two players in a given game to have far more advanced skills than the other players. In this instance, though, it looked like an NFL player was on the field with the other twelve-year-olds. Dylan overwhelmed the defense with his speed, shiftiness, quick feet and sudden changes in direction. The defenders could barely touch him, let alone tackle him. Dylan carried the ball eleven times and scored eight touchdowns.

After the game, they all went to Skyline Chili for lunch, and to Graeter's Ice Cream for dessert, two iconic Cincinnati institutions. As they entered Skyline Chili, Brandon noticed with amusement that Dylan and Ryan were having a very animated discussion. Once they were seated, Brandon asked them, "What were the two of you talking about as we were coming into the restaurant?"

Dylan, looking a little sheepish at first, said, "We were trying to decide who is better."

"What do you mean?" asked Brandon with a smile.

"Me or you," replied Dylan.

The others at the table giggled, and Brandon asked, "So, what did you decide?"

"Me!" exclaimed Dylan.

Brandon then looked at Ryan, who was cradling his football, and pointing at Dylan with a smile.

"That makes three of us," said Brandon. "I guess it's unanimous."

As the group was leaving Skyline, Patrick and Brandon lingered and chatted in the parking lot.

Brandon asked, "How are your classes going? Your engineering major must be pretty demanding."

"They're going well. I feel like this field of study is such a good fit for me. Now that I've got some of the introductory classes out of the way and can get more into the engineering

CHAPTER 44

courses, I'm really enjoying them. How is school going for you, Brandon?"

"I'm getting back in the groove again myself, and it's a big adjustment after being away from the classroom for several years. Now that I've declared a major in kinesiology, I'm trying to balance upper-level classes with my football commitments. Plus, with planning a wedding, my plate is pretty full. I'm seeking God for wisdom on how to manage it all."

"That reminds me of the verse in Philippians that says, 'I can do all things through Christ who gives me strength'," said Patrick.

"Amen, brother. That's the best way, if you ask me."

Chapter 45

THE NEXT MORNING, AS Brandon was walking to class, he got a call from Antonio Alvarez.

"Hi, Antonio! How're you doing?" asked Brandon warmly.

"I'm good, Brandon. Great game on Saturday. You put on quite a show."

"I didn't know you were a Buckeye fan."

"I wasn't until I learned that you play for them," said Antonio with a laugh. "Hey, I wanted you to know that I've been meeting with our mutual friend and your former cellmate, Carlos Flores. We've had some good conversations about faith, and after I invited him to the Christian retreat, he agreed to attend the one next month."

"That's fantastic news, Antonio. Thank you for listening to God and being obedient."

"I'm so thankful to you, Brandon, for investing in me and helping me get back on the right track. I hate to think about where I'd be without your guidance. It's a pleasure to pay it forward with Carlos."

"I'm really proud of you."

"Thanks, man. Hey, can I ask you for a favor?"

"Of course, Antonio. What can I do for you?"

"I need a job. The church has been so generous to me in allowing me to stay in the rectory as well as working at the

CHAPTER 45

church. I don't want to wear out my welcome, and I'd also like to work somewhere that leads to a career path for the rest of my life. The challenge, though, is that I need some flexibility in my schedule because of Sofia. She's my number one priority."

"What kind of work do you like?"

"I've always loved the food industry, and I'd really like to become a chef someday."

"I have a friend, Angelo, who owns Angelo's Italian Restaurant. He's very successful, and he takes great care of his employees. I know he has a number of staff members who have young children, so he offers child care at the home of one of his family members. I could let him know that you're willing to do anything at the restaurant, but that eventually you'd like to learn to be a chef. What do you say?"

"That sounds like an answered prayer!"

"I'll call him right now and see what he says."

"Thank you so much!"

About five minutes later, Brandon called Antonio back. "Hey, Antonio, good news. I just talked with Angelo, and he said that anyone recommended by me is hired automatically. He asked if you could drop by his restaurant anytime tomorrow afternoon so he can show you around and iron out the details. He said you're welcome to bring Sofia along if you'd like."

"Thanks again, Brandon!"

"You're welcome, but I do have an ulterior motive. Because I eat regularly at Angelo's, this way I can hopefully see you more often. One other thing. As you transition from moving from Cincinnati to Columbus, you and Sofia are welcome to live with me while you're trying to get settled here. I have an extra bedroom in my apartment."

"Wow, this is incredible. Your kindness and generosity are amazing."

"It's all about showing others the glory of God and inspiring them to do the same thing," exclaimed Brandon joyfully.

Ohio State's second and third games were non-conference games. The next one was at home, and the following game would be on the road. This week's home game would be against a stiffer opponent than their opener. With a week to study the film of Brandon and the Ohio State offense, the opponent would certainly make some adjustments that would make life more difficult for Brandon. For that reason, Coaches Caldwell and Pittman once again installed the halfback option pass back into the offense from Brandon's former playing days at Ohio State. They practiced it from a variety of different formations, including the one with both Tristin and Brandon in the backfield at the same time.

The defensive coaching staff also spent a lot of extra time with Manny Garcia this week to make up for the time he'd missed practicing over the summer. He was steadily improving, and he was convinced that he played better without Adderall, which he had abandoned forever.

The day of the game was sultry and overcast with a temperature in the high eighties. It was the sort of weather that favored the fit. In spite of the conditions, the Ohio State fans were stoked because of what they'd witnessed in the

CHAPTER 45

opener. The legend of Brandon Campbell had returned to Ohio State.

During Ohio State's first offensive possession, the strategy of their opponent was obvious. They loaded up their defensive line with eight players, and they keyed on every move of Brandon. Ohio State suspected that they could counter the strategy through passing plays, using Brandon as a decoy for Tristin, and their secret weapon – the halfback option pass.

On the second play from scrimmage, Coach Anderson dialed up the halfback option pass, hoping both to catch his opponent off guard and to get in their heads early. The ball was snapped to the quarterback as Brandon started sweeping to his right. Multiple defenders started toward Brandon before the quarterback had even shoveled the ball backwards to him. Fortunately, the offensive line did their job, giving Brandon enough time to launch a thirty-yard perfect spiral to the wide-open receiver, who caught it in stride and raced untouched the additional forty yards to the end zone. Brandon once again pointed to where Dylan and Ryan were celebrating in the stadium.

During the remainder of the game, the Ohio State offense mixed up their plays to keep their opponent off-balance. They would fake a shovel pass to Brandon sweeping around either the left or the right end. As the defense collapsed on Brandon, Tristin would receive the handoff and run up the middle with success. They'd sprinkle in enough passing plays to keep the defense honest. As the defense would begin to recognize that Brandon's role was largely as a decoy and pay less attention to him, Brandon would get the ball and make them pay. At the conclusion of the game,

Tristin had rushed for over one-hundred yards, Manny defended a pass and got a tackle, and Ohio State achieved a second decisive victory.

The same group of Brandon's friends gathered at Angelo's that evening to celebrate. The only difference was that Antonio was one of the staff members who took care of the guests. His joy added to the fun and camaraderie of the evening. The arrangement of Antonio and Sofia temporarily living with Brandon was going well. At one point during the evening, Brandon pulled Antonio aside and said, "Antonio, this entire group is traveling to Cincinnati tomorrow afternoon to cheer for Dylan at his football game. Would you and Sofia like to join us?"

"We'd like that very much, Brandon."

"Great. I'll fill you in on the details later, but don't say anything to Dylan because we're going to surprise him."

The next day, Dylan's mobile cheering section again surprised and motivated him at his game. During the first half, the other team put all their attention on Dylan and kept him in check. At halftime, Brandon went down to the field and showed Dylan how to do a spin move and a jump cut. Now armed with two new weapons in his arsenal, Dylan scored three touchdowns in the second half.

The next week, Ohio State had their first away game. Their opponent's strategy was to blitz from a variety of different positions on nearly every play. Although they occasionally had success, Ohio State simply had too much

CHAPTER 45

firepower and eventually overwhelmed them. The result was another solid victory for the Buckeyes.

Ohio State's fourth game was another away game, against their first Big Ten opponent. They provided the most difficult test for OSU so far this season. The opponent's fans in the previous away game viewed Brandon with respect and curiosity, but this week, the fans of Ohio State's opponent assumed the role of trying to disrupt Brandon's concentration. As Ohio State's team buses arrived at the stadium, there was a line of hostile fans holding posters awaiting the players as they disembarked. Examples of the messages included:

- TROJANS WILL HANDCUFF CAMPBELL

- NEW UNIFORMS FOR BUCKEYES: ORANGE JUMPSUITS

- OUR D GONNA ARREST CAMPBELL

- BAT DOWN CAMPBELL

The last one, showing a drawing of a baseball bat, was directed at both Manny and Brandon, and was especially malicious.

As Brandon walked by the line of posters, he laughed at the ones that were particularly clever. The fans generally yelled taunting remarks at him as he strode by. At one point, buried in the line of hostile, poster-waving fans, a little boy, wearing a Brandon Campbell Ohio State jersey, was spotted by Brandon much to the chagrin of the boy's parents standing nearby. Brandon stopped and asked his young fan if he'd like Brandon to sign his jersey. The little boy enthusiastically agreed, as television cameras captured Brandon adorning the jersey with his autograph as the sour-faced parents observed.

Much like their fans, the opponent of Ohio State thought they could successfully rely on their own strength and grit to overcome the Buckeyes. Ohio State countered their arrogance by giving them a heavy dose of Brandon Campbell. The game concluded in a hushed stadium with Brandon rushing for 275 yards and four touchdowns, and passing for a fifth.

Chapter 46

THE FIFTH WEEK OF the season marked Ohio State's second game against a Big Ten opponent. The competition would gradually get more formidable as the season progressed. Although the team was proud of what they'd accomplished in the first four games, the players followed Brandon's example. They remained humble and recognized that their season wouldn't be measured by wins and losses, but rather by how well they reflected the glory of God. They all sensed the influence of the Holy Spirit growing stronger each week.

The national media was also beginning to pay more attention to Ohio State. The Buckeyes had risen to fifth in the polls, and Brandon was at the top of early Heisman Trophy watch lists. The media was also noticing more subtle attributes of the unique Ohio State team. There was joy in how the players approached the game. They were also frequently observed helping not only their own teammates up off the ground, but also opposing players. Brandon often congratulated defensive players of their opponent for making good plays, especially when he was the recipient of the tackle. The camaraderie between Ohio State and their opponent was infectious, although it didn't dampen the usual competitive fire.

INSPIRING GLORY

On the day before the game, Ryan Fisher was admitted to Nationwide Children's Hospital with pneumonia. Because his immune system was suppressed from the chemotherapy, his pneumonia was very serious, and there was concern that he may need to go on a ventilator. That evening, Brandon, Tristin, Manny and Dylan, who was in town for tomorrow's game, went to visit Ryan in the hospital. When the guys entered Ryan's room, his mood noticeably brightened immediately, although they all recognized how Ryan was struggling to breathe.

"How are you feeling, Ryan?" Brandon asked.

"I'm sad because I'm not going to see you, Tristan and Manny play in the game tomorrow."

"At least you can watch it on TV," said Dylan while nodding toward the television in Ryan's room. "I remember watching the Ohio State games on TV lots of times while I was in the hospital. One time, Brandon broke his leg in the game, and I told my dad that I'd share my hospital room with Brandon." The others all laughed.

Tristin asked Ryan, "Is there anything I can do for you to help you feel better?"

Without hesitating, Ryan said, "Yes, you can score two touchdowns in the game tomorrow." Tristin was increasingly fulfilling his potential by becoming a more dynamic runner. He was steadily racking up yardage. He had scored a touchdown in each of Ohio State's first four games, but he hadn't yet scored more than one in a game.

"You've got it," responded Tristin confidently.

"And Manny," said Ryan while turning towards him, "You would help me by getting an interception in tomorrow's game."

CHAPTER 46

"Sure thing, Ryan," said Manny while trying to sound more confident than he felt.

The next day, it was a perfect early autumn afternoon for a football game, with sunny skies and temperatures in the upper sixties. Although the weather was ideal, Ohio State's play on the football field certainly wasn't, especially their defense. Late in the fourth quarter, Brandon had executed another dominating performance with over two-hundred yards rushing. He had run for three touchdowns and had thrown a pass for a fourth. Tristin had also scored a touchdown. In spite of Ohio State's offensive output, they trailed by four points with their opponent having the ball around midfield. The other team had experienced success all day by moving the ball with short passes.

Manny was in the game at right cornerback, largely because the starter at his position had been ineffective all game. It was third down and five, and Manny was beginning to get a sense of the tendencies of the wide receiver he'd been covering. With time running out, Manny knew that he may need to gamble if he was going to give Ohio State a chance to win. His instinct was that the receiver was going to run a short route into the flat to try to gain just enough yardage for a first down. Another first down would effectively put the game away.

As the ball was snapped, the receiver took several steps downfield, and then faked as if he was going to run a route across the middle. He then changed direction suddenly and angled outside toward the sideline. Manny was waiting for him, and adeptly snatched the ball just before it reached the receiver's hands, and then wisely stepped out of bounds. Manny didn't want to waste any of the precious remaining seconds, and he knew that it was better that Brandon carry the ball the rest of the way. He was elated to fulfill Ryan's wish, something Manny had prayed for.

The Ohio State offense called the play on the sidelines before they trotted onto the field. The play was one where Brandon and Tristin were lined up side-by-side in the backfield, with Brandon on the left and Tristin on the right. Brandon would receive the handoff and sweep around the right side, and Tristin was responsible for blocking the defensive end on that side. Brandon would be able to step out of bounds to stop the clock if he thought he was going to be tackled.

When the ball was snapped, Brandon received the handoff and swept around the right side at full speed. The defensive backs were playing deep to prevent a big gain by Ohio State. After advancing about ten yards, Brandon saw the cornerback on that side and both safeties converging to make the tackle. Brandon initially considered running out of bounds, but then glanced over his left shoulder and saw Tristin trailing the play about five yards behind him.

Brandon yelled at Tristin, "Follow me!", as he tossed the ball backwards to Tristin and then lowered his shoulders and hit the three defenders like a skillfully thrown bowling ball splintering three upright pins. Tristin danced through and around the bodies strewn on the ground and crossed the goal line just as time expired, sealing the Buckeye win. He said a silent prayer of thanks for scoring the second touchdown for Ryan.

At Nationwide Children's Hospital, Ryan, joyfully watching the game on the TV in his room with his parents,

CHAPTER 46

screamed, "Mom! Dad! Manny and Tristin did the favors they promised me!"

Tristin was interviewed on the field by the television crew immediately following the game.

"What was it like scoring that touchdown with time running out?" Tristin was asked.

"First of all, our opponent played a great game today, and we were very fortunate to get the victory. On that last play, all the credit goes to our offensive line and to Brandon Campbell who made the final block which cleared the way to the end zone. I'm just grateful and blessed to be a part of it, and to play the game that I love with such godly men," answered Tristin humbly.

After the game and before heading to Angelo's for their post-game celebration with their friends, Brandon, Manny and Tristin went to Nationwide Children's Hospital to visit Ryan. When they entered his room, he was sleeping peacefully, but his parents received the three teammates with joyful enthusiasm.

"I can't believe you guys pulled that game out! What an exciting finish!" exclaimed Ryan's mom.

"You should've seen how excited Ryan was, especially when Manny got his interception and Tristin scored his second touchdown. It was as if we could almost see Ryan turning the corner right before our eyes," said Ryan's dad.

Hearing his name, Ryan groggily awakened, but quickly came to life when he saw his three visitors. He became quite animated as he recounted the final events of the game.

Brandon said, "We came to see how you're doing, Ryan, and to let you know how much we'll miss you and your mom and dad at Angelo's this evening. We also came to bring you some presents." Ryan's eyes began to sparkle even more brightly.

Manny stepped up to Ryan's bedside and, while handing him a football, he said, "Here's the ball I intercepted that I promised you I'd get. I wrote on it a message that includes the date and the significance of this ball." Ryan accepted the ball gently and looked at it as though it were the most valuable thing he'd ever seen.

"I can't wait to show this to Dylan," exclaimed Ryan.

"While you're showing Dylan that, you might want to show him this as well," said Tristin while stepping to Ryan's bed and holding out another football.

"Is this the one you used to score the winning touchdown?"

"That's right, Ryan, and I signed it similarly to how Manny signed his."

Ryan beamed as he cradled both of his new treasures.

After the three players left to go to Angelo's, Ryan's parents sat cuddled together in the couch in his room watching Ryan sleep peacefully while holding the two footballs. They tearfully shared the same thought, "Regardless of God's plan for Ryan's medical course, Ryan would always know how much he was loved."

Chapter 47

FOLLOWING THEIR DRAMATIC VICTORY, an inexplicable peace, like the morning dew, fell upon the Ohio State players. They recognized that they were a team of destiny, not necessarily by winning every game, but by how they reflected God's glory to the world. They saw God's hand in their most recent victory, but they knew that remaining faithful and keeping their eyes on God was a much higher priority than winning games.

Even opposing players recognized that playing Ohio State was like no other game on their schedule. There was still fierce competition, but there was no foul language exchanged by the players in the trenches between the offensive and defensive lines. They congratulated each other over an exceptional play. The games were fun for the players, like they used to be when they played as kids in the backyard with their friends.

The next week's game was another home game for the Buckeyes. Ryan was out of the hospital, having recovered from his pneumonia, and was joyfully back in the stands sitting next to his friend, Dylan. Both of them, as usual, were adorned in their Brandon Campbell jerseys, as were about two-thirds of the fans at the game.

As Tristin had emerged as an exceptional running back to complement Brandon, the offensive coaches had further expanded their playbook to make it even more difficult for defenses to stop them. On one play, Brandon and Tristin were lined up side-by-side in the backfield. Brandon swept around the right side and received the backwards shovel pass from the quarterback like on a usual halfback option pass play. Brandon pump-faked to the receiver downfield. He then threw the ball across the field to Tristin for a screen pass. With an army of blockers in front of him, Tristin streaked to the end zone.

Just after Brandon had thrown the pass to Tristin, one of the defensive linemen was nearly successful in tackling Brandon before he threw it. The two of them stood together and watched Tristin race down the opposite sideline for the touchdown. After Tristin scored, the opposing player patted Brandon on the helmet and said, "Nice play!"

"Thanks, but I thought you were going to get me before I got rid of it," responded Brandon, smiling.

"I'll get you next time." The player, whose name was Cole Arnett, didn't know Brandon personally.

"Hey, Cole. I read this week that your dad died recently. How are you doing?"

"Thanks for asking, Brandon. I'm getting by, but I'm worried about my mom. She's having a really hard time. Would you pray for her?"

"You can count on it! Actually, I've got a little time right now as I jog back to the sideline," said Brandon, smiling. Amidst a stadium full of fans wildly celebrating Ohio State's touchdown, Brandon blocked it out and prayed for peace

CHAPTER 47

and God's loving comfort for Cole's mother as he trotted across the field to his own sideline.

On another play, Ohio State had the ball on third down with five yards to go for a touchdown. Ohio State's right offensive tackle reported as an eligible receiver to the referee. When the ball was snapped, Brandon rolled to his left and received the backwards shovel pass from the quarterback. The defense quickly shifted to stop Brandon's run, but before he reached the line of scrimmage, Brandon stopped suddenly and lofted a gentle pass to the opposite corner of the end zone where his tackle was patiently waiting all alone. Brandon was the initial player to congratulate him on the first touchdown of his life. It was the final score of a dominant Ohio State victory in which the Buckeyes had given their future opponents much more to contemplate for their upcoming games.

The celebration that evening at Angelo's was especially joyful, in large part because Ryan and his family were there after being absent the previous week because of Ryan's hospitalization. After dinner, as the group was mingling and enjoying their desserts, Jalen stood beside Jasmine in the center of the room and asked for the attention of the guests.

Jalen began, "I've lived a very eventful life, and God has blessed me richly. I have never experienced a year like this one, though. I've returned to Ohio State, a place that I love, as a coach, and this football season has been like none that I've ever experienced. Because of some preseason challenges, the team has bonded through their common faith in God. Oh, what a ride it's been!"

Jalen continued, "But the biggest blessing for me this year has nothing to do with football. One year ago tonight,

I met Jasmine, and she has captured my heart. We share a mutual love for Jesus, and she is my soulmate. As we have gotten to know each other through the four seasons and all the holidays and other celebrations of the past year, God had made it very clear to me that she's the one he wants me to take as my wife. In this room are many of my closest friends and the people whom I love the most. I want to share this moment with all of you." Slipping a ring box out of his pocket, opening it and dropping to one knee, Jalen looked up at Jasmine and said, "Jasmine, my beloved, will you marry me?"

Jasmine, overcome with emotion, said quietly, "Yes, I will, Jalen. I love you."

Jalen slipped the ring on her finger. He arose, kissed her, then embraced her while their friends clapped and cheered.

About ten minutes after Jalen's proposal, Mike Nelson approached Brandon and said, "Hey, Brandon. Can we find somewhere private to talk? I have something I'd like to discuss with you."

Brandon replied with a slight grin, "I haven't seen you this serious since you asked me if I'd be willing to share my story with you for publication."

They found a private meeting room that wasn't being used and closed the door.

"Brandon, as you know, I've always admired your dad. Ever since we went to UC together, he's been one of my closest friends. I never shared this with you, because I knew you were having struggles of your own, but it was really tough on me when your dad died. It was especially difficult because I'd lost my wife about four years earlier to cancer. We never had any children, and I felt really alone

CHAPTER 47

after she died. I threw myself into my work, and your dad and mom really came to my rescue in getting me through that heartbroken time. I was convinced, though, that I'd never remarry. When I began teaching your mom about the love of Jesus, it was as though God simultaneously began softening my heart. I have such respect for you, Brandon, and what I'm about to tell you may be difficult for you. I've fallen in love with your mom, and I'd like your permission to ask her to marry me."

Brandon wasn't sure where Mike was going until the very end, and he said, "I need to go buy a lottery ticket, because God just keeps showering me with blessings today. First the game, then Jalen's proposal and now this. I'd love for you and my mom to be married to each other. I know that you'll love each other more deeply each day with God in the center of your marriage. Although my dad can never be replaced, I can't think of anyone else I'd rather have at my mom's side than you."

Chapter 48

A FEW DAYS LATER, EMMA and Brandon had dinner at Sweetgreen. It was casual, and the food was healthy and delicious. Best of all, the other patrons respected Brandon's privacy. After purchasing their salads, Brandon and Emma found an open table. Brandon prayed a blessing over them and their meal.

Emma began, "Now that you've had a few days to think about it, how do you feel about Mike Nelson marrying your mom?"

"I'm really thrilled about it. Mike is such a faith-filled man, and I know that he'll treat my mom like a child of God. Besides, he's been a friend of my dad and mom for decades, and he's just a really solid, classy guy. When my dad died, he looked after me like a surrogate father. If I hadn't kept him and others, like you, Jalen and Sam, from connecting with me during that difficult period of my life, things may have gone much differently for me."

"The path you took was all part of God's plan," reassured Emma.

"Sometimes I think about the course that my life's taken since my dad died. Although it's been very eventful and mostly wonderful," Brandon said as he squeezed Emma's hand, "I'm not sure I understand God's plan and what

CHAPTER 48

he's trying to accomplish with all that he's allowed me to experience."

"Obviously, none of us completely understand God's plan, but I can give you some insights on part of what I believe he's accomplishing through you. Do you remember when we were in high school and Sam first started teaching us about Jesus? One of the things he said was that he believed God was actively pursuing you because he had big plans for you."

"I remember that," replied Brandon.

"I believe God allowed you to get to such a deep, dark, desperate place so he could demonstrate his power to the world by redeeming you. God didn't just stop after he redeemed you, though. He also wanted to reveal how his power could be manifested through one of his faithful children."

"I hadn't thought of it that way before."

"Look at what's happened to you—and through you—since you dedicated your life to Jesus. Your story of redemption has been published in *Sports Illustrated*, your former drug dealer has given his life to Christ, your mother has accepted Jesus into her life, and your long-sleeping love of football has been awakened through a series of events that began with a car accident that occurred right in front of you. Your return to football has given you the platform of Ohio State to demonstrate super-human grace to Manny and Tristin in the face of your own wrongful incarceration. Your grace has drawn not only Tristin and Manny to the Lord, but also many of your teammates and coaches. As a result, your team as a whole is demonstrating what it looks like to be living in faith. The victories are only part of it, but what's even more inspirational is the way the team conducts itself with joy, respect and sportsmanship."

"Thank you, Emma. That helps me to appreciate the big picture. I could feel the power of the Holy Spirit working in me and the team, but I guess I was just too close to the details to really see what God's doing."

"Sometimes I think we need to take a step back to get a fresh perspective on what God is accomplishing in our lives. I shared with you all the things I see that God has orchestrated through you, but there are countless other positive impacts of your actions that I'm not aware of or haven't even come to fruition yet." Emma paused as her heart was stirred by the realization of so many blessings, and she looked deeply into his eyes and said, "Brandon, I'm really enjoying being engaged to you. Every time I look at my ring, it still gives me a thrill. Should we start thinking about potential dates when we could have the wedding?"

"From my standpoint, Emma, the sooner the better."

"I agree. Obviously, we want to avoid the football season. If Ohio State goes to the National Championship game, the season will be over about the second week of January. What would you think of planning our wedding about a month afterwards, in February? That will give you enough time to recover from the season and also for us to organize the final details."

"I love that idea. Do you think that gives us enough time to pull it off?"

"That's only about four months away, so it will be tight, but I think we can accomplish it with God's help."

CHAPTER 48

The next day, as Brandon was entering the locker room to prepare for practice, Coach Anderson approached him and said, "Hey, Brandon. I have something I'd like to discuss with you. Can we slip down to my office for a few minutes?"

"As long as you promise that I won't have to run extra sprints for being late to practice," Brandon replied with a chuckle.

"I promise."

As they were walking the short distance to Coach Anderson's office, Coach said, "I heard on ESPN today that you're the clear frontrunner for the Heisman. What's more, they said that Tristin is also getting some attention."

"Wow, that's great, Coach. I'm really glad to hear about Tristin being considered too, because I know that winning the Heisman Trophy has always been a dream of his."

They entered Coach Anderson's office, and he closed the door behind them. "What you just said is a great transition into why I wanted to talk with you. Although you're the clear star of our team, you're so humble and selfless. You put all of your teammates first, and your approach has rubbed off on the entire team. I know you're driven by your faith and your desire to glorify God. The way that God has led this team through you is something I've never experienced in all my years playing and coaching football."

"Thank you, Coach. That means a lot."

"That brings me to what I wanted to talk with you about. Because of our success this season, particularly on offense, I've been getting a lot of interest from other college teams to be their head coach next year. I've also received some inquiries as to my interest in being an offensive coordinator in the NFL, which has always been my dream. Please keep all of this confidential."

"Of course, Coach, and congratulations! That interest in you is well deserved."

"The reason I wanted to talk with you, Brandon, is to see if you have made any decisions about your future. Because of you and your influence on this team, I'd delay my career advancement if I thought there was any chance that you and I could remain together at Ohio State. Why would I do anything differently when I'm so clearly in God's will right now?"

"Coach, I'm so honored that you'd share this with me and that you'd take my plans into consideration for your future. I've been so focused on this season that I haven't given much thought to what comes next. I promise you, though, that I'll begin praying fervently for God's direction. Also, I'm planning to marry Emma after this season, and I'd like to get her input into my future. As soon as she and I discern God's will, I'll let you know immediately."

"Thanks. I just want to stay on the Brandon train as long as possible. There's one more thing I want to share with you. A moment ago, I mentioned being clearly in God's will, and something happened earlier today that demonstrated God's involvement in your life. I'd call it a miracle."

"I can't wait to hear where you're going with this, Coach."

"Do you remember when we talked on the phone last spring when you told me of your desire to return to Ohio State as a player?"

"Of course, I remember."

CHAPTER 48

"At the time, I thought there was no way that the NCAA would grant you any additional eligibility. The usual rule is that you must use your four years of eligibility within five years. There are special cases around military service, as well as religious exemptions such as an extended mission trip, which is common with BYU students. The NCAA sometimes considers extraordinary medical events, and that was the approach I used with them regarding your circumstances. Right after my call with you, I phoned an NCAA official, whom I know well, and discussed the details of your situation. Immediately after the call, I sent him an email which contained all the details. I was very surprised when he contacted me less than two days later with approval for your eligibility."

Coach continued, "About three weeks ago, on the Monday after our third game, I got a call from my contact at the NCAA. He shared with me that the NCAA had made a mistake in granting you additional eligibility, but they hadn't yet decided how to handle it. He advised me that you could continue playing until they made their final ruling. I was hesitant to tell you because I didn't want you to worry needlessly. Anyway, my contact reached out this morning and said that the NCAA concluded that the initial ruling on your case was completely their mistake and that it wouldn't be fair to terminate your eligibility mid-season. Call it what you like, but I say it was a miracle."

"Wow! Thanks, Coach, for sharing all of that with me. In the future, please don't hesitate to be forthright with me about what seems to be bad news. I've put my faith in God, and I trust that he'll work out the details for the best."

As Coach Anderson and Brandon embraced at the end of the meeting, Coach said, "I really admire your faith, Brandon, and I'd definitely remain at Ohio State if you'd agree to return next year as a coach."

Ohio State's opponent on Saturday would, by far, be their toughest challenge up to this point in the season. They were also undefeated and ranked nationally, just below the Buckeyes at number five. Adding to the difficulty was the fact that it was an away game for Ohio State. The contest would match the Buckeyes' offensive strength, especially the running game, against their opponent's defensive strength in stopping the run. Their opponent ran frequent stunts with their defensive linemen and blitzed from multiple different positions. Consequently, it was very difficult to block them, and they often were able to get unblocked defenders into the backfield, resulting in tackles for significant lost yardage.

Ohio State's plan was to mix it up enough with their offense to keep the defense off-balance and to prevent their opponent from setting the tone. On obvious passing plays, they would keep Brandon in the backfield to help protect the quarterback. They also intended to lean heavily on plays where Brandon blocked and Tristin was the primary ball carrier. Ohio State also planned to liberally use the halfback option pass, depending on how their opponent tried to defend it. One final twist that the Ohio State offense would consider was inserting Brandon as wide receiver. They had been practicing some plays, and Brandon was faster than

CHAPTER 48

any of the Buckeyes' receivers. It could be just the wrinkle Ohio State needed to confuse their opponent.

On OSU's first offensive possession, the other team stacked nine players along the line of scrimmage, but when the ball was snapped, three of them withdrew. They continued that strategy through the first half, varying only on which three players withdrew on a given play. It made it very difficult for Ohio State's offensive linemen to create holes for the running backs.

Ohio State attempted two halfback option pass plays in the first half. On the first one, the defense didn't vigorously pursue Brandon as he rolled right. Instead, they guarded the line of scrimmage with three linemen and double covered the downfield receiver. Brandon's pass was knocked down by one of the defenders. On the next option play, Brandon was determined ahead of time that he would run. This time, however, the defense pursued him aggressively and tackled him after a short gain.

At halftime, the score was tied, 7-7, and it was a game of wits. Ohio State decided to put Brandon at wide receiver to start the second half. It was the key that brought their opponent's defense tumbling down. On the first play with Brandon at wide receiver, their opponent was clearly confused. Brandon did a simple out pattern ten yards downfield, and it put him in the position where he thrived. He easily outleaped the defender to catch the ball, and then used his superior speed, strength and athleticism to overwhelm the defensive backs for a long touchdown.

On Ohio State's second offensive series, as they expected, the defense double-teamed Brandon, which allowed the receivers on the opposite side to make easy catches and drive the ball down the field for another touchdown.

With the Buckeyes' next possession, they anticipated that their opponent would shift a defensive back away from Brandon and over to the other side of the field. Instead, they brought an additional defensive back into the game to stop Ohio State's passing attack, but leaving them vulnerable to the run. On the first play, Brandon lined up at wide receiver, but then went in motion to line up at the halfback position. When Brandon received the handoff, he was like a thoroughbred race horse who had been kept in the barn for several days. He danced and darted through defenders with glee until he hit the open field, where he sprinted to the end zone for a seventy-two-yard touchdown, effectively putting the game away.

Chapter 49

TWO DAYS LATER ON the following Monday, Brandon had just finished his first class of the morning. He had an hour before his next class and was walking to the library to study when he got a call from Hank Fisher.

"Good morning, Hank, how're you doing, man?"

"I'm good, Brandon. You played a heck of a game on Saturday. I can't believe that you even snuck in some plays at wide receiver. Is there anything you can't do on a football field?"

"I'm a lousy kicker," Brandon chuckled. "How's Ryan?"

"That's actually why I called. Healthwise, he's doing fine, but he's having a little problem I was hoping you may be able to help him with. You know that he adores you, and his friendship with you has brought him so much joy that completely keeps him from thinking about his cancer. Part of the fun for him is sharing what you do for him with his first-grade classmates. He's a bit of an outsider because of all the days he's missed with his cancer and also because of his frailty. Recently, for show-and-tell, he took the two footballs that Tristin and Manny gave him, but some of his classmates accused him of making it all up. It seems to me that the accusations are being led by a kid named Max Borchert, and he's influencing some of the other kids to join in. I've heard that Max's parents are in the middle of a divorce, so maybe his mistreatment of Ryan is arising out of his own hurt. Anyway, Ryan has been inconsolable for the last several days, and he's breaking my and Pam's hearts. I was wondering if you could write a short letter to Ryan or something that would verify that the two of you are pals."

"I've got a better idea, Hank. Text me the name of Ryan's school and his teacher, and I'll take care of everything. Also, please tell Ryan to wear his Ohio State jersey to school on Wednesday."

"That won't be a problem, because he wears it every day," replied Hank, laughing.

On Wednesday morning, two days later, Ms. Swanson said to her first-grade class, "Before we go outside for recess, Ryan Fisher has arranged for three guests from the Ohio State football team to join us." She opened the door to the hallway, and Brandon, Tristin and Manny, all dressed in their Ohio State jerseys, stepped into the classroom. They immediately found Ryan, who was seated in the first row, and greeted him by name while giving him a high five. The children were excited but also a little intimidated by the three large men standing at the front of their classroom.

After introducing himself and his two teammates, Brandon said, "The three of us play football for Ohio State. Ryan is our friend. He comes to all of our home games that he can, and then has dinner with us after the game. I understand that some of you don't believe that we are who we say we are and that we're friends with Ryan. What can we do to prove it to you?"

Several of the students gave sidelong glances at Max Borchert, and he spoke up somewhat sheepishly, "You look

CHAPTER 49

like the pictures of Brandon Campbell that I've seen, but my dad says that Brandon Campbell is the fastest player ever at Ohio State. Show us how fast you are on the playground, and then I'll believe that you are who you say."

The three football players, Ms. Swanson, Ryan, and his classmates filed out to the open athletic field adjacent to the playground. Brandon asked, "Who's the fastest in your class?"

Immediately, Max Borchert raised his hand and said, "I am!"

Brandon looked at the rest of the class and said, "Is there anyone who wants to join Max in racing against me?"

After some cajoling from Max, several of his accomplices agreed to also participate in the race. Brandon then set up a starting line for him, one for the students, and a common finish line. The students would have an approximately twenty-yard head start in a forty-yard race for Brandon.

Brandon asked his competitors, "Does that look fair?"

Max responded confidently, "There's no way you can beat us."

Brandon asked Ms. Swanson to be the starter, just in front of where Max and his friends would start. Twenty yards behind the students and unbeknownst to them, Brandon had Ryan climb on his back, piggyback style, before the start.

Ms. Swanson called out, "Ready—set—go!", and the students ran as hard as they could. Besides the sound of their footsteps and their own labored breathing, all they could hear was the sound of Ryan's giggling converging on them rapidly from behind. Brandon and his jockey passed all of the students with about four yards to go, and he and Ryan easily crossed the finish line first, amidst the cheering of the rest of Ms. Swanson's class stationed at the finish line. Everyone was laughing joyfully after the race, including Max and the other student competitors.

Brandon approached Max and asked, "Have I proven that I'm Brandon Campbell?"

Without hesitating, as he tried to catch his breath, Max replied enthusiastically, "Yes! That was amazing!"

"Let me also prove to you what good friends Ryan and I are. I'll arrange for you to sit with Ryan at Saturday's game and then go to dinner with us after the game. What do you say?"

Max didn't know what to say. The protective layers of toughness that had built up on him because of his situation at home suddenly melted, and Max could only nod affirmatively as the tears streamed down his cheeks. Brandon wrote his mobile number on a piece of paper, handed it to Max and said, "Have your dad or your mom call me, and I'll arrange the details." Brandon knew that Patrick would gladly give up his ticket that day for such a good cause.

On Saturday, Ohio State's opponent didn't have the skill on defense to match the Buckeye's offensive firepower. It may possibly have been Brandon's most spectacular game as an Ohio State player, and he only played the first half. His elite skills were never better exhibited than on one play in particular. Brandon and Tristin were lined up side-by-side in the backfield. When the ball was snapped, the quarterback faked a handoff to Tristin, who rushed into

CHAPTER 49

the middle of the offensive line. The quarterback then handed the ball to Brandon as he swept around the left. As he made the turn and just got back to the line of scrimmage, he saw the approaching outside linebacker. Brandon cut to his left to avoid him. The linebacker flailed with his right arm, grabbed the right side of Brandon's jersey and caused Brandon to spin 180 degrees so he was now facing backwards. Fortunately, the linebacker's momentum caused him to lose his grip on Brandon's jersey. Brandon, still backwards, glanced behind him and saw a tackler coming in low from behind. Brandon launched himself backwards and upwards, much like a high jumper doing the Fosbury flop. The tackler missed Brandon, and as he reached the climax of his jump, parallel to the ground and with his back facing downward, Brandon did a half twist in the air. With the ball in his left hand, he landed simultaneously on his right hand and both feet and immediately popped up. Brandon quickly did a jump cut to the right to evade the next tackler. He now only had the safety between him and the goal line. He faked right, cut left, and sped the fifty-five yards down the sideline for the score.

The Ohio State fans, long accustomed to Brandon's feats of athletic prowess, were stunned by his mid-air twist that would have made any feline proud. The fans wildly cheered Brandon's efforts.

By halftime, Brandon had rushed for 171 yards and four touchdowns, and had thrown for a fifth touchdown. After each touchdown, he pointed to the part of the stadium where Ryan was sitting between Dylan and Max. Max was overwhelmed by the pomp and circumstance of the game, the exuberantly celebrating fans, the offensive fireworks of Brandon, and Ryan's dear friend, Dylan. The day got even better for Max over dinner when he could eat all the delicious pasta he could hold while celebrating with his heroes and their families and friends. Max had no difficulty sleeping that night after living a nearly perfect day for a seven-year-old. Needless to say, he had become an avid Ohio State football fan for life. In addition, Max and Ryan had become best friends.

Chapter 50

EARLY IN THE MORNING on the following Monday, while Brandon was preparing a high-protein fruit smoothie for breakfast, he received a phone call from Carlos Flores.

"Hey, Carlos, what a pleasant surprise!"

"Hi, Brandon. Sorry for calling so early, but I just couldn't wait to talk with you. I attended the Christian retreat in Cincinnati this past weekend, and it was so moving. I heard so many dramatic testimonies, and it helped me to understand how God moves in our lives. I was thinking about you all weekend because it became so clear to me that it was no coincidence that you were my cellmate last summer. God used you to set me on his desired course for my life. Thank you, Brandon, for being obedient to God and giving me the guidance you did when I was at a very vulnerable crossroads in my life. You stood in the gap for me, and I'm so grateful."

"I'm happy I could be there for you, Carlos. Also, I don't know if I ever formally thanked you for your role in catching the guy who assaulted Manny Garcia. I understand you provided a key lead which led to his arrest."

"That's the least I could do for the guy who saved my life."

"Congratulations, Carlos. I'm so happy for you, and I'll continue praying for you."

"Thanks, Brandon. I love you, brother."

Carlos's call about his retreat experience reminded Brandon that he hadn't talked with Sam recently. It was early enough that he might be able to catch Sam before he began his day at the hospital, so Brandon called him right away.

"Hi, Sam. It's Brandon. Do you have a minute to talk?"

"I sure do, Brandon. I'm driving to the hospital now. What's up, man?"

"I just got a call from Carlos Flores. He was telling me about his experience at the retreat this past weekend, and it reminded me of you. I realized that we haven't talked in a while, and I just called to see how you're doing."

"I'm good. And busy. I'm in the middle of interviewing for residency positions right now."

"What type of residency are you hoping to get into?"

"Emergency medicine. After rotating through all the various areas of medicine, my time in the emergency department seemed like the best fit for me. I really enjoy the fast pace, the variety, and the occasional opportunity to actually save someone's life."

"What schools are you looking at?"

"I've applied to programs all over the country, but the majority of them are in the Midwest."

"When will you know where you're going?"

"I'll need to rank order my preferences and submit them to the residency match system in early March. After discussing things at length with Grace, I'll get to convey our choices of programs, and the programs also rank the potential candidates. Then, through a computerized match, in mid-March, every fourth-year medical student in the

CHAPTER 50

country finds out at the exact same time where they'll be going for their residency."

"Wow, that sounds stressful."

"As you know as well as anyone, Brandon, it's all about having faith in God's plan. Grace and I are praying that we will be able to clearly discern God's will for us in this next chapter. By the way, I just wanted you to know how well Grace is doing. When you got arrested last summer, her anger and pain were rekindled about Joshua's death. However, when you were found innocent and set free, she was also released from her guilt, shame and anger. The former joyful Grace, who I knew when we were first married, has returned in full, and I'm so thankful to have her back."

"That's great news, Sam. I know you need to get going, but it sure has been great catching up with you. Please give Grace and the kids my love."

That evening, Brandon had dinner at Emma's apartment. She prepared baked salmon, garlic mashed potatoes and corn.

As they sat down at the table to eat, Emma said excitedly, "Brandon, I heard some wonderful news about Ryan Fisher today. He had another CT scan, and the tumor in his lung is completely gone. He is officially in remission!"

"That's such an answered prayer. It's been so much fun to have Ryan and his family be part of the journey with the Ohio State team this season. And to think it all started when I met his dad while handcuffed in the back of his police car. Speaking of children who've battled cancer and are devoted Buckeye fans, Dylan was named as the MVP of his league yesterday."

"That's fantastic! It's hard to imagine that the sickly little boy laying in a hospital bed seven years ago would grow into what he's become on the football field."

"It just goes to show that all things are possible with God."

"Amen! Speaking of that, we can really use God's miraculous powers to solve a dilemma with our wedding planning."

"Oh, really? What's going on?"

"It's about the guest list. We need to figure out how many people we can invite. Our options are to have a small, elegant wedding, or a bigger wedding that would need to be more modest. A great example of how we need to decide where to draw the line is with the football team. I'm sure you want to invite some of your teammates, but how can we prevent hurt feelings unless we invite everyone? What do you think?"

"I think that the most important objective of our wedding day is that we glorify God through the demonstration of our love and commitment to each other. With that in mind, I think that having lots of guests participating in the celebration would be more important than having an elaborate wedding."

"That makes sense. Thanks for helping set our priorities."

"Speaking of the priorities in our wedding planning, I was thinking of asking Jalen to be my best man. Are you okay with that?"

"Of course! I imagine that was a tough choice for you, with Sam, Patrick and even Tristin being such close friends to you."

CHAPTER 50

"The most difficult one was Sam. Besides you, he's been with me the longest of my current friend group, and he had such a major role in bringing me to Christ. But I know he's so busy with medical school, residency interviews and his young family, and I didn't want to burden him with the responsibilities of being best man. Besides, Jalen and I see each other every day, and we've become really tight."

"You've sold me. Jalen it is!"

At the conclusion of practice the next day, Brandon found Jalen before heading to the locker room and said, "Can I talk with you after I shower and change? There's something personal I'd like to discuss with you."

"Sure, Brandon. I'll be in my office."

When Brandon entered Jalen's office about thirty minutes later, he said, "What do you think about strolling around campus for old time's sake? Do you remember giving me advice as we walked around campus during my freshman year?"

"I sure do. What a great idea. It's a beautiful afternoon, and the fall colors on campus are on full display right now."

As Brandon and Jalen walked out of the Athletic Center, Jalen said, "It's funny that you just used the expression 'for old time's sake', because recently, I've been reflecting on my football career and trying to put this season in perspective. I've never experienced anything like this year, and I'm not saying that just because we're undefeated. I've had other undefeated seasons. What makes this season so different is the chemistry and camaraderie of the players, the selflessness, the work ethic, and the focus. I believe it's because of the love that we have for each other, and that love comes from God. I've never had an experience in football or any other sport that was anything like this team. Do you feel it, Brandon?"

"I do. It seems like our team has experienced what it feels like to be sheltered from our broken world. It's been a little slice of heaven, where everyone is in harmony with God."

"Well said. I don't know about you, but I wish this slice of heaven that we're enjoying would never end."

"That would be nice," said Brandon, "but God has asked us to tell others about Jesus so that everyone who believes can experience the joy of heaven on this side of life. That likely means that we need to immerse back into our broken world again someday."

"You're right, but I'm going to enjoy this season to the fullest while it lasts. By the way, what did you want to talk with me about?"

"Jalen, I'd like you to be my best man. What do you say?"

"I would be honored, Brandon," said Jalen, smiling widely.

"Thank you, Jalen," and the two men embraced.

Ohio State had four games left in the regular season. They won their next three games without being challenged significantly. The only team remaining which stood in the way of Ohio State's undefeated regular season was their arch rival, the Michigan Wolverines, who were also undefeated.

Chapter 51

AS WAS THE CASE most years, the University of Michigan would provide the toughest test of Ohio State's season. Regardless of the records of the two teams coming into the game, it was generally a close, intense, hard-fought contest. Their bitter rivalry dated back to the days of Woody Hayes and Bo Schembechler, the fiery, legendary coaches of The Ohio State University and the University of Michigan, respectively.

In this particular year, Brandon and his Buckeye teammates would have an especially difficult challenge against Michigan. The talent level of Michigan's team was very comparable to that of Ohio State. Notably on defense, they had the athleticism, speed and strength to effectively neutralize Ohio State's weapons, and they were very well coached. Michigan would have a game plan that would minimize all of the Buckeyes' strengths, and their players were very disciplined. In addition, the game was being played at the University of Michigan in front of their 107,000 rabid fans. The outcome would likely come down to which team made the most big plays, including turnovers.

Even though Brandon had previously played in parts of three Ohio State football seasons, he had never played in a storied Michigan game, either because of injury or the sudden death of his father. Although he had played in plenty of big football games, including the high school state championship game, he had never before experienced any comparable intensity as the emotional fervor of this game. Brandon, as usual, turned to God and led his team in prayer in the locker room prior to taking the field before kickoff. As they marched onto the field in enemy territory, they felt a peace which surpassed all understanding.

During the first half, it was clear that the one edge that Ohio State possessed was Brandon Campbell. He rushed for 125 yards and one touchdown. Unfortunately, two of his passes were dropped by wide-open receivers in the end zone. In addition, the Buckeyes had two goal line fumbles, both recovered by the Wolverines. One was a fumbled snap by their quarterback, and the other was a fumbled handoff to Tristin. Even though Ohio State was down 20-13 at halftime, they had reason to be optimistic, if only they could execute better on their upcoming scoring opportunities. Also, Ohio State would receive the kickoff to start the second half.

Unfortunately for the Buckeyes, the second half began with a disaster. Their kickoff returner fumbled the kickoff deep in Ohio State territory, and Michigan once again recovered the fumble. Three plays later, Michigan scored another touchdown, making the score 27-13 in Michigan's favor.

Whenever he had the opportunity, whether he was on the field or on the sidelines, Brandon instructed his teammates to have faith. He reminded them that this was all part of God's plan, and their role was to glorify God regardless of whether they won or lost the game. Brandon's words

CHAPTER 51

calmed his teammates and caused them to focus on God rather than on the seemingly impossible task at hand.

With a two-touchdown lead, Michigan anticipated that Ohio State would rely heavily on Brandon Campbell to lift them out of their hole. Instead of countering Michigan's strategy by using Brandon as a decoy, they elected to give Michigan exactly what they wanted, because after all, Brandon was largely responsible for Ohio State's undefeated season, as well as for their limited success in the game up to this point.

On the Buckeye's first possession after Michigan's touchdown, Brandon carried the ball on nine consecutive plays, grinding away at the Michigan defense and steadily moving the ball down the field. After each play, it seemed that Brandon got stronger as the Michigan defense became more fatigued. On the tenth play of the drive, with the ball on the Michigan three-yard-line, Brandon received the handoff and ran into the hole created by his left offensive tackle. The hole quickly closed with linebackers and defensive backs as Brandon entered it, and he carried three defenders with him into the end zone.

Regrettably, Ohio State's offense was undermined by turnovers most of the rest of the second half. Their quarterback threw two interceptions, both of which led to Michigan field goals. The score was now 33-20 in Michigan's favor, with a little more than three minutes to go in the game. Michigan was now punting the ball, hoping to bury Ohio State deep in their own territory. After a brief discussion between Coaches Anderson and Pittman, they decided to put Brandon into the game as their punt returner, even though he had never previously played that position.

As the teams lined up for the punt, the Michigan coach noticed that Brandon was on the field to receive the punt, and he immediately called a timeout. When his punter came to the sideline, the coach instructed him to punt the ball as far as he could, but to make sure the ball went out of bounds along the left sideline so that it was unreturnable. As the punter went back onto the field and lined up to receive the snap, all he could think about was how Brandon had battered his defensive teammates the entire game and what would happen if he was the only player between Brandon and the goal line. The punter was so unnerved by the thought that his punt barely missed carrying out of bounds.

Brandon made an acrobatic catch along the sideline while keeping his feet inbounds. He immediately began sprinting in a long arc for the opposite sideline and effectively outraced most of Michigan's punt coverage. As he sped up the sideline, he stiff-armed one defender. Then he faked toward the sideline and cut inside past a second defender. The only player left to beat was Michigan's punter. Brandon lowered his shoulder as if he was going to bowl him over, but at the last instant, he cut left, leaving the punter grasping only air as Brandon scampered to the end zone.

With the score now 33-27 and about three minutes to play, the Ohio State coaches elected to kick it away on the ensuing kickoff and trust their defense to get a stop. Their faith in their defense was rewarded as Michigan punted with one minute and thirty-two second remaining.

As Ohio State huddled before their final opportunity for an offensive touchdown, Brandon led a quick prayer with his teammates. "Dear Father, thank you for giving us the

CHAPTER 51

opportunity to play this game we so enjoy with brothers that we love. We ask you to help both teams to play to the best of their abilities, and that, regardless of the outcome, we may glorify you today. In Jesus' name. Amen."

Everyone in the stadium expected what would come next—that Ohio State would repeatedly hand the ball to Brandon Campbell on various running plays, and they were correct. Ohio State had all of their timeouts remaining, and by effectively managing the clock, Brandon Campbell gained fifty yards on six carries. However, they still needed twenty more yards and only had ten seconds left. The Ohio State coaches knew that conventional wisdom would be to throw a pass in this situation, but they had seen Brandon perform so many spectacular feats in these scenarios over the course of the season that they decided to keep the ball in his hands. This would very likely be their final play of the game. They decided to have Brandon run around the right side, because the offense had had consistent success on that side and it gave Brandon space to maneuver. There was also a chance for Brandon to step out of bounds if he was in trouble and give the Buckeyes one more play before time expired.

After the snap, Brandon received the pitch as he ran around the right side. He surveyed the defense as he headed downfield. The blocking was perfect, but he'd still need to beat two or three defenders on his own. As he gained about five yards, three defenders encircled him with no chance for his escape. Just before impact with his tacklers, Brandon alertly glanced behind him and saw the 350-pound Ohio State right offensive tackle catching up to try to help Brandon spring loose. Brandon tossed him the ball and then barreled into the three defenders, knocking them all down.

The offensive tackle was as surprised as anyone that he found himself with the ball in his hands, and miraculously, he hung on to it as he began stumbling in slow motion the final fifteen yards to the end zone. A safety hit him at the five-yard line, but bounced off of him like windblown autumn leaves against the windshield of a moving car. He crossed the goal line as time expired, and the extra point was good. Buckeyes win!

The Buckeyes celebrated joyfully but considerately. In the post-game interviews, the Ohio State players and coaches complimented the skill, tenacity and coaching of the Michigan team and how much respect they had for them.

One week later, Ohio State played in the Big Ten Championship game in Indianapolis, and won easily against their over-matched opponent. They could now look forward to the college football playoffs which would begin in about a month, but there was one additional relevant event first.

Chapter 52

ONE WEEK AFTER THE Big Ten Championship game, the Heisman Trophy presentation occurred in New York City. Brandon Campbell, as one of the four finalists, was invited to attend the ceremony which was televised nationally on ESPN. Brandon had not been following the Heisman race. He didn't even know who the other finalists were, let alone how his statistics compared to theirs. Brandon was completely unaware that he had set a new Division I college single season rushing record, which was ironic given that his pursuit of the comparable record in high school almost cost his team the state championship. He had also set the single season record for combined rushing and passing touchdowns.

Although Brandon's statistics should have made him the clear choice as the Heisman recipient, doubt arose because some of the voters had misinformed impressions of Brandon's character. They remembered him leaving Ohio State abruptly after his father died. They were also aware of his opioid, alcohol and gambling addictions from the *Sports Illustrated* article. They recalled the headlines earlier this year when he got embroiled in a fight with a teammate in practice and was arrested the next day, accused of assaulting that teammate with a baseball bat. Many of the voters felt that a player of questionable character shouldn't be honored with the Heisman Trophy regardless of his on-field performance. The controversy over the misunderstanding of Brandon's character had created much interest in the Heisman Trophy presentation, with over thirty million viewers, about triple the usual number.

Brandon, resplendent in a classic black tuxedo with a scarlet bow tie, sat in the front row of the venue along with the other three finalists. After some initial formalities, Chris Fowler, the emcee, introduced each of the four finalists individually and shared their highlights and accomplishments. Brandon was overwhelmed when he learned that he had set a new collegiate single season rushing record, and it reminded him of his dad. When doing their workouts together in high school, Brandon would often share with his dad that breaking the Ohio high school rushing record was one of his dreams. His dad would humor him by listening, but always cautioned him that team goals were much more important than individual accomplishments. The memory of his dad brought a tear to Brandon's eye, especially as he thought of often telling his dad that winning the Heisman Trophy someday was also one of his goals.

After completing the introductions of the finalists, Chris Fowler said, "It is now time to introduce this year's winner of the Heisman Trophy. Our winner is… Brandon Campbell from The Ohio State University."

As Brandon arose and climbed the steps onto the stage, he relished this incredible opportunity to glorify God. As he stood at the podium, the screen behind Brandon featured a slideshow of photos, selected and provided by Jalen Pittman, many of which Brandon had been unaware of at

CHAPTER 52

the time they were taken. The photo gallery showed a new photo about every three seconds and included:

- Brandon entering the stadium during Ohio State's season opener arm-in-arm with Tristin Garner and Manny Garcia

- Brandon visiting Ryan Fisher in the hospital and giving him the football autographed by the team

- Brandon visiting Manny Garcia in the hospital, along with his teammates and coaches

- Brandon presenting Dylan and Ryan each a football at Angelo's after the first game

- Brandon on the field at halftime of Dylan's second game, showing him how to do a jump cut

- Brandon baptizing his teammates

- Brandon with Ryan on his back during the race at Ryan's school

- Multiple photos of Brandon scoring his various record-setting touchdowns

As the photos rotated and the crowd applauded, Brandon took a moment for a quick, silent prayer that God would give him the words to speak that would glorify God. As the slideshow was completed and the audience began to settle, Brandon leaned toward the microphone, and said, "Please bow your heads and pray with me. Dear Heavenly Father, we praise you for the magnificence of your creation, and we thank you for the gift of your beloved son Jesus who died on a cross for the forgiveness of our sins. We also thank you for his resurrection three days later that promises eternal life with you for those who believe in him. We also thank you, Father, for the coaches, players, media and others who dedicate their lives to football at all levels. May you inspire them to use their platform to spread the word about you. In Jesus' name I pray. Amen."

After his prayer, Brandon concluded, "Thank you so much for this honor. It's certainly been an eventful path in my football career to achieve this recognition. I wouldn't be standing before you today without the support of many people who've encouraged me along the way. I especially want to acknowledge my late father for instilling in me the love of football. My times practicing with him are among the fondest memories of my life. But even more, I hope that my efforts please and bring glory to my Heavenly Father, and that I might inspire others to know and follow Jesus, his Son. Thank you, and may God bless you."

Amidst thunderous applause, Brandon glanced at the left wing of the stage, smiled and nodded. He continued, "Because of the substantial weight of the Heisman Trophy, I have asked two assistants to help me carry it. On cue, Ryan Fisher and Dylan Hubbard, both dressed in identical tuxedos to Brandon's, confidently entered stage left and excitedly high-fived Brandon. Together, Brandon, Dylan and Ryan carried the Heisman Trophy and exited stage right, much to the delight of the audience.

Chapter 53

TWO MONTHS AFTER THE Heisman Trophy presentation, it was Emma and Brandon's wedding day. In the interim, Ohio State had won the National Championship, and an affluent Ohio State alumnus was so impressed with the football team's performance and influence, as well as with Brandon earning the Heisman Trophy, that he made a generous donation to Ohio State's NIL fund. The additional money allotted to Brandon allowed Emma and Brandon to invite 700 guests, as well as to host the wedding and reception in a beautiful venue, The Walter Commons at St. Charles in Columbus. The guest list included family and friends, as well as all the players, coaches, trainers, managers and anyone else associated with the football team.

The venue was elegant, featuring unique architectural details, high ceilings, dramatic lighting and lavish floral arrangements. The seating for the wedding was set up theatre style, and as soon as the ceremony was completed, the room would be converted to the reception space while the guests enjoyed a cocktail hour in an adjacent room.

At the start of the ceremony, Brandon entered the stage from the side, along with the officiant, Mike Nelson. As the bridesmaids and groomsmen came up the aisle in pairs, Brandon scanned the guests, and the enormity of the moment hit him. He saw members of his and Emma's extended families, his football teammates, coaches and staff, Ryan and Dylan and their respective parents, many close friends, and finally his mom, looking radiant in the front row. Brandon realized how much he wished that his dad was here.

As the matron of honor, Grace Gilmore, and his best man, Jalen Pittman, entered the cavernous room, the doors where they had entered in the back were closed. Once Jalen was in his place on the stage next to him, Brandon glanced at the groomsmen to his left—Patrick Cutler, Sam Gilmore, Antonio Alvarez, Manny Garcia and Tristin Garner. He looked to his right at the bridesmaids, and they included Grace, Jasmine, three of Emma's cousins and one of her co-workers.

As Brandon looked at the rear doors, expectantly awaiting Emma, his bride and soulmate, his mind began rapidly recounting the events of his life—workouts with his dad in middle school, winning the high school state championship, all the halfback option passes which he always associated with his dad, his dark period of addiction and homelessness after his dad's death, his redemption and baptism which was almost exactly a year ago, his love of football returning after the accident of Patrick and James Cutler, the *Sports Illustrated* article, his arrest and incarceration, baptisms of his teammates and his mom, the undefeated National Championship season, winning the Heisman Trophy, and the single season collegiate rushing record, which also reminded him of his dad.

The music changed from soft classical music to a jubilant processional melody, signaling that it was time for the

CHAPTER 53

bride to make her enchanting entrance. Brandon's sentimental reflections faded, as he took a deep breath and returned to the present, wonderful moment. The doors at the back of the room opened, and there was his stunning Emma, escorted by her beaming dad. Brandon's eyes filled with tears as he thought about how long he had dreamed of this moment. Once again, Brandon felt a tiny twinge of loss as he wished that his earthly father, who had loved Emma, could be here. Then he realized that his path to Emma had been orchestrated by his heavenly Father, who was always with him and loved him completely. Brandon felt only joy.

Acknowledgements

I AM VERY APPRECIATIVE OF my wife Lisa who collaborated with me to develop and refine the plot as we took long walks while training for a half marathon. She also typed the manuscript from my hand-written pages and meticulously helped me edit, suggesting many astute changes which enhanced the story.

I would also like to thank multiple family members and friends, including Cathy Campbell, Dave Cullom, John Fencl, Lyn Fencl, Christopher Lee, Evan Lee, Susan Lee, Chuck Reed, Dana Reed, Bridget Rogers and Mark Rogers. They all reviewed the initial manuscript and suggested valuable modifications that significantly enhanced the final version of this book.

About the Author

DAVID T. LEE, M.D. grew up in Dayton, Ohio. He majored in chemical engineering at the University of Cincinnati, went to The Ohio State University School of Medicine, completed his residency at Indiana University School of Medicine and served as an internal medicine physician in a thriving practice in Indianapolis, Indiana. Later in his career, he became a healthcare executive. In retirement, he is joyfully pursuing his desire to glorify God through creative writing. He is happily married to his bride of thirty-three years, and is the proud father of two adult children.

Printed in the USA
CPSIA information can be obtained
at www.ICGtesting.com
LVHW090812041224
798134LV00003B/4